AF422160

GOOD LOOKING

Good Looking

Lucy May Lennox

Copyright © 2023 by Lucy May Lennox

All rights reserved. No part of this book may be reproduced in any manner whatsoever without written permission except in the case of brief quotations embodied in critical articles and reviews.

First Printing, 2023

Contents

1

NICK

1993: Somewhere in the Midwest

My brother and I have always been the center of attention. When we were fourteen, all kinds of doctors and researchers spent over a year studying us, because Nate had gone blind and I could still see, even though we're identical twins. I don't know what they were hoping to find, exactly. It's not like we have secret psychic powers, and I could transmit images to him. Most of the tests seemed boring and pointless, like having us try to solve a Rubik's cube and see who could do it faster, me with colors or Nate with Braille. Nate always won, but that's just him. I bet if we raced now he'd still win.

Sometimes the researchers would ask hesitantly how it affected us, like if Nate was jealous or resentful or anything, and they always seemed surprised when he said no. But this wasn't because Nate's such a great guy. I had already shown symptoms of the same condition. We had always had trouble seeing in the dark, and by the time we were ten or so we both had blind spots. It's just that his were bigger than mine. The way he figured it, he was more advanced, and it was only a matter of time before I caught up.

Nate was right. By the time I was sixteen, I could hardly see anything at all except a few pinholes in big static-y gray patches, like a badly tuned TV set. The studies stopped.

I guess by then we were just two blind kids, identical twins or not. I never did find out if the studies came to anything. A few of the researchers sent us copies of their essays once they were published, but in print. How lame is that? They knew we're both blind now, but they didn't even bother to send the results in an accessible format. Our dad offered to read one out loud to us but even listening to the title, "A Study in Differential Visual Acuity in Monozygotic Juveniles with Retinitis Pigmentosa Blah Blah Blah," we could die of boredom.

Still, all that made our time at Knob Park High School kind of eventful for us, and we weren't sure what we wanted to do after so we ended up for two years at Onasca Community College still living at home. But by then life in our boring little Midwest town with hovering parents was unbearable. So that's why we transferred to Calstock State University in Allenville, living on our own for the first time as juniors, two guys squashed into one tiny dorm room.

We move into the dorm two weeks before classes start, long before the other students. Predictably, things pretty much suck at first, and it's only the thought of Mom hanging around behind us saying "Are you suuuuuure you're okaaaaaaaay?" that keeps us from going back home.

Our first day on campus, someone from the Center for Students with Disabilities takes us on a tour so we can get oriented. We follow along behind three whirring electric wheelchairs as the student worker says the names of various campus buildings in a bored voice. I assume he's gesturing at things we can't see. Then we all crowd into the tiny CSD office at the edge of campus to register for the upcoming semester.

The admin lady who insists on meeting me and Nate together instead of one at a time pushes us to take all the same classes. I think it's so the CSD would have half as much work with arranging for note taking, transcribing and textbook ordering. We tell her no way. Nate goes for psychology and I choose computer science.

The next day, everyone else moves into the dorm. We're the only juniors in the dorm. Everyone else is younger. Calstock doesn't have nearly enough dorm rooms for all the students, so most people only live on campus for freshman and sophomore years. After that, they take their chances with sketchy rental houses. It's kind of a tradition for juniors and seniors to get together with five or six friends and rent a house, put a couch on the porch and party all the time.

The other students in the dorm think we're creepy. That's the kind of thing that Mom would get mad about if she heard me say it.

"How do you knooooow?" she'd say.

Well, I know because I hear the asshole in the room across the hall say so. The day he moves in, he knocks on our door to introduce himself, and Nate answers while I'm hanging up our clothes in the closet. They talk for a minute or so before I go over to introduce myself.

"Hi, I'm Nick."

"Woah, there's two of them!" the asshole says. "Are you both blind?"

"Yeah," we say at the same time.

"Ugh, creepy!"

"Asshole." Nate slams the door in his face.

A few days later, people on our hall find out we're twenty-one, and suddenly we become the most popular guys in the dorm. That year of high school we had to repeat for O&M training doesn't seem so bad after all. That's short for Orientation and Mobility, but basically it means blind skills like using a white cane and how to cross the street without being run over.

The asshole across the hall knocks on our door one afternoon.

"Hey man, got any beer? I'll pay you for it."

"No," says Nate, "but I could go get some."

"Woah, no way!" says the asshole, whose name is Carson. "But dude, how do you have an ID? Aw man, don't tell me they gave you a driver's license?"

This is just one of the stupid questions we get all the time. People assume that because we can't drive, we don't have any ID at all. On the other hand, we hardly ever get carded, which was handy when we were younger.

"Of course I have an ID, dumbass," says Nate. "It's issued by the state. It's just an ID, not a driver's license. If you're paying, come on, let's go."

I hear Nate groping around in the closet for a jacket. We try not to wear the same clothes at the same time but we don't exactly have separate clothes either, just a bunch of interchangeable stuff we share. It's easier that way.

"Are you coming or what?" Nate asks me.

"Ok, fine." It's not like I have anything else to do.

We walk caravan-style, with Nate holding Carson's shoulder and me holding Nate's shoulder, both of us with our white canes, trying not to trip each other. I hate doing the caravan. I'm sure it's quite the spectacle, but there's no other way unless I'm willing to risk wandering off after the wrong set of footsteps. Which has happened more than once, but anyway.

We walk out the back of the dorm, left to the intersection, then right two more blocks to Village Mart. I'm trying to get better about remembering things like that. The student worker from CSD who gave us our tour had been very emphatic about showing us the way there, although at the time we weren't sure why.

"Are you sure Village Mart has beer?" Nate asks as we straggle across the intersection, tires squealing on all sides as Carson leads us straight into traffic.

"Dude, are you kidding me? That's like mainly all they have."

Nate turns back to me. "You hear that, Nick? We've been cheated! These past few days, we've only been buying chips and candy. Shit! Why didn't that asshole from the CSD tell us?"

When we get to the door, Carson stops. "Uh, one of you has to buy it on your own. If they see me with you, they'll try to card me too."

"Gotcha. Whaddaya want?" Nate replies confidently.

Carson hesitates. Did he think this all the way through? "A case of Natty Light, I guess?"

"Ugh, gross," I say.

"Hey, it's his money," Nate says. "Nick, go get a case of Natty Light."

"What? Why me? No!"

"I'll stay by the door with Carson and wait for you."

"That's a stupid plan. You think they won't notice the guy who looks exactly like me hanging around with the underage dude? If we fuck this up, they'll never let us buy beer here again."

"Yeah, cuz Village Mart's so close to the dorm, they're super strict," Carson adds.

"Whose side are you on?" Nate asks irritably. "Ok, fine, we'll go in together. You wait outside, genius."

"Ok, so where's the beer?" I ask, already dreading this outing.

"In the refrigerators along the back wall, I think?" Carson's answer does not inspire confidence. "And there's always cases stacked up in the aisles in the middle. The second from the end. No, maybe the third?"

"Fine. Let's get this over with." I push the glass door open, not waiting to check if Nate is following me or not. He's pretty good at getting around on his own though, better than I am, even though he can't see at all and I still have a few blurry pinholes. Two, maybe three on a good day.

We walk in the door and those pinholes vanish. I mean, I assume the store has some lights on. The other customers are not stumbling around in the dark. But for me, it's like walking into a pitch-black cave.

I listen for the impatient tapping of Nate's cane as he pushes ahead of me. Instead of heading for the farthest aisle like we usually do, he turns suddenly into the unknown middle of the store. The tapping slows down as he runs the tip along the floor, poking at something.

"Think this is it?"

I reach down and feel the edge of an object that is definitely a cardboard box with metal cans of something inside.

"Sure, why not."

We're going to feel awfully stupid if we go through all this just to buy case of pop. Nate picks up the box and we both sort of shuffle together to the front of the store. It's not hard to locate the cash register, chattering away, printing out receipts.

"Can I see some ID," the cashier says tonelessly, not even making it a question. We both pull out our cards and hold them up. At least now we know we're buying some kind of alcohol.

"That'll be $6.99," he says in the same bored voice.

I stand there, not really paying attention. I assume Nate will hand over the money, but I don't hear anything.

"$6.99," the cashier says again, now with a slight edge in his voice.

"C'mon, pay and let's go," Nate adds.

"Me? I didn't bring my wallet."

"What? Didn't—" I can tell Nate is about to say, *Didn't that asshole give you money to buy beer for him?* but he catches himself just in time, before the cashier can guess what's actually going on.

"Didn't you bring money?" I ask, feeling increasingly nervous. I like buying chips here in the afternoon. I don't want to get banned for life.

"All I have is coins," Nate says. He pulls off his backpack and I can hear him rummaging around, then the sound of an avalanche of coins being poured out onto the counter.

"Why are you carrying all that around?"

"Shut up. I was going to take it to that counting machine in the bank but we came here first. I'm not sure it's enough. You don't have anything in your pockets?"

I dig through my pockets. Behind me I can hear several people in line, sighing and shifting around impatiently. I know Nate can hear them too, because he turns to face me and as he does, he knocks some of the coins onto the floor. I hear the tink-tink-tink of pennies hitting linoleum.

"Oh, did I drop something?" Nate says, speaking a lot slower than usual, and I know he did it on purpose, just to mess with the people behind us. If they're going to get impatient, he's going to slow things down even more. He knows they won't yell at a blind guy, even if they really want to.

"Nick? Are you there? Can you give me a hand?" He plays up the fake helplessness outrageously, but of course everyone takes him seriously.

I don't move. There's no way I'm touching that gross floor to search for a few pennies. I'm about to tell him to cut the crap but in the second I hesitate, some other dude pushes in front of me.

"Hey man, no problemo. I got it," says a voice from near the floor. "Here ya go." He has the slow, mellow tone of a pothead. "Lemme help you count it." Now the voice is back at normal standing height.

So Nate, some random hesher, and the cashier meticulously count out $6.99 in coins, including two extra nickels from the floor, plus three dimes and a quarter from my pockets.

The chattering register spits out a receipt. Nate grabs the case and pushes the back of one hand against my elbow. We shuffle slowly out the door, ignoring all the other customers who are surely staring at us.

"Ugh, Michelob Lite! Blech!" It's the first thing Carson says when we get outside.

"What are you talking about?" Nate says loftily, as if he knew what he bought and didn't just grab a case at random. "This is *my* beer. You didn't even give us any money for it, asshole. If you carry it back to the dorm, I might let you have one. *Might.* Unless you don't want any."

"Hey, hey, I didn't say I wouldn't drink it. Fine, I'll carry it."

So that's how Nate and Carson become best friends.

My first week of classes is a disaster. That one tour with the CSD doesn't keep me from getting lost every five minutes.

Monday morning I get up extra early so I know I'll be on time for my first class. But I don't even make it to the dining hall for breakfast. I go down the stairs, but I can't get across the lobby to the cafeteria entrance. There's some kind of barrier that makes a metallic clang when I hit it with my cane. All I can see is a white blur. What the hell is this thing in the middle of the hallway? I'm sure it wasn't here yesterday. I try to walk around it but I can't find the end. I go back in the other direction, same thing.

"Um, excuse me?" I can hear a few people walking nearby. No one answers. "Excuse me?" I say even louder. "How do we get in the dining hall?"

A guy answers. "Dude, just go around to the other entrance."

There's another entrance? Shit! "Where is it?"

"It's right over there," a girl says, sounding annoyed. Right over where? But already their footsteps are getting further away. Now I really feel like an idiot.

I retreat back up to our room.

"That was fast." Nate's brushing his teeth at the tiny sink in the corner.

I tell him what happened.

"Oh yeah, Carson said there's some kind of welcome event in the lobby tonight. They must have set up something for that."

"What the hell, man!" I can't believe I retreated so easily. We've both been excited to come to Calstock, to live on our own for the first time, but the reality is intimidating.

"Come on, let's go get breakfast. I'm sure we can figure out the other entrance. Never give up, right?" Good ol' Nate, at least it's easier with him here. That's how we got through high school. He was always there to push me on when I got discouraged.

We wander around the sprawling maze of the dorm and eventually the smell of bacon and burnt coffee leads us to the dining hall via the scenic route.

"You got this, man," Nate says after I bolt down my breakfast. "No retreat. Show 'em what you can do."

"Thanks. You too."

I'd give him a fist bump or high five or something, but we'd probably fumble around or slap each other by accident, so I just say goodbye.

My first class is Numerical Analysis, which I'm already dreading because I'm not great at math. I walk across campus on the route I've already learned, but end up in the wrong classroom. Luckily before class starts I overhear students around me talking about booking time on the telescope and realize I've wandered into Astronomy 101 by accident. I check the room number and some guy tells me to go two doors down to the left.

At least the guy gives me decent directions. I try what I hope is the correct room.

"Ah, you must be Nick Bauer," a deep voice at the front of the classroom booms as soon as I walk in. "I'm Professor Agarwal. Come, let us review the CSD requirements before I start the class."

Prof Agarwal is on top of things. Apparently there was another blind student a few years ago majoring in computer science, so Prof Agarwal already has the assignments on floppy disks. I'll get them from the CSD then use them on my computer with a screenreader. I can submit homework through the campus intranet.

After that first class, I start to think that I've got a handle on things. But the rest of my classes don't go as smoothly.

The CSD was supposed to contact all my profs in advance and help them prepare accessible materials and other accommodations for me, but their service is, shall we say, spotty at best.

Aside from Prof Agarwal, my other profs sound shocked and annoyed when I tell them what I need: assignments on disks or submitted in advance to the CSD so I can access them with a screenreader, note takers, and a list of textbooks sent to the CSD to order on tape. But when I go to the CSD to pick up my required texts, the bored work study student at the front desk informs me that half the tapes they ordered are delayed for some reason.

The worst is my British literature course. I thought I finished my general education requirements at Onasca but apparently my one semester of world history wasn't good enough for Calstock. I'm forced to pick a humanities class, and British literature seems promising. I like to read, although lately I've been listening to books on tape since reading print has gotten harder.

The first lecture, I sit there doing nothing because the CSD assigned note taker doesn't show up, or if they did, they never identify themself to me. Who does that?

I grow increasingly anxious as Professor Roesman reads through the syllabus. How am I ever going to get through so much reading and writing?

2

———

ABBY

There's this guy. I can't take my eyes off him.

The first day of my Brit lit class, I'm sitting there quietly, looking over the syllabus and thinking about how I'm going to manage all the assigned reading and writing with my rehearsal schedule when there's a clattering along the side of the lecture hall. Somehow I just know what that sound is. A second later, I look up to see a white cane hitting the backs of the fixed chairs and my attention is drawn like a magnet to the guy holding the cane, the most arrestingly, strikingly handsome guy I have ever seen. I mean, most girls might look at him and see an average looking white guy with brown hair and brown eyes, but they would be so, so mistaken. His hair is slightly curly and he has that clean-cut, boyish look that I always go for. But it's not only that.

It's because he's blind.

I watch him walk halfway down the lecture hall then whack his cane against the chair on the end of my row and sit down a few seats away from me. I feel a flush ripple over my entire body, and even while I'm enjoying it, I also feel a stab of resentment for how much I'm reacting to this guy I don't know at all.

Down at the front of the lecture hall, Professor Roesman introduces himself and starts lecturing, but I hardly hear a word. I'm watching this guy, but trying not to be too obvious about it. It's rude to stare, even if the person you're staring at can't look back at you. Maybe even more so in that case. And anyway, I'm pretty sure this guy can see at least a little. His eyes are clear, no scarring, and he sometimes seems to be focusing on things, even though he doesn't take out a notebook and start writing like everyone else, but sits with his hands in his lap, running them over and over his thighs.

Why is he here? It feels like a sign of something, although I'm not sure exactly what. Here I am, trying to get through my senior year, certainly not expecting anything from this lit class I'm taking as an elective, and this hottie sits down practically next to me.

Just let him go, I tell myself. He probably has a girlfriend already. Or a boyfriend, who am I to judge? He doesn't want to be bothered with some random girl in his class. But I already know that I'm going to find a way to talk to him after the lecture. I can't let this opportunity pass me by. There are so few guys I'm attracted to like this.

I'm a devotee.

Hardly anyone even knows what that word means, or that people like me exist. I thought I was the only one until a very kind therapist talked me through it when I was eighteen. I'm attracted to people with disabilities. Blind guys most of all. I'm not a sadist; I don't want to make anyone suffer or watch them struggle, but there's something about a blind guy that is endlessly fascinating and oh so sexy.

Professor Roesman reads through all the assignments for the class, including two essays. The guy at the end of the row gets more agitated listening to this, shifting around in his seat nervously. Where is his note taker? The CSD should have assigned someone to him for each of his classes. That's what Ted had.

No, I can't think about Ted. I try my best to banish all thoughts of him from my mind. Ok, so I will talk to Mr. Sexy sitting almost next to me, but I can't let him know that I'm a devotee, and I absolutely can't ever let him know that my ex-boyfriend is also blind. I'll just say hello to be friendly, then let him go on his way. He probably doesn't want to talk to me at all anyway.

At the end of class, though, he surprises me by getting up and walking down to the front of the lecture hall. By the time I've gathered up all my things and followed him down, he's already in the middle of a conversation with the professor.

"...so the CSD should have contacted you..." I hear him say as I edge toward the lectern, pushing against the tide of other students leaving.

"The what?" Prof Roesman sounds impatient and irritated.

"The Center for Students with Disabilities. They were supposed to send you an email?"

"I never read my email," Roesman declares, as if that's a sign of how important and smart he is. What an asshole. Would it kill him to be even slightly accommodating?

"Ok...well, um...they were supposed to order me the novels on tape but only the ones for the second half of the semester have come in, the ones for the first week aren't here yet. And, uh, I was supposed to have a note taker in class with me but they're not here, I don't know why, and um, I don't know what I should do."

"I don't know, try talking to this 'center' or whatever again." Roesman gathers up his papers and puts them in his bag.

"But I really need this course to graduate."

"None of this is my problem. If you'll excuse me, I see the next class is coming in, so we all have to leave now."

I can't believe Roesman is giving this guy the brush-off. What is he supposed to do? If the prof won't help him, I have to do something. I step forward and put my hand on his arm. He startles slightly.

"Um, excuse me? I can share my notes with you, if you want."

"What?" He turns toward me, frowning in confusion. His eyes swim around and my stomach does a flip-flop.

"I mean, I'm taking this class too and I can help you out if you want. Let's go in the hallway to talk about it. The next class is coming in. Here, take my arm." I push my elbow into his hand and he follows me up the stairs out to the hallway. My heart is hammering wildly. No, I tell myself, this is not flirting. He needs help and I'm in a position to give it. I'm not going to be creepy or expect anything in return.

"This ok?" I ask when we reach the hallway. He shrugs. It's noisy and crowded but there isn't anywhere better nearby. "I can share my notes with you," I say again.

"Sure, thanks." He doesn't sound too enthusiastic.

I plow on anyway. "And you said you're missing the first few books? Do you want me to read them to you?"

"No, it's ok, I couldn't ask you to do that." He slides his eyes around, and now I'm sure he has some vision. Is he trying to see me? I feel all fluttery being so close to him.

"I really don't mind," I insist. "I have to read it myself anyway. And I'm a theater major, so it's good practice for me. I'm Abby, by the way."

"Nick." He sticks out his hand, waiting for me to take it. "Nice to meet you." I give his hand a firm shake, holding just a second longer than usual. Does he feel that little spark too? Maybe, because for the first time he smiles, just the cutest grin. It nearly strikes me dead on the spot. I will never forgive myself if I don't get to know this guy. Isn't that what college is for? I have to shoot my shot.

"Hey, it's almost lunchtime and I'm starving. Wanna go get something to eat?"

"I'm on the dining plan..." I know exactly what he means by this. His parents are paying a shit-ton of money for him to eat every meal in the dorm cafeteria. Eating at a restaurant means effectively paying twice for the same meal.

"Which dorm?"

"Probus Hall."

"Oh, cool! I lived there my first two years but now I'm off campus. Let's eat there! I can pay for a single meal. It'll be fun to go back. I've been missing it." This is a bald-faced lie but only the last part. I really did love living there, even if the food is mediocre. I can't think of any other way to keep this connection going, but Nick goes along with it.

"Ok, sure, if you don't mind." He smiles again and puts his hand out for my arm. "Let's go."

Oh lord, what am I getting myself into?

3

NICK

What is up with this girl?

Abby. Her name is Abby. Her voice is loud and brassy, and her hands are firm, confident. I'm not sure quite how it happens, but before I realize it, I'm crossing campus with my hand on her elbow. It should feel weird, but it doesn't. Is she cute? She sounds cute. All I can see of her is a girl-like shape, kind of short, and what might be a mass of dark hair. Or maybe there's a cloud around her head, who knows. But I like her already.

When most people meet me for the first time, they're nervous and awkward, or try to guide me by pulling my hand or pushing my arm. But Abby knows how to do it right. Talking to her, walking with her, it all feels so easy and natural. She must know some other blind person, I figure, maybe a family member. Like a grandma with cataracts or something.

The weather is warm and sunny as we cross the quad. The trees are still leafy green. It's more late summer than early fall, and the fresh air feels good after the stuffy lecture hall.

"So I'll give my notes to the CSD every week and they give them to you in an accessible format, right?" Abby says as she leads me through the echoing stone archway at the edge of the quad. For a moment I'm in total darkness.

"Yeah, that's right. Thank you."

"But what about the books? The first assignment is to read all of *Moll Flanders* by next week. Come on, let me read it to you. What are you going to do otherwise?"

"But it's going to take a really long time." I don't say, listening to her read aloud will be unbearably slow. Usually when I have an audio book, I listen at three or four times normal speed. Nate goes even faster. Although the idea of spending so much time with Abby is starting to seem not so bad.

"I really don't mind," she insists. "I have to read it myself anyway. And I'm a theater major, so it's good practice for me."

We come out of the archway, and the bright sunlight gives my few remaining pinholes a boost. As we walk down the street towards the dorm, I try to get a better look at her, without moving my head around too obviously. I get a glimpse of a figure dressed all in black, topped with wild brown hair. When we pause at an intersection to wait for the light to turn, she looks back at me. The sun catches her full in the face and I see the flash of a big silver hoop earring, then as she keeps turning her head, the biggest, sweetest smile. A second later, she's turning her head away again as she leads me across the street. I would follow her anywhere just to see more of her face.

I start to get more nervous as we line up outside the dining hall. I really don't want to embarrass myself in front of her by tripping or dropping something. Getting in is easy—go in a straight line, follow the metal rails with the plastic tray and let the attendants serve the hot food, in a little front room. Most of the workers are also students who live in the dorm and know us, so they're pretty chill about telling us what's on the menu. But it's chaos beyond that, in the main dining hall. Chairs and tables with people walking around randomly everywhere, drink dispensers along the wall, and in the middle, a huge buffet of cereal all day, trays of stuff to make sandwiches, and dessert.

It's almost impossible to hold my tray flat with one hand and use the cane with the other, so I usually skip the buffet and settle for whatever I get served on the line, whether I like it or not. Today it's mac and cheese, thank goodness. I shuffle over to the closest table I can find and set my tray down. Luckily it's still early so no one else is sitting there. It wouldn't be the first time I tried to put my tray down on top of someone else's, or almost tripped over someone's feet.

I have no idea where Abby went. She'll have to find me. A few minutes later, she smacks down a tray that sounds heavy, then offers to get me drinks.

"Here," she says when she comes back. "I got you three glasses of water and two glasses of soda." The glasses in the dining hall are notoriously tiny so they can fit between the stacked trays on the dish-washing carts. Everyone gets lots of glasses rather than jumping up every two minutes for more.

"You're not from around here, are you?" I tease her.

"What?"

"It's pop, not soda."

"Pahp, pahp," she says. "Lemme guess, you're in-state?"

"Yeah, from Chesterford Hills."

"Never heard of it."

"It's only two hours from here. Where're you from?"

"New York City."

"No kidding? Is it just like in the movies?" As soon as the words leave my mouth, I'm already regretting them. God, I sound stupid.

"You ever see *The Muppets Take Manhattan?*" she deadpans. "It's exactly like that." Then she gives this throaty, raspy laugh and I laugh too. She tells me more about how she's an only child, grew up in Manhattan, right near Central Park, and she describes her family as a bunch of hyper-intellectual neurotic Jews.

I love her sarcastic, self-deprecating humor. I come from boring nowheresville. New York always seemed like the most amazing place. I've always wanted to go, and I'm stoked to meet someone who's actually from there. Already she seems like the coolest person I've ever met.

We chitchat some more, and somehow I manage to avoid saying anything too stupid again. Guess I got it out of the way early. Abby is easy to talk to. I like how she laughs a lot, and makes me laugh.

Turns out, we're both twenty-one, even though she's a senior and I'm a junior, because I repeated a year of high school. I tell her a little about me being a transfer student, how it's my first year on campus even though I'm a junior.

Abby is going on about the one time she took the train home during winter break instead of a plane and how she'll never make that mistake again when a shadow crosses by our table.

"Hey asshole, why're you eating so early?" It's Carson, with Nate on his arm. They both sit down at our table, and I introduce them.

"Nice to meet you," Abby says, her voice sounding a little strangled.

I feel my heart sink. Everyone always freaks out around me and Nate together. One of us is weird enough but two is beyond comprehension. I was hoping Abby might be different, but no.

In a lame attempt at small talk, I tell Nate about how Abby volunteered to read me *Moll Flanders.*

Nate snorts. "What're you thinking? That's a terrible idea."

"It's only until the CSD gets the tapes in." I surprise myself at my sudden desire to defend Abby's plan.

"No," Nate insists. "Do you have any idea how long it'll take? Don't waste your time."

"What's it to you?" Abby bristles, sounding more like herself. "What do you care if I waste my time?"

Nate ignores her. "Hey man, I'm sorry the CSD screwed you over, but just cut your losses. You don't need this class for your major. Drop it and take something else before you get so far behind you can't catch up."

"It'll be fine," I insist, waving my fork around the plate to make sure I got most of the mac and cheese. "Never give up, right? I don't want to drop just because it will take another week or two for the books to come in."

"Ok, I just don't want you to tank your GPA in your first semester."

I ignore Nate's warning and arrange to meet Abby on Saturday morning to start the novel. Just as soon as I get off the phone with our parents. They're still calling every morning to check in on us. Hearing how anxious I am to end the call, Dad hesitantly suggests that we scale back the calls to once a week.

"Ok, yes! Thanks! Bye!" I hand the phone to Nate and take off downstairs. I don't tell them that my books didn't come in and a girl is going to read to me.

The class isn't until Wednesday but Abby has rehearsals through the week, so we decide to get the reading done over the weekend. When I get to the lobby by the main entrance of Probus Hall, there she is already, a dark fuzzy smudge calling my name.

We find a spot in one of the lounges on the first floor. Actually "lounge" is too fancy a word. It's basically some couches in the hallway by one of the entrances. According to campus lore, back in the 1950s when Probus Hall was built and it was men only, this is where any visiting females had to wait to meet their dates.

The lounge isn't the best spot for reading, with people are coming and going all around us, but I couldn't think of anyplace else. It feels weird to invite someone I hardly know to my dorm room, and anyway Nate is studying there. She can't read out loud in the library. A café is too noisy. So we settle into one of the ledges by the big bow windows facing the street.

She sits down right in the middle of a bright sunbeam, and I can't resist trying to get a look at her.

"What are you doing?"

"Nothing," I say, feeling like I've been caught out.

"You're moving your head all around." She leans back and disappears from the sliver of light.

"Sorry." I try to hold my head still in what I hope is a normal position.

"It's ok, don't be sorry. You have some vision, right?"

"Yeah, a couple spots where things are clearer, but the rest is vague shadows, even in really bright light." I don't mind answering, but she catches me off guard. Sighted people don't often ask me questions like that. They usually assume "blind" means seeing nothing at all.

"I thought I saw you making eye contact, but I wasn't sure. So were you looking at me?"

I feel my cheeks heat up. "Sorry, I didn't mean to be creepy."

"It's not creepy. I didn't mean to make you embarrassed. It's ok, you can look." Her voice is suddenly lower, huskier. She leans forward again so her face is in the sunbeam.

I swing my head around, trying to focus. She's gorgeous, at least what I can see of her. The pinhole is too small to see her whole face at once, but one at a time, I can see big brown eyes with long lashes, full red lips, a silver necklace with a circular pendant, a v neck t-shirt…

I force my gaze back up, fixating on her curly dark hair. I'm never going to be able to get any work done like this.

"Do you have retinitis pigmentosa?" Her words jerk me out of my horny daydreams.

"Um, yeah." How the hell does she know that? I've never met anyone who wasn't a medical professional who's even heard of RP.

"And your brother too?"

"Yeah, it runs in families. We're identical twins, so we both got the same defective gene."

Usually people respond to this information by saying something like *that sucks*, or *how sad*, or *God must have a plan for you* (barf). I'm so glad she doesn't say any of those things.

"But he can't see at all, right?"

"Is it that obvious?"

"I can tell you're sometimes focusing on things but he doesn't do that."

"Yeah, he always says he's more advanced than me."

She laughs at my joke, and it feels so good. I've never had a conversation quite like this with a girl. It's kind of exciting how interested she is in me. I want to ask her how she knows all this, but I can't quite figure out how without being rude. Maybe there's someone in her family who also has RP.

"Ok, sorry I'm wasting time." She disappears out of the sunbeam again. I hear her rustling through her backpack. "We should really get started." She pulls out her copy of the first assigned book and starts reading.

"The Fortunes and Misfortunes of the Famous Moll Flanders, &c. Who was Born in Newgate, and during a Life of continu'd Variety for Threescore Years, besides her Childhood, was Twelve Year a Whore, five times a Wife (whereof once to her own Brother), Twelve Year a Thief, Eight Year a Transported Felon in Virginia, at last grew Rich, liv'd Honest, and dies a Penitent. Written from her own Memorandums..."

"Hey, don't spoil the whole story!"

"That's just the title."

"What!"

"That's the way people wrote back then. The title is like a summary so you know what you have to look forward to. And by that I mean sexy times. That's what you have to look forward to: sexy times, plus a little accidental incest. Do you want me to keep reading or what?"

"Oh, by all means, continue." I settle back in the window seat and listen.

Abby is an amazing reader. I've been listening to speeded up tapes so much I've almost forgotten how nice it is to hear nuance, pauses, inflection, dramatic interpretation. Even with the flowery archaic language, she gets what the words mean and makes the sentences sound like modern speech. Listening to her, I almost feel like I'm watching a movie, seeing the scenes play out in my mind.

And of course, I'm enjoying sitting near her and letting her voice wash over me. Her raspy New York accent makes everything she says sound smart and funny. She tones down her natural accent as she reads, trying to sound a little British, but even so, her voice is like warm honey. I could listen to her forever.

Except I'm kind of getting my wish, because this book is taking literally forever. It's been three hours but we're not even a quarter of the way through. Abby has some things she has to go do, but she promises to come back.

In the late afternoon, we're back in the same window seat again, this time sadly in shadow. She promises to skip over some of the wordy monologs to get to the action and hopefully make it go faster, but our progress is still so slow. We take a break for dinner, and she joins me in the dining hall, where we eat mostly in silence. I'm worried she might lose her voice.

After dinner, it's back to the lounge again. Now her voice is noticeably hoarse, and she's speaking a lot more softly. I keep telling her it's ok to stop, she doesn't have to continue, but she won't quit. And the truth is, I'm still enjoying listening to her. I don't want to stop, even though my back is aching and my butt has fallen asleep. She seems to be enjoying reading, even as her voice dwindles down to a whisper.

"I think I have to take a break for today," she rasps out finally. "Oops, I mean for tomorrow."

"What?"

"It's one AM."

"Shit! I'm sorry! Are you ok?"

"I'm fine," she whispers. "It's been fun."

I'm sure by now that we're almost done with this book, but no, there's still a lot more. Abby is all for going on, but I'm worried she's going to hurt her voice.

In the end, she goes home, we both get some sleep and continue on Sunday afternoon through the evening. All together, I think she reads to me for about fourteen hours in two days.

"Wow." That's all I can say when she closes the book at last. It's a weirdly intense, intimate experience, focusing on nothing but her voice for so long. She's so close I can hear her breath going in and out. She smells amazing too, kind of smoky and musky, like incense, something I can't quite name. I'm longing to touch her, to wrap my arms around her and kiss her. But I can't say any of that, so instead I just say "wow" again.

"Yeah, it's a surprisingly entertaining book for being written almost three hundred years ago," she says. That's not what I meant, but I'm glad she doesn't guess the unseemly thoughts I'm having about her, to use word like what I just spent fourteen hours hearing her read. Her voice is nearly gone. I feel slightly guilty.

"I don't know how I can ever thank you enough," I say.

"Take me out to dinner," she whispers cheekily in her hoarse voice. I hear her putting the book back in her bag.

"What?"

"Come on, don't be so oblivious. If you want to thank me, buy me dinner next weekend."

"Yes, of course! Wherever you want to go. But that doesn't seem nearly enough."

"It's a start." She laughs. "See you in class on Wednesday."

She brushes my arm slightly as she gets up to leave, and I wave goodbye. Did she touch me on purpose? I mean, she did just ask me out, but there's always that bit of doubt. Is she serious or what? I really hope she's serious.

And as much as I enjoy listening to her read, I realize with a sinking heart that Nate is right. There's no way we can do this a second time, let alone every week for half the semester. I've got to figure something out, because there's no way I'm dropping this class now.

4

ABBY

I get back late on Sunday night to find the house mercifully silent, dark and empty. Reading to Nick was beyond intense. I had to keep reminding myself to look back down at the page before I lost my place. Watching his expressions come and go, seeing him listen to my voice, was even more of a turn-on that I could have imagined. The excitement of being near him helped me power through, but oh man was that book long. Now I'm utterly used up. I got nothing left in me.

My two housemates must still be at rehearsal. We're all theater majors, and being in a play is required every semester.

As soon as I walk in, I see the light blinking on the answering machine in the front hall. Three messages. I press play.

The first two messages are from my housemate Jennifer. We're in the same production of *The Crucible*. She asks when I'm coming, then tells me the director is asking why I'm not there.

I didn't tell Nick, but I skipped rehearsal to read to him. I didn't want him to worry, or think it was weird that I wanted to spend so much time with him. Also, and this is the honest truth, I severely underestimated how long it would take me to read that book. But really, it's no big deal. My part in the play is the most nothing role. My character doesn't even have a name. I'm just one of the "afflicted girls," third from the left.

Despite Jen's messages, skipping this weekend is no biggie. What are they going to do, throw me out? It's a student production. The director is required to cast us. And believe me, if I could get out of this stupid play, I would. The prof let the students decide on everything about the staging and whatnot, so to be edgy they decided to make all the girls skater punks. I get what they're going for, but nothing else in the script is changed. It feels stupid to be holding a skateboard and saying "Goody so-and-so." We've only had a few rehearsals so far, but already I hate this production. Also Jen is cast as Abigail. Not that I'm bitter about that or anything.

Anyway, my rehearsal schedule is only going to get more crazy as the semester goes on. If I'm going to skip any, it might as well be early on. And there's no way I was going to say no to reading to Nick. My back is killing me from sitting in that window seat and I think I've almost completely lost my voice, but damn, it was worth it.

I get a warm flush thinking of Nick. That intent expression on his face, the way he turned his ear ever so slightly toward me to listen, his lips slightly apart. I wonder what it would feel like to kiss him.

I erase Jen's messages and go on to the third one.

It's from Ted. My heart sinks when I hear his voice.

"Hey Abs." I hate when he calls me that. Why not say Abby like everyone else, is that so hard?

"Sooooo," he continues, "I'll be blowing through Allenville tomorrow on my way to Iowa City and I thought we could meet up. I mean, if you don't still want to perforate my liver with a steak knife. Also, you have my tape recorder and I'd like it back. I'm going to need it while I work on my MFA. I'll call again when we get to town to set up a time to meet, ok?"

"No it's not fucking ok!" I shout at the machine as it beeps at the end of the message. "Ted, you asshole!" I jam my finger on the erase button.

Upstairs in my bedroom, I throw my backpack on the bed. Mood officially ruined.

Why can't people disappear after a breakup? Especially when it's the person who dumped you. Despite his overly dramatic phrasing, I don't wish Ted lasting physical harm. I just wish he would vanish from the same plane of existence as me, and go live in a different one.

Every word of that message fills me with rage. "I'm" coming to Allenville when actually he means "we." His parents are driving him. I don't judge him for that. He's blind, of course his parents are driving, but there's no way in hell I'm going to meet him for the first time after the breakup with his parents in tow.

And of course he doesn't really want to meet me. He only wants that recorder back. But even though he called it "his" actually it's on loan from the National Library for the Blind. It's a special kind of tape recorder for making transcriptions of print materials, with more precise back and forward controls than most tape decks. I borrowed it from him when we were dating and I offered to record a book on astrology for him. I got about halfway through and quit, because it was so boring. He never listened to it.

I know for a fact that he has at least one more recorder exactly like it, and can easily order more from the NLB. He's looking for an excuse to remind me that he has already graduated and been accepted to grad school at Iowa State. In the answering machine message he took that word "MFA" for a walk, drawing out each letter.

I lie on my back in my bed, staring up at the blank white ceiling as the past two years with Ted flash before my eyes. He was a creative writing major, one year ahead of me. I fell hard for him. He seemed so cool and intelligent, confident despite his disability. I thought we would be together forever. He would write plays and I would act in them. We were perfect for each other, I thought.

Being with him was such a thrill to my little devotee heart. I wanted everyone to know I had a blind boyfriend. Walking around town with him on my arm, seeing people staring at us, I was in heaven. I wanted to shout, "That's right, I'm with him! This guy has a hot girlfriend!"

Then he dumped me because I'm a devotee. Not right away, but after I told him, things were never the same. At first he said it was ok with him, but gradually he kept making these little digs, saying things like I only loved him because he's blind. Refusing my help with anything. Assuming that anything we did together was playing into my "weird fetish." I realized that what I had taken for confidence was actually fronting and ego tripping. And not only about the devotee thing. He kept talking about how he was older and wiser than me, did better in his classes, had a more creative mind.

"Anyone can read words on a page," he used to say. "It takes a *real* artist to write those words."

After he got accepted to Iowa, it was so much worse.

"I'm going to write the Great American Novel, the first one by a blind person," he said. "But I'm not going to let you read it. You'd be reading it for the wrong reasons."

I wish I'd said something or yelled at him or stormed out when he said that. But I was so shocked, I just went home quietly and cried. Then right before graduation, he dumped me and I never got the satisfaction of telling him off.

So no, I'm not going to rearrange my day for him. I'm going to mail that recorder back to NLB. Ted can kiss my undergraduate ass. He can go off to his Mother Fucking Artist program without meeting me on the way, and I never want to speak to him again.

I roll over and stare out the window, looking at the green leaves of the trees. In a few weeks, they'll all turn red and fall.

I wonder if I hadn't met Nick, if I would have had the courage to say no to Ted.

Maybe not.

Fucking Nick, man. He shows up in my class with his hotness as if it's nothing. When I met his brother, I thought I was going to fall down dead right there. If anything, Nate is even more handsome, with his wavy brown hair and eyes that wander around and never focus on anything.

But I could tell from the minute he opened his mouth that he's another Ted. Huge ego to make up for the shitty, infantilizing way people treat him. I'm staying far away from him. Nick isn't like that. He's sweet, easy-going.

But no. I'm not getting involved with either of them. If they knew the truth about me, they would hate me, just like Ted did. I never want to hear again that I'm only interested in a guy because of his disability.

And also, every single person I know, from my friends and house-mate to my thesis advisor to my parents know about Ted. What will they say when I show up with blind guy number two?

No, there's no way I can be with Nick. I'll enjoy being friends with him, but it can't go any further.

5

NICK

On Monday we're eating lunch in the dining hall, Nate sitting across from me and Carson sitting next to him. Getting to the table with all three of us was kind of a disaster because Carson offered to help us with cereal at the self-serve station and it got all over the floor but anyway.

Out of nowhere, Carson says around a mouthful of sugar cereal, "You know I'm Chinese, right?"

"Duh," Nate says in his usual sarcastic tone.

Carson's silent for a minute, then asks, "Ok, but how do you know?"

"I can tell by the way your elbow feels," Nate says without missing a beat.

"Really?"

"Oh yeah, totally, Chinese elbow for sure."

Nate and I have a kind of running joke between us about how stupid sighted people like to imagine that we don't "see" race. As if your ethnic identity is nothing more than a few superficial features and not, you know, an actual culture. It's freaking insulting, and not only to us.

"He's joking. We heard you talking to your parents on the phone in Chinese," I say hurriedly, worried that Carson might be taking Nate's nonsense seriously.

"I think the entire dorm heard you talking on the phone," Nate adds.

"You have to shout when you speak Chinese! There are four billion of us."

"But you grew up here, right?" I say, trying to make polite conversation. He has a pretty standard Midwest accent like we do.

"Yeah, my parents are from Taiwan but I was born here. Grew up in Anterfax. What about you?"

"Ah, the usual boring white bread mix. From Chesterford Hills."

These are both small towns a few hours away, neither one with any distinguishing features to speak of.

Carson munches on his cereal.

"So..." he drawls after a while. "The Burr Oak Theater is playing *Rocky Horror Picture Show* on Sunday night. Wanna go?"

When neither of us answers immediately, Carson hurriedly adds, "I mean, if you watch movies...?"

"Of course we watch movies," Nate says scornfully. "I watched TV with you last night, dumbass." Carson is one of the lucky few with a single dorm room, no roommates, so no one to complain if he watches TV or plays video games.

"Oh, right."

"Sorry," I say. "I already have plans."

"Gotta hot date?"

"He's going out with that Abby chick," Nate says before I can answer.

"Oh hey, good for you man. She's hot."

"Really?" I mean, I think so already but it's nice to have confirmation from someone with more than 10% vision. I can't stop thinking about Abby.

On Wednesday, I go to class as if I didn't make one of my classmates spend two solid days reading to me just to get the bare minimum of work done. Even though I still think Professor Roesman is kind of a pompous asshole, I like the way he makes connections and gets us thinking about the book in new ways. I even put my hand up and answer a question about how Moll finds her perfect match in a man who's as much a criminal as she is. Abby has to poke me in the ribs to let me know he's pointing at me, but I'm still proud of myself for speaking up.

"Nice," she whispers to me, after Professor Roesman says I got the right answer. Her breath tickles my neck as she leans toward me. She smells amazing, a kind of rich, musky scent I can't quite place, maybe sandalwood. I take a deep breath.

This class has become the highlight of my week. I just have to figure out a way to get the readings.

The next day, I march into the CSD office with an angry speech prepared and vague threats about suing under the Americans with Disabilities Act if they don't get my books for me. But before I can even get one word out, the student worker at the front desk says, "You're Nick Bauer, right? Just a minute," then walks off.

I'm still fuming but a minute later he comes back and shoves a giant cardboard box in my hands, containing tapes with complete audio transcriptions of all the assigned novels. I'm so stunned I nearly drop it all.

Holding the box in one hand and my cane in the other is no easy feat but I'm so relieved I don't even care. I walk very slowly and carefully back to the dorm.

"I can't believe it all came in so fast," I say to Nate and Carson over dinner. Meatloaf, ugh. "They told me it would be like six weeks at the soonest."

"Yeah, well, I went there last week and yelled at them," Nate says.

"Wow, thanks man!" Of course Nate has my back. It was the same when we were kids. He's the one who fought Knob Park High School to get us on the wrestling team when the principal tried to say we were a liability.

"Come on, dude. It's obvious you have a thing for that girl. I knew you would never drop that class. I couldn't stand by and let you get an F in your first semester because you're thinking with your dick."

"Yeah, you should have heard him," Carson chimes in. "He was all, 'You're failing in your responsibility to provide barrier-free education' and 'I'm going to the school newspaper with this story.' It was impressive."

And here I thought I was being a bit more smooth about Abby. But wait, Carson was there too?

Anyway Nate does go to the school newspaper with the story, even though the CSD came through with my tapes. I don't know how, but he finds out that this sophomore girl named Cricket who lives down the hall writes for the paper. He tells her about what happened, and she interviews me and a few other students who use the CSD.

Well, "interview" is kind of a fancy word for what actually happens, which is that she drops by our dorm room unannounced Thursday afternoon, asks me a bunch of questions, then leaves. On Friday there's a big article on the front page of the student paper with the headline, "Is the CSD Doing Enough to Help Disabled Students?"

"Dude, you guys are famous!" Carson says excitedly, waving the paper over our lunch trays as we sit down together in the dining hall. Sloppy joes today, blech.

"Whatever." Doesn't he get that we're already famous? I doubt there's anyone on campus who hasn't noticed the two identical blind guys. I can hear people whispering as we walk down the street or through the dorm hallways. The crowd always parts like the Red Sea, bodies moving away from us, saying things like, "Oh, it's those guys again."

"It should be 'Students with Disabilities,' not 'Disabled Students,'" Nate says. "People-first language."

"What? Where did you get that?" I ask. He never talked like this before.

"I'm taking that sociology class, remember?" he says. I don't remember, but before he can elaborate, someone pulls out the empty chair next to me.

"What do you think of the article?" It's Cricket, plunking her tray on the table and sitting down.

"I wouldn't know. The paper isn't published in an accessible format," Nate snaps back.

She gives an audible gasp. "Oh! Oh no! I never even thought of that! I'll definitely bring it up at the next editorial meeting."

With many more apologies, she reads the article out loud to us around bites of salad. It's ok, I guess. I mean, it was nice of her to write about the CSD which I'm sure no one else on campus cares about. But I wish she didn't make me and Nate sound so pathetic. Things like, "Nicolas and Nathaniel Bauer were like any other boys until age fourteen, when tragedy struck." That's not what happened at all. Our eyesight was always pretty bad, and our grandfather had RP too so it wasn't like a sudden shock. I don't like to think of my life as tragic, but I can't bring myself to criticize Cricket with her sitting right next to me.

Besides, I think she's kind of cute. I get a sudden flash of long blonde hair as she flips it over her shoulder. She has this intense way of talking, like she's so excited to share her ideas, and it makes me want to listen to her.

But Nate doesn't give a shit about that, and as soon as she finishes reading, he starts lecturing her about ableism and people-first language, which I swear to God are words I have never heard pass his lips before this very day.

Cricket goes very quiet, all her manic energy suddenly drained out. "I see. I mean, I uh, I understand," she says in a strangled voice. "Thank you for the feedback. I really appreciate it." I hear the scrape of her tray on the table and her chair pushing back, then she's gone.

"Dude, I think you made her cry!" Carson says, laughing. "Why are you such an asshole?"

6

ABBY

I meet Nick for dinner on Sunday night, but it's not a date, ok? I'm just letting him pay me back for reading to him. Sunday is the only choice, since it's the one night a week that the dining hall is closed and everyone living in Probus Hall has to find their own food.

Nick is waiting for me on the steps outside the dorm's main entrance, standing there holding his white cane, bathed in the golden light of the setting sun, with the green leafy trees beside him. I slow down as I approach, taking it all in. God, he's gorgeous. He must've gotten a haircut. His brown hair is neat and smooth on the sides, and just long enough on top to curl. The shorter hair makes his brown eyes look even bigger. His eyes kind of wander back and forth and I wonder if there's enough daylight for him to see anything.

I'm only a few feet away but he doesn't notice me, so maybe not? If I don't say something, he won't know I'm here. But of course I'd never do that.

"Hey Nick, it's Abby," I call out as I trot up the steps. "How ya doin'?"

Almost in slow motion, he turns toward my voice and a huge grin lifts his face. That flash of straight white teeth gets me right in the chest.

"Hungry." His smile turns slightly wolfish.

"Ok then, let's go!"

He reaches out with the hand that isn't holding his cane, and I shove my elbow into it.

"I want to go to Langar," I say as we walk across campus. "It's my favorite restaurant. You don't mind vegetarian, do you?"

"Sure, sounds good." I glance back and see he's still smiling but now in a more nervous, fake kind of way. I wonder if he knows how transparent all his expressions are. It's one of the things I like best about him, how all his emotions are always plain to see.

"It's ok if you'd rather have meat."

"Nah, it's fine! I can't think of even one time that I haven't had meat for dinner. Why not try something new? That's what college is for, right?"

I lead him up the wooden stairs to the restaurant. It's crowded because the dining halls are closed. I hope the long wait doesn't make him regret his choice. I really do like this place.

"What's seitan?" he asks, once we finally get a booth and I read the menu to him.

"I dunno, it's a kind of fake meat."

"Why would you want to eat fake meat when real meat is cheap and plentiful?"

I laugh. "Don't ask me! Look, just get the curry. It's what I always order."

When the curry arrives, Nick wolfs it down.

"Wow, this is amazing!" He gives the cutest grin of pure delight. "I dunno if it's from weeks of nothing but bland cafeteria food, but this is seriously delicious."

As we're eating, I tell him about my stupid lame play.

"Can I come to the performance?" There's that grin again. Damn.

"Sure, but did you miss the part where I said it's going to be terrible?"

Nick scoffs, and for a second I feel like he's making eye contact with me. "I read *The Crucible* in English class in high school. It'll be fun to see it actually performed."

I promise to give him a ticket when I see him in class next week, but I don't expect him to actually show up. Surely he has better things to do, like organizing his sock drawer, or listening to paint dry.

I don't want to be talking about any of this. I want to know more about him. For a second I get a flashback of Ted telling me that I'm interested in him for the wrong reasons, but just as quickly, I shove that down the memory hole.

Nick is almost done with his curry. This is my only chance to ask him about himself. I'll never forgive myself if I chicken out. I wait for the conversation to peter out, then before he can change the subject to something else, I blurt out, "So you used to be able to see more, right?"

Nick pauses before he answers, the spoon halfway to his mouth. Oh no, was that too personal?

"Sorry, you don't have to answer if you don't want to," I add hastily.

He resumes eating, looking thoughtful.

"How do you know that?" he asks.

"I read that article about you in the student paper."

"Oh, that."

"Yeah, that. It pissed me off so much! Such ableist bullshit. If I ever meet the author, I'm going to tell her a thing or two."

"Cricket's not so bad."

"Oh, you know her?"

"Yeah, she lives on our hall."

"But that's even worse! If she knows you guys, she should know better than to write about you as if your lives are so tragic."

"I guess so," he mutters, twirling his spoon around his now mostly empty bowl. I watch him feel around the bowl with the spoon, searching for any curry he might have missed. Why is he defending this girl?

I change the subject back to what I'm really interested in. "Ok, but you used to see more, right? Do you still picture things in your mind?"

He twirls his empty spoon, looking thoughtful.

"Yeah, I do. Actually it's kind of an argument between me and Nate. He doesn't and he says that it's better not to. He's always trying to convince me to go what he calls 'deep blind.'"

"What's that?"

"I think he means not only not relying so much on my tiny bit of vision but also not thinking in terms of visual memory."

At this moment, the server stops by our table to ask if we want anything more or if we're finished, except instead of addressing both of us like she normally would, she only talks to me.

"Nothing for me, thanks," I say, but she doesn't take the hint.

"Does he want anything?" She looks only at me, not even glancing at Nick.

"Hey!" he says angrily, sitting up straighter. "I'm right here!"

The server, a very young-looking blonde girl who I bet is a freshman working part-time, gapes at him but doesn't say anything.

"And yes, I want some dessert!" Nick blusters on, not waiting for her to figure out how to apologize. "What do you have?"

The server mumbles that the only dessert they have is a carob tarte, and Nick orders a slice, before I can warn him that carob is not actually an acceptable substitute for chocolate, and that tarte is going to taste terrible. I order a coffee to keep him company.

"I'm sorry she was rude to you," I say as the server leaves with our orders. "Does that happen a lot?"

He shrugs and leans back in the booth. "Sometimes. She must have seen me come in with the white cane and all. Not everyone notices."

"When did you start using it?"

"Nate started at thirteen. I was fifteen. Then when we were sixteen we did a whole residential training program and missed so much school we had to repeat our junior year."

"Ah, that sucks. Was the program good?"

"I dunno, I guess we learned a lot but it was weird. All these blind kids in a dorm together hooking up."

"No way! Really?" My voice comes out as a kind of squeak. "Did you get lucky?"

He doesn't answer, but from the way he kind of freezes up and goes red, it's obvious the answer is yes.

"Never mind! Scratch that! Forget I asked!" Man, after tonight he's never going to want to speak to me again. I can just imagine him going back to the dorm and telling his brother what a pushy weirdo I am.

The server comes back silently with our dessert and Nick takes a bite then turns his mouth down.

"Is it supposed to taste like that?"

I try a bite. "Yeah, sorry, I was going to warn you that desserts are not their strong suit here."

"It's ok, at least I tried something new. And that curry was delicious."

I flag down the server . As we're both pulling out cash to split the bill, I glance at my watch. Shit! Late already.

"I really want to stay longer, but actually I'm supposed to be at a rehearsal right now."

"Wait, what? Why did you agree to dinner?"

I shrug into my coat. "Sunday night is the only time you can eat out, right?"

He takes my arm and I lead him around the tables then outside and down the wooden steps. We walk halfway across campus together, until we're near the theater.

"I'm really sorry. My rehearsal schedule for the next month is crazy. But we can do this again after the show."

"Ok, yeah."

"I'll see you in class."

I turn and run down the hall to the green room, hoping I won't be yelled at for being late. That look on Nick's face just now almost killed me. If I had stayed a second longer, he would have leaned forward and tried to kiss me, I'm sure.

Only because he doesn't really know you, a little voice that sounds like Ted whispers in my ear. So no, I can't kiss him, no matter how much I want to. Anyway I'm not lying, I really don't have any free time until after the play is finished.

I dump my bag and coat in a corner and try to put Nick out of my mind.

7

NICK

I can't stop thinking about Abby. Does she like me or not? Every week in class I spend more time listening to the scratch of Abby's pen on the notebook than to the professor. I thought our dinner at Langar was a date, until she ran off at the end. If I could see better, I would have kissed her where we stood out in the middle of the quad. Instead I hesitated because I didn't want to crash into her by accident, and a second later she was going to rehearsal. What if she's only being polite? Maybe I need to take the hint already and move on.

The weather turns colder. Walking across campus to class, I hear the crunching and skittering of fallen leaves all around me. I draw in lungsful of dry, clear autumn air, thinking of the flash of her smile, that throaty laugh, even though I also have to concentrate on not wandering off the sidewalk or getting run over or crashing into a street sign.

Mondays I have Numerical Analysis with Professor Agarwal. He's the one who had another blind student a few years ago, so he's been the most organized about getting my assignments to me through the CSD. He even lets me submit my homework electronically through the university intranet. It's one advantage to being a computer science major. I'm sure Professor Roesman doesn't even know what the intranet is.

The math is kicking my butt but I don't mind. At least it's because the material is intellectually challenging, not because I can't see well. In our junior year of high school, a teacher threatened to fail me and Nate in biology because we couldn't dissect a gross frog and make a drawing of its insides. I got detention for saying a swear word to the teacher, but Nate went to the principal and our parents got involved, then the next thing I knew we were transferred to a different class. That was the worst, but there were lots of other times where teachers acted like I was personally insulting them when I asked for accommodations.

But not Professor Agarwal. He even checks up on me after each class to make sure I'm keeping up. It makes me want to try even harder. Show him I can do it.

The air outside is cold as I walk across the quad. Damn, I really need to get some gloves. My right hand on my cane is freezing, but I don't want to switch hands because it throws off my sense of direction.

When I get back to our dorm room, Nate is in Carson's room playing video games. Carson must have left his door open. I can hear them trash-talking each other.

Everyone on our hall is curious about how Nate plays video games. It's not a big mystery, he just listens for the sounds and memorizes what they mean. We have a Super Nintendo at home and I used to play against him sometimes but we left it behind because we thought we'd be studying all the time. But it turns out Carson has the same system. I hear the two of them playing *Street Fighter II* and *Legend of Zelda* every day.

"Nick!" Carson calls out to me as I pass his doorway. Nate asks if I want a turn, but I say no.

"Dude, what's wrong with you?" Carson asks. His voice is distorted, probably because he's still working the controller. Electronic punching sounds fill the room.

"Nothing." I slump against the doorframe.

"He's still pining for that Abby chick," Nate says.

"Still?" Carson sounds incredulous. "Dude, if you haven't hooked up yet, you gotta move on. We're going to a party on Friday. You have to come with us."

"Is it a frat party?"

"Of course it's a frat party," Nate scoffs, as if there isn't any other kind.

I haven't been to any parties yet but walking across campus on a Friday or Saturday night, the noise coming from fraternity row is unmistakable, and the freshmen and sophomores living in the dorm brag about which houses have the most messed-up parties that they went to. It all sounds kind of gross.

But maybe Carson is right, so I agree to go.

"What are we supposed to wear?" I ask Nate on Friday night. Before he can answer, Carson bangs the heavy door to our room open.

"Frat parrr-TAAAAY! Let's GO!"

"Nick wants to know if we look ok," Nate says, hopping down from the top bunk.

"You look like a couple of faggots," Carson replies without missing a beat.

"Hey, don't use that word," I mumble.

"Oh sorry," Carson says in a mocking tone. "You look like a pair of identical homosexuals. You're wearing the exact same clothes."

"We are?" we both say in surprise at the same time.

"Ugh, don't talk at the same time, it's creepy." Carson rummages around in our closet and makes Nate change but I guess I look ok because he doesn't say anything more about me. Whatever. I try to wear plain colors that can't be mismatched. I don't want to use Braille tags on my clothes because they're stiff and bulky, and it's too much work to keep track of. And I don't want to have to ask someone else to put the tags back on every time I do laundry.

I pull on a jacket, grab my cane, and we all head out the door together.

The frat house is down the street from the dorm, only about four blocks away. I can hear it before I'm close enough to make out the blurry glow of the front porch lights. They're blasting Beastie Boys to the whole neighborhood, with an undertone of loud chattering voices, as everyone shouts at each other to be heard over the music.

Carson leads us up the front steps and pushes through the crowd. We go into one big room then another. I try not to think about how everyone must be staring at us, going caravan style, as usual. Are there cute girls here? Are they staring at me? There's really only one girl I want to be with, and she's not here.

Finally we get to the room where the beer is.

"Keg stand!" Carson shouts over the noise.

"Hell no," Nate shouts back at him.

I'm jostled on all sides by the crowd, and the lights are so dim I can't make out anything beyond a few unhelpful shadows. Nate detaches his elbow from my grip and disappears. Carson shoves a plastic Solo cup in my hand then he also vanishes.

Not knowing what else to do, I chug the beer.

"Hey!" A girl shouts in my ear, making me jump. "Hi!" She puts her hand on my arm.

I smile in the direction of her voice. "Hi!"

"Wanna dance?"

"Ok, but I have to warn you, I'm not a very good dancer." I hold up my cane meaningfully, in case she hasn't noticed it yet.

"Whoa, no way! Are you really blind?" Good thing I mentioned it, then. She sounds pretty drunk.

"Yeah, I really am."

"You sure? You don't look blind."

Argh, this again. I'm not nearly drunk enough to put up with this bullshit. There's nothing wrong with the front part of my eyes, the part that other people see. The damage to my retinas is invisible from the outside. A lot of people think it's their business to tell me I don't look disabled enough to be for real, or that I must be faking.

Normally I try to laugh it off, even though it's fucking annoying. But I'm pissed at Nate and Carson for abandoning me, and irritated that I can't get my bearings in the crowd. I've got nothing left over to be polite to this random chick.

"Yeah, I'm really fucking blind!" I shout, rattling my cane again.

"You don't have to be rude! Sheesh! Some people! I was just trying to be nice." She flounces off.

I drain the rest of my cup, still stuck awkwardly in the same spot, but at that moment, some drunk frat dude sees that my cup is empty and refills it for me, with a sloppy one-armed hug like we're best friends. We chug it together, and he gets me another, then drags me into one of the front rooms where everyone is dancing.

The drinks finally start to hit me, and I flail around for a while, pretending to dance. I'm starting to think maybe this isn't so bad after all, when some other drunk dude plows right into me from the side and we both crash to the floor.

"Sorry, man!" He's laughing so hard he can barely stand, but he helps me up, apologizing over and over.

I tell him it's ok, it was an accident, but now I'm covered in beer and my left hip is sore from where I landed on it. I don't feel like pretending to dance anymore. As an extra gesture of apology, the idiot who knocked me over presses another plastic cup into my hand, and I drain it without thinking.

I sway on my feet, the beer hitting me hard now. I realize with sudden clarity that what I want to do more than anything else is take a piss. This poses a major problem because I have no idea where I am, or where the bathroom is.

I'm now too drunk to care what people might think of me, so I start grabbing at random around me, asking for directions.

"Over there," they all say.

I get fed up after the third person does this. "Hey, I can't see! Can you say it in words instead of pointing?"

But instead of helping, the girl gets huffy with me for criticizing her. "I said, it's right there! Sheesh!"

Finally, some dude drags me by the hand through more crowded rooms, then stops suddenly in what I guess is a hallway.

"Here's the line," he shouts in my ear, then disappears.

I have to endure some of the world's most boring small talk with the dude ahead of me in line, but at least I know when it's my turn. Now here is the real problem, because there's no way in hell I'm putting my hands on anything in this bathroom, which already reeks. I swing my cane around until I find the toilet, and aim as best I can, which is challenging under the best circumstances, even more so when the room seems to be ever so slightly spinning. Whatever. I'm sure I'm not the first one to miss the target tonight, and I won't be the last.

I wash my hands then stagger out of the bathroom. The noise and crowd make it impossible to get my bearings, and I don't feel like talking to anyone here, much less flirting. And from what I can tell from randomly bumping into people or overhearing shouted voices, the ratio of guys to girls is like ten to one.

I decide it's time to go home, but where the hell is Nate? I guess I could find my way back on my own, but I wouldn't leave without telling him. And Nate wouldn't leave me here, right? Before coming to Calstock State, I would have said of course not, but now I'm not so sure. I feel a tiny bit of distance opening up between us, like I'm no longer entirely sure what he's thinking. It doesn't feel good.

I should find Nate, but how? Grab strangers again and ask, *Have you seen another blind guy who looks exactly like me? Can you lead me to him?* I'll get laughed around the block.

The only thing I can think to do is to edge slowly to the side of the main room where people are dancing. I find a wall and lean awkwardly against it, wondering if I'm going to have to spend the rest of my life here.

"Hey, asshole!" Beefy fingers poke me painfully in the shoulder. "What the hell you looking at?"

I put my hands up in surrender. "Nothing, dude! I'm blind, man. I swear, I'm not looking at anything."

"What?" For a second, the frat boy leans back in surprise, but then he's up in my face again. "Bullshit! Don't fucking lie to me. I saw you staring at my girl."

He sounds super drunk, but then again, so am I. I've had it with this party.

"Get your hands off me." I slap away the fingers still poking my shoulder aggressively.

"Fuck you!" A sudden smack on the side of my head makes me stagger. "Stay away from my girl!"

"No, fuck you!" I shout. "No one's looking at your ugly ass girl!" I'm about to take a swing at him when someone grabs my arm.

"NICK!" A beery voice shouts in my ear.

"Fuck you, Carson! Where the hell have you been!"

"What's going on?" Nate must be right next to Carson.

"Holy shit, there's two of them!"

"Ok, let's go. Time to leave!" Carson puts a heavy arm around my shoulders, pulling me away.

"Where do you think you're going?" Frat boy lunges at me again, even though Carson is trying to pull us apart.

"Hey, Mike!" Another frat boy comes between us. "Dude, what's wrong with you? Don't hit a blind guy, man."

"He isn't blind! Look at him!"

"Yeah, they both are. I've seen 'em all over campus."

Embarrassing him like this doesn't calm him down, just the opposite.

"Blind asshole! I didn't know Calstock was letting in retards!"

I lunge at him again, but Carson pulls me back. He's surprisingly strong.

"We're leaving." Carson puts an arm around each of our shoulders, mine and Nate's.

He drags us through the crowd and out the front door like some three-headed monster.

The cold air and quiet of the outside hit me in the face. It's awkward with Carson in the middle still gripping each of us around the shoulders because he's a few inches shorter than we are, but he keeps his grip on us like a vice. His arm is muscular and heavy.

"Nick, what the fuck were you thinking?" Nate says as we stumble up the street towards the dorm.

"What're you talking about? You heard what he said."

"Oh, so you were going to strike a blow for inclusion by getting punched in the face?"

"Dude, you ruined a perfectly good party," Carson complains.

"That party sucked! All those smug assholes and their shitty attitudes. I'm sick of it."

We've reached the dorm. Carson leads us to the closest stairwell, but someone must have puked there, because the smell is overpowering. We quickly turn back and head to the opposite end of the dorm to a clean stairway.

Later, as we're lying in bed in the dark, Nate says, "I know it's rough. I hate hearing that shit too. But getting in a fight isn't going to solve anything."

I roll over angrily and curl up into a ball. "Fuck all of them. I just want to be included."

"Yeah, me too. But not with those assholes."

"I know! But why does everything have to be so fucking hard?"

"Because we're tougher than all of them. Don't forget that."

Saturday morning, all three of us wake up feeling like shit, but Nate and Carson drink a ton of orange juice at breakfast and seem to recover, while I feel worse and worse as the day goes on. By the evening, it's clear this is more than a hangover.

I have a cold.

I wake up Monday morning with my throat on fire and my eyes glued shut. I feel like the whole front of my face has been filled with cement, from my nose to my ears. I stagger down the hall to the bathroom, feeling even more disoriented than usual. At least the lights in the bathroom are bright enough that I can figure out where things are. I stand under a blasting hot shower for a good half hour, and return to my room feeling sufficiently recovered to take on the day.

"What are you doing," Nate says flatly as I rattle around in our shared closet.

"What do you think I'm doing? I'm getting dressed. I have a class at ten."

Nate snorts loudly. He's sitting at his desk for once, rather than lounging on the top bunk. "Dude, you're sick. Take a few days off."

"I'm fine. It's nothing." I pop an antihistamine and head off to Numerical Analysis.

But as usual, Nate is right. I should have rested. By the time I get back from class I feel like utter shit. I spend all of Tuesday lying in bed in a drugged-up haze.

The next day I'm still not feeling any better, and now I have a problem because my lit class with Abby is on Wednesdays. A part of me wants to sleep in. But an even bigger part of me wants to hear her voice. In my weakened state, I can't resist her any longer.

I dial her number from memory, then stretch the cord across the room to lie in bed. I listen to the ringing at her end.

"Hello?"

"Hey, it's Nick. So, um, I seem to have a cold or something. I won't be in class today."

"No problem. I'll submit my notes to the CSD and I'll see you in class next week."

"All right. Thanks. I appreciate it."

"Get some rest, ok?"

"Thanks." I pause, gathering up my courage. "Then maybe next week we could go to dinner again?"

But it's too late. I hear the click as she disconnects. She didn't hear me. I drop my head back against the pillow. Idiot! Why did I hesitate? I don't even have it in me to get up and put the receiver back. I vaguely hear the silence replaced by the pinging tone of a busy signal, but under the influence of weapons-grade cold medicine, I drop off to sleep without even realizing it.

The next thing I know, I'm woken up by Nate shouting.

"Nick! What the fuck!"

I jerk upright as the phone is ripped out of my hand. Nate is still crashing around and cursing. I stumble blearily out of bed with my hands extended, feeling around until I collide with Nate. He's gotten his cane wrapped up in the phone cord. The receiver is right next to the door, so when I stretched the cord to lie in bed, I effectively clotheslined him as he came in.

It takes us way longer than it should to get the cord untangled and the phone put back. In my defense, I'm still drugged up and disoriented from sleeping in the middle of the day.

"Dude, I get that you're not feeling good, but you're driving me crazy," Nate says, once the phone is finally put away neatly. "Just ask her out already."

"How do you know I was talking to Abby?"

"Who else do you talk to on the phone?" I hear his wristwatch saying the time, six o'clock. How long was I asleep?

"Come on, it's dinner time," Nate says.

"No, I'm not hungry. Go without me."

"Don't be dumb. You need to eat."

The last thing I feel like doing right now is wandering around the dining hall like an idiot, but Nate insists, so I give in and follow him downstairs. As we're waiting in line to go in, we run into Cricket.

Or more accurately, Cricket is ahead of us in line and turns to talk to me, otherwise I would never know she was there.

"Nick? Are you ok? You don't look so good."

"Cricket, right? Yeah, I caught a cold. Sorry, don't get too close."

"Oh no, it's definitely going around. I had it last week. Hey, the line is moving."

She takes my hand as everyone moves forward one pace, and as she does so, she steps under one of the ceiling lights and for a second I catch a glimpse of shining long blonde hair and bright blue eyes.

Cricket keeps guiding me along, into the dining hall, through the line and around the buffet trays. Carson cuts the line to join us and Nate goes off with him so I guess Cricket doesn't feel like she has to help him too. Ordinarily I would shake off her hand and tell her I'm fine on my own, but I'm so exhausted, it's easier to let her guide me. The truth is I never feel confident in the dining hall, with so much noise, and trying to hold my tray with one hand and my cane with the other, and keep the tray flat so the food doesn't slide off. It's kind of nice to have help this one time.

All four of us sit down together, and Cricket chatters away about her classes and how much homework she has. She's an English major, so I mention my class, and it turns out she took it last year.

Even though I have a crashing headache and still can't breathe through my nose, talking with Cricket is the most normal thing I've done all week. It feels almost good.

8

ABBY

I don't expect to see Nick at my performance of *The Crucible*. I mean, he did ask me for a ticket so I gave him one a while back, but I figured he was just being nice.

Nick didn't even come to class this week. He said he was sick, but that's what everyone says when they reach that point in the semester when they realize they'd rather sleep in than drag themselves across campus for yet another boring lecture.

The play is in a lecture hall, one of the bigger ones that has a stage with curtains at the front. But it doesn't have a proper backstage, just a closet that becomes a makeshift green room. We all have to change our clothes and put on makeup in the bathroom down the hall, which is the same one people attending the play also use. Our "costumes" are our regular clothes, so at least putting them on isn't such a big deal.

I slouch on stage with the other girls, holding skateboards and chewing gum even though everything else in the play including all the dialog is colonial times. All the leads have this shouty way of delivering their lines that is so grating and pretentious. I thought for sure the director would tell them to tone it down but no, he dials it up even more. Come on, even in the 1600s no one talked like that.

This isn't art. What the hell am I doing here? I look straight out from the stage, scanning the audience. We're not supposed to do that, but I don't care.

The glare from the spotlights contrasts with the darkened lecture hall making it hard to see out into the seats, but I can tell we're at best half capacity. I recognize some of the attendees as other theater majors, here to be supportive. The rest are friends and family members of the cast.

I go through the motions on stage, following the other girls as our blocking moves us to the opposite edge. And there, sitting right in the third row on the aisle is Nick. I wonder if he can see anything at all on the stage. From what he's said, probably not, maybe only a vague blur of light, shadow, and a few colors.

My one line is in the trial scene when all the girls pretend to be attacked.

"No! Please don't hurt me!" I shriek, covering my head with my hands.

As I say my line, I see Nick sit up straight, a big grin on his face at the sound of my voice. God, he's so hot. I feel a flash of desire thinking of him listening to me from the audience. It's enough to carry me through the rest of the ridiculous play.

After the curtain calls, everyone rushes into the hallway to see their friends, as if we needed any further proof that this is not a serious performance and no one is pretending this is real theater.

All around me are the shrieks of girls congratulating and violently hugging each other. I let myself be hugged by girls I know, and tell Jen what a good job she did as Abigail.

"Thank you." Her voice is a whisper, almost completely gone after two plus hours of shouting. "You got the Jagermeister, right?"

Oh shit, I totally forgot I promised her I'd get it for the cast party which is at our house right after the show. She already drove out to Meijer in her car yesterday and bought cases of beer, chips and stuff but she forgot this one thing. Over breakfast I told her I'd get it.

"I'll swing by Village Mart on the way home." I give her an apologetic smile as she glares at me.

Behind her, I see Nick picking his way carefully through the crowd. He's holding his cane crosswise close up against his body, weaving around as people bump into him. I push past Jen and move in his direction.

"Nick! Hey, Nick!" I'm kind of proud that even with all these other loudmouth theater kids around us, I can still be the loudest.

He freezes in surprise as I struggle through the crowd to him and put my hand on his arm.

"Hey, you. I didn't think you'd come." I try to sound neutral, but it's hard when you have to shout to be heard.

He smiles uncertainly. "Of course! I wouldn't miss it. It was really cool to see it performed and not just read it."

I sock him on the shoulder playfully. "You're sweet."

"I'm sorry I didn't bring flowers or something. I know how hard you worked on this play. You were good."

"Please. This was risk-free theater." It's nice of him to come and all, but I don't need him to lie to me. I don't even care if my castmates hear. Whatever, they're not listening anyway.

"No, it was good," he insists. "So do you wanna go out and get a drink or something to celebrate?"

Oh shit! Now what? Yes, I want to say yes, let's run away together and leave all this bullshit behind. It's obvious he likes me. But only because he doesn't know. I can't get too close. And I promised Jen I would get the gross Jaeger she has her heart set on for the party. I've been jealous that she got the lead and I didn't. We've been friends since freshman year. What kind of friend would I be if I ditched her for some guy I just met?

"I'm sorry!" I blurt out "There's a cast party tonight. I can't skip out."

His face falls. "Oh, ok, well, have fun then. Seriously, you were great. I'm glad I came."

"Thanks. I'm…glad you came too."

He turns to go, and the disappointment written on his face just about crushes me. "See you in class."

"The door is that way." I nudge his shoulders around ninety degrees from where he was facing.

9

NICK

The whole way home, my mind is a blank. I concentrate on the tip of my cane swinging back and forth, back and forth, carefully controlled arcs, scraping lightly over the pavement. Straight to the corner, turn left, then follow the sidewalk straight straight straight, across ten side streets, the busy sounds of the major road to my right, until the traffic sounds decrease, and the road leads up to campus. Then feel for the button to turn the traffic light, listen for the cars to stop, cross the road and onto the quiet, leafy quad. Follow the sidewalk diagonally across campus, past the looming lecture halls, empty at this time of evening, past the library, through the arch of the engineering building, with its sharp, stony echoes. Across one more intersection, turn right and down the street until I come back to the dorm.

I thought for sure Abby liked me. Reading that book to me, taking notes, going out to dinner, was it all out of pity? I cycle through anger, frustration, embarrassment, but with no outlet for any of it. I don't tell Nate that I asked Abby out and she shot me down. He doesn't ask how her play was.

The week goes by in a haze. I go to my other classes, do homework, go to the dining hall, all of it on autopilot, like my body is a ship I'm steering from a distance, like I'm standing outside myself. At least ten times a day, I catch myself wanting to call Abby on the phone, or saving up some interesting fact to share with her, then feeling crappy all over again when I remember. I feel weird talking to her.

I still can hardly believe it all got spoiled so quickly. Nate was right. I gotta move on.

Somehow, without noticing how or why, I find Cricket joining us for almost every meal in the dining hall. Which is nice, although she does talk a lot. She's very into what she calls reparative justice, and goes on and on about the need for prison reform, workplace protections, minority rights, queer representation, blah blah blah. I mean, I agree with all of this in principle, but what can I do about it? I feel a bit guilty, but whenever she gets into the details, I zone out.

I suspect Nate and Carson find her a little annoying but they never say anything when she meets up with us in the line or sits down next to us. Whatever, it's good to have someone's arm to hang on to as I'm trying to navigate around the tray carts and steam tables, or who can warn me where there's cereal spilled all over the floor.

Sunday evening, Cricket stops by our dorm room and asks if I want to join her for dinner at the local Ethiopian restaurant.

"It's really cool," she says. "They serve the food on a giant piece of bread and you eat with your fingers. It's delicious."

I've been so caught up with homework all day that I've barely left the room except to do laundry, so I'm glad for an excuse to get out. The cold air on the walk over clears the cobwebs out of my head, and she's right, the food is delicious.

But for once, Cricket is unusually quiet, almost shy. She hovers around me in the restaurant, checking every few minutes if I like the food, if I know where everything is on our shared giant bread platter. It's exhausting, and I wish she would be more normal with me.

Suddenly, like a flash of light opening up my tiny pinhole of vision, I realize that maybe this is a date, and her weird hovering is a kind of awkward flirting. Is that what's going on here?

"Don't forget, you can eat the bread plate. Do you like the bread?" Cricket asks nervously.

"Yeah, it's really good." I give her an encouraging smile. That seems to work, because she launches into a long story about how last summer she was a counselor at a Girl Scouts camp and took the girls on these grueling hiking trips which sound horrible to me but apparently she loved it.

I smile and nod along, concentrating on trying not to drop food on my clothes as I eat curry with my fingers. Could Cricket be interested in me? That would explain why she's been hanging around so much lately. I was so focused getting a date with Abby, but somehow I fell ass backwards into a date with Cricket instead. I'd rather be with Abby, but Cricket is nice. Maybe I should give her a chance.

"So do you ever go hiking?" Cricket asks, finally pausing in her story. Before I can answer, she continues, "I mean, I'm pretty sure you could. We had a camper who had Down syndrome and she was an amazing hiker, just kept up so well and never got tired."

Knowing how earnest and well-intentioned she is stops me from rolling me eyes so hard and giving her a sarcastic answer. But I fucking hate it when people compare me to an intellectually disabled person. Even aside from that, the constant need to mention the one other person with a disability they have met and compare us even when we have nothing in common is also super annoying.

"Maybe if you had a guide dog," she continues. "Do you have a dog?"

I smile tightly. "I live down the hall from you. Have you seen me with a dog?"

"Oh!" She sounds mortified, and instantly I feel bad. "I'm sorry. I thought all blind people would have a seeing eye dog."

"It's actually pretty complicated to be matched with a dog. You have to do special training and everything. A dog is a living creature, not a machine. Anyway, our dorm room is so tiny, can you imagine me and Nate there with two dogs? And having to walk them all the time? There's no way."

"I had no idea. Wow, maybe I should write an article about seeing eye dogs."

I wish she wouldn't. Instead of answering, I smile and tear off a piece of flatbread with my fingers.

Cricket goes back to the topic of hiking and how I could join her.

I swallow hard and say, "I'm not really the outdoorsy type."

"Oh, but the feeling of being out in the fresh air is so amazing! I'm sure you could do it. There are some amazing trails not far from here...." She's off again, while I just nod. I'm not going hiking, especially not when it's about to start snowing any day now.

I'm not sure how I feel about Cricket but then when we get back to the dorm, as she says goodnight, she gives my hand a squeeze and says in that shy voice again that she had a nice time.

I walk back down the hall to my room in a daze. For once, the dorm is relatively quiet, no blasting music or the pixelated shouts and grunts of video games, no gangs of students running up and down yelling or partying in their rooms. I have our room to myself. Apparently Nate is still out getting dinner. For the first time in forever, I feel peaceful and relaxed. Thinking of Cricket giving my hand a squeeze makes me feel like maybe I do like her.

"You missed it last week, I gave a whole speech about ableism in class," Abby says as I sit down next to her in the lecture hall. The book last week was *Jane Eyre*, which I didn't read because I was sick. I don't admit that, though.

"You know how at the end of the novel, Jane only gets to marry Rochester after he goes blind?" she continues. Actually I didn't know that, but I nod as if I did. "So I pointed out that's ableist bullshit, that blindness symbolizes a loss of masculinity and status, which is the only reason they can be allowed to be together. Then some freshman bitch puts up her hand and is like, 'But it's so romantic how he saves her from the fire,' and I was like, we shouldn't be valorizing these novels that use blindness as a metaphor for something else, instead of thinking about it as simply part of the human condition."

Wow, she's sounding like Nate now but I don't have anything to add, so I just nod.

The lecture starts, and I try to concentrate but my mind keeps wandering.

We're reading *Frankenstein* this week, which I've been looking forward to all semester, but I'm so distracted by Abby, I can hardly even think about the novel. Ok, so she seems to want to be friends, nothing more. I can do that. I'm not going to be a creepy asshole who drops her as a friend just because she won't go out with me. And maybe I'm going out with Cricket now? I'm still not sure how I feel about her.

Halfway through the lecture, as Professor Roesman is droning on and on about doppelgangers and the loss of self as the modern condition, I recall that there is a blind character in *Frankenstein* too, the old man who makes friends with the monster. Will Abby go on another tirade about ableism? I don't get what she's talking about and I don't want her to bring it up with me sitting right next to her. I feel like I should be the one talking about it in class but I really don't want to. I don't see any connection between me and the characters in the novel, and I have zero desire to talk about anything so personal in front of these students I don't know at all.

Thankfully, she doesn't say anything.

Professor Roesman ends the class with a reminder that the first paper is due next week. Shit! I had forgotten all about that.

"Five pages double-spaced on a classic conflict in one of the novels assigned so far," he says. "And try not to make it too boring, ok? At least make an effort to be original."

I have no idea where to even start with this paper.

"Hey," I say to Nate, as we're both studying in our room.

He pulls off his headphones with annoyance. "What?"

"What's an example of a classic conflict?"

"Sphincter versus dilator," he deadpans without even pausing to think.

"Ugh, gross! Come on, I mean something I can write a paper on!"

"Do your own homework. I told you not to take that class."

I hear him click his tape player back on.

I pound out a paper on man versus man in *Moll Flanders*, and get a C+. Passing, but just barely. Even worse than the sinking feeling that I am in fact going to tank my GPA in this class is the thought of Nate telling me *I told you so* at the end of the semester. Just once, I want to do my own thing and prove him wrong.

10

ABBY

Now that the stupid play is behind me, I feel like I can coast through the rest of the semester. Except now I've got to start thinking about my senior thesis next semester, my final performance to show the world I've actually learned something about THEATRE and ART. To show that I've done something important and real. Not that I've spent my four years here chasing after guys who will never accept me if I show them who I really am.

I want to do something big, something totally original. But I have no idea what.

I'm so screwed.

Every time I start to think about my thesis, I realize I have some other assignment due that I have to work on first. I toss off that short paper in Brit Lit and scrape by with an A-. Not too bad, but I'll have to step up for the final paper.

I don't know what grade Nick gets because for the first time he doesn't ask me for help. I'm seized with a sudden wave of jealousy. I'm sure this means he's seeing some other girl.

Stop it, I tell myself. This is what you wanted. He deserves to be with someone normal, someone who'll like him for the right reasons.

I force myself to concentrate on the lecture, to take good notes for him. He's sitting there right next to me with his hotness. I can't help staring at him. His brown hair has grown out slightly, making perfect curls at the crown of his head. He's frowning slightly as he listens to the lecture, his dark eyes unfocused. He looks tired, with shadows under his eyes.

It's getting to the busy time in the semester. I think about how much longer it takes him to do his work for this class, then multiply it by four.

"Getting busy, huh?" I say as we're packing up to leave after class.

Nick sighs. "Yeah. Feels like every minute I'm not in class, I'm either in my room listening to tapes or at the CSD using the CCTV."

"The what?"

"The closed circuit television. They have a thing where I put in a book and it puts the text on a screen, where I can make it really big."

I stand up and shoulder my backpack. "Does that actually work?"

Nick stands up and puts his hand on my elbow. "Eh…" I glance at his face as I lead him up the shallow stairs out of the lecture hall. "It's slow."

"What, are you reading one letter at a time on the screen?"

"Basically." He sounds slightly embarrassed.

"But why?" I know I shouldn't be so up in his business, but I can't help it. "I thought you were getting these notes transcribed into Braille."

We reach the hallway outside and he drops my arm. "Actually, I kind of suck at reading Braille."

"But you can read Grade 2, right?"

Nick's eyebrows go up in surprise, and I swear he's staring at me. Oh shit! I said too much, revealed that I know more than I should.

I know all this from Ted, who was proficient in Braille and used it all the time. Grade 1 Braille is every print letter spelled out with a Braille cell. But doing that is freaking huge—each sentence takes way more space than in print, and reading is slow. Grade 2 Braille is a system of abbreviations to make it more compact and efficient. Basically every Braille book for adults uses Grade 2.

But whatever he's wondering about me, Nick doesn't say. Instead he admits with some embarrassment, "I can read the letters fast enough but I'm not great at Grade 2."

"Dude! No wonder you're having trouble keeping up with your classes. You've got to get on this!"

"Lay off! I get enough of this from Nate."

"Sorry! Sorry! But I could help you memorize the contractions if you want."

"Maybe," he says, and even I can tell that's a lie.

Nick goes back to Probus Hall for lunch, and I watch him go. If I hadn't blown it already with him, I certainly have now. What is wrong with me?

I've got to move on with my life and stop obsessing over Nick. I have a lot of papers due, and throwing myself into my work helps moderately. On the weekend is the monthly poetry slam at Hot Cups, a tiny café with a truly awful name located in a dank corner of the basement of Probus Hall. Most of the poetry is godawful but there's one guy at the end who's really funny, kind of a local celebrity. I think he's a grad student in philosophy or something but he's been doing this act for years and I love how raw and hilarious it is. I used to go all the time with Jennifer. She invites me to go again with her but then cancels at the last minute. Do I go on my own? Watching him always perks me up.

But the café is in the basement of the dorm where Nick lives. It's a conundrum.

Screw it. I decide to go and enjoy myself and not think about Nick. I arrive early and get a seat at one of the tall stools by the bar. The spaces around me fill up quickly and I think I'm in the clear but a minute before the slam starts, the giggling sorority girls beside me suddenly leave. A second later, who files in through the crowd but Nick, on the arm of some hippie chick with long blonde hair dressed in earth-tone corduroy.

He sits down right next to me, so close we're actually touching. Fuck my life.

"Oh hey, it's you." I try to keep my voice as neutral as possible.

Nick gives a little start, his head jerking up and his eyes kind of swimming around in my general direction, but then he breaks out in a genuine grin.

"Hi." He's happy to see me, I can hear it in his voice. "This is Cricket."

I wave to her and introduce myself. So this must be his date. I guess. I mean, she has a kind of outdoorsy vibe that I associate with women loving women, but on the other hand there's no mistaking the dopey look she gives Nick.

Dammit. I will not be jealous. I'm sure she's perfectly nice.

"Do you come here every month?" Cricket asks, making small talk before the show starts.

"Not every month. Mostly it's just girls going on and on about their boyfriends, but sometimes it's people I know from my major. Mainly I'm here for the Meat Poet."

"The what?"

Before I can answer, there's an ear-piercing squeal of feedback from the microphone onstage. Everyone covers their ears. After more excruciating wrestling with the mic, at last a girl thanks us for coming.

"This is what you get when you don't hire a proper tech crew and leave it to the baristas to set up the mic," I whisper to Nick and Cricket. "It's always like this."

First up is a girl named Tiffany. "This is called 'His Hands,'" she whispers shyly into the mic. Her poem is all about how amazingly huge her boyfriend's hands are. Her nervous rocking and swaying as she reads off her notebook into the mic causes a weird doppler effect. I feel seasick watching her.

"Wow, you weren't kidding about the boyfriend poems," Nick remarks.

Next, a guy with a squeaky voice shouts his way through a poem about how modern life is bullshit and he wants to go join the Sandinistas.

"That's just wrong," Cricket mutters angrily. "Does he even know what he's talking about?"

The aspiring Sandinista is followed by three more girls reciting boyfriend poems, then two other guys with the same spiel on the bullshit of modern life, punctuated with occasional mic feedback.

I tune out the poems and watch Nick out of the corner of my eye, trying not to be too obvious. He shifts around on the uncomfortable bar stool, looking nervous. His arm is pressed right up against me. He feels solid and warm, and I want to lean into him. I can see curls of brown hair at his wrist below his sleeve. He runs his hands lightly up and down his thighs. With an effort, I tear my gaze away and back to the stage.

There's a particularly painful squeal from the mic, prompting howls of protest from the audience. A short, skinny guy lopes onto the stage and grabs the mic from the MC.

"HEY HOT CUUUUUUUPS! Are you ready for some MEAT POETRY!!"

He has buggy eyes and a beard that looks like he dipped his chin in a bowl of glue and hair, but he makes up for it with some intensely expressive eyebrows. He's wearing a t-shirt he silkscreened himself with MEAT POET in ransom note letters.

"Fucking finally!" I whistle through my fingers, a sound almost as ear-piercing as the mic.

"What is this?" Nick asks.

"You know beat poetry?" I say. "Well, this is meat poetry!"

The Meat Poet's act is mostly yelling a lot of curse words and also talking about poop, but he delivers each line of potty talk as if it's the most profound statement known to man. What can I say, it's hilarious. And it's fucking original. I can't think of anyone else who has the guts to get on stage and go crazy like this. Certainly not any of the poseurs in the theater program. I have deep respect for his fearlessness.

"And now," the Meat Poet declaims, "I present to you a little ode entitled, 'Hot Dog.'" Everyone screams like crazy, including me. This one is my favorite.

"Hot dog

Hot dog

Hot *dog*

HOT dog

Oh shining hot dog

Oh phallic hot dog…"

As he goes on like this, he opens up packs of hot dogs and starts throwing them into the crowd. The room fills with a smoky, porky scent. This is always the best part.

"Over HEEEERE!" I stand up in my chair and wave my arms.

"What a horrible waste," Cricket sniffs. "Those poor cows and pigs suffered and died just to be a fucking joke?"

"Aw, I missed." I slump back down. "I think it fell behind the bar."

"Art should be sustainable and cruelty-free," Cricket insists more loudly.

"No, art should push you out of your comfort zone." I lean around Nick to make my point. I try not to sound too pretentious, but I'm not sure I succeed. "Anyway, I know him, and he's actually a vegetarian."

"At least it's less pretentious than any of the boyfriend poems," Nick says. Cricket shoots him an angry look that is of course lost on him.

The Meat Poet shouts the final lines of the Hot Dog poem, then screams some more obscenities, and the show is over. The audience cheers.

"Wow, that guy is hilarious!" Nick grins as he pulls his cane from his back pocket and lets it snap open. Cricket is still frowning. I admit, the Meat Poet is, shall we say, an acquired taste.

"He's here every month, although it's more or less the same each time."

I'm ready to call it a night but to my surprise, Cricket invites me to join them for coffee. Maybe the best way for me to get over my nascent jealousy is to make friends with Cricket. She seems nice. Why the hell not?

Nick also looks slightly surprised that Cricket wants to get coffee. Was he also planning on leaving? So this isn't a date?

"Ok, but there's no way I'm drinking coffee here with hot dogs all over the floor," he says. "It smells like a cafeteria."

Cricket suggests going to the café on the corner across from the dorm. But then instead of letting Nick take her arm, she speeds off toward the exit without even looking behind her. Nick takes a hesitant step after her, but Hot Cups is packed with students pushing in various directions, chairs and tables scattered randomly through the crowd.

He takes another step, and crashes into a beefy frat bro in a Calstock State sweatshirt.

"Hey, watch it, asshole!" Nick frowns in annoyance. The frat bro turns red and backs off without saying anything.

"At least apologize!" I shout at the guy's back as he disappears through the door back into the dorm.

I stifle my unkind thoughts about Cricket and instead offer Nick my elbow to guide him out into the street and down the block.

"Oh hey, Cricket," I say when we catch up to her outside the café, so Nick knows she's there.

"Don't do that!" he snaps at her.

"What?" Cricket looks stricken at his tone, but also totally clueless about why he's upset.

"Don't just run off like that."

"Oh! Sorry!" Cricket's blue eyes go big and round. "The café is right here." So now she overcorrects by saying too much, and takes his hand like a child. But if they're dating, it's normal to hold hands, right? Are they dating?

We sit down together around the tiny marble-topped table with our overpriced cappuccinos.

"So you're a theater major?" Cricket asks, politely making small talk.

"Yeah, but it's not what I thought it would be." I take a sip of mediocre coffee. "I'm tired of the theater kid bullshit."

"Aren't you a theater kid?" Nick smirks at me, like he's enjoying needling me about this.

"Please. There's a difference between theater with an e-r and theatre with an r-e. Not one of those poseurs is ever going to be a working actor. They're going to graduate and go to work in a bank, then do community theater productions of *Our Town* and *Pippin*."

I don't know why I'm unloading on these two but pretty much all my friends are in the same major, so it's not like I can vent to them. Honestly, Jen was good in *The Crucible*. It's not her fault the direction sucked. But every semester I get more and more frustrated with this program.

"I'm sick of these risk-free productions," I say. "They think they're being all edgy and shit, but they don't have a single original idea."

"And you can do better, right?" Nick says.

"Yes! No. I dunno. I only have one more semester to do something meaningful, not this fake crapola."

"Ok, so do something!"

"It's not that easy! I can't pull something out of my ass. It has to be, like, *real*."

"Like the Meat Poet." Nick runs his finger around the rim of his coffee cup. "All those girls were talking about their real boyfriends but their poems came out exactly the same. The Meat Poet yelled a bunch of stupid nonsense but he made it sound real."

"Yeah, exactly!" It makes me so happy that Nick gets it. "I wish I could be as fearless as he is."

"I'm sure you can."

If only he knew.

11

NICK

Going to the café with Abby and Cricket was not as awkward as I feared. Maybe this is a sign that Abby and I are better as friends, and I'm meant to be with Cricket.

"Oh, hey! Check it out!"

I'm standing in line to go in the dining hall with Cricket, Nate and Carson. This has become our daily routine, except tonight Nate and Carson got back late from the gym so now we're at the height of the dinner rush, at the back of a line that snakes down the hallway and around the corner.

"Check what out?" I have no idea what Cricket is talking about.

"There's a flier up for a free massage class in the lounge on Saturday," she explains.

There are activities in the dorm all the time, movie and TV nights, game nights, lectures, things like that. Our mailbox is constantly stuffed with fliers, which we usually throw away rather than asking someone to read them to us.

"'Learn basic massage techniques for relaxation and health,'" Cricket reads. "'No experience or equipment necessary. Just bring a partner.' Sounds fun! Wanna try?"

All four of us end up going to this free massage class together. I'm secretly worried it might be weird, but it turns out to be surprisingly normal. The instructors are two kinesiology majors, a guy named Mike and a girl named Stephanie. So many people turn up that there's barely enough room for everyone to lie down.

Mike talks us through each of the big muscle groups, and how to move our hands so it's exactly the right amount of pressure. I lie down first, while Cricket practices on me.

I've never felt anyone touch me quite like this before. I lie on my back, and she starts at the shoulders, then works down to my hands. At Mike's direction, she massages each of my hands, rubbing the palms, then pulling each finger in turn. It's not sexual, but it's the best I've felt in weeks. By the time she's done, I'm so relaxed, I feel like I could sink into the floor. Who knew that having your hands massaged could feel so good?

Then it's my turn to practice on her.

Copying how Cricket massaged me, I massage her scalp as she lies on her back, then move on to rub her shoulders, then her arms and hands. It's oddly intimate, feeling her ears, her collarbone, her elbow, her fingers. I only had the vaguest idea before of what she looks like, long blond hair, average height for a girl. Now I can tell she's slender, almost wiry, small hands, long, bony fingers. Crouching on the hall floor, the industrial carpet under me, surrounded by at least fifty other people including my brother right next to me, it's far from sexy, but I feel somehow closer to her. She keeps giving these little sighs as I work on her. It's cute.

It might have been more than that, if I didn't have to listen to Carson and Nate arguing the whole time.

"Ow! What the hell! What are you doing?"

"That's how Mike said to do it!"

The whole experience makes me realize how wound up I've been lately.

Later, while I'm listening to endless speeded-up tapes of textbooks and lecture notes, I rub my hands, trying to get the tension out, and remembering the pressure of Cricket's fingers. I want to touch her, to be touched by her like that again.

"Are you really going out wearing that?" Nate is hassling me because I'm going to a party with Cricket.

"Shut up, ass-face!"

Well, "party" makes it sound more exciting than it really is, namely, some of Cricket's friends hanging out in their dorm room. But it's a Saturday night, why shouldn't I have fun? Nate is just jealous that I'm going out with Cricket. Sort of.

I know he has no idea what I'm wearing, and he doesn't actually care. He's just being a dick. It's not my fault his whole social life revolves around playing video games and working out at the gym with Carson.

"Hey, are you ready?" I jump slightly when Cricket's voice comes from the direction of the door. Damn, we have to stop leaving the door open for anyone to wander in.

"Yeah, do I look ok?"

I turn towards her, a blurry figure topped with a halo of long blonde hair.

"Sure, I guess."

Not what I was hoping for, but ok. I'm wearing the same jeans and t-shirt I've been wearing all day. I figure as long as I'm not stinky, that's good enough.

"Ok, this way." Once again, Cricket takes off without offering me her arm. I race along after her with my cane, trying to keep up with her shadowy form. I want to tell her to give me her elbow, or at least slow down, but I already told her once.

She speed-walks down the hall, then stops suddenly in front of the door to the stairwell, and I run right into her.

"Oh sorry!"

"Hey, you gotta let me hold your arm!" I hate how my voice sounds like I'm scolding her.

She apologizes several more times, which makes it worse. She takes my hand and I follow her down the stairs, across to the opposite side of the dorm, up more stairs, down more long hallways, until at last she stops in front of a room with an open door.

The sound of many voices raised over loud music filters out. The room itself is like a black box, compared to the relatively well-lit hallway. I clamp my hand more firmly onto Cricket's arm.

She introduces me to her friends, a bunch of English majors like her. They call out greetings, four guys and a girl. Three of the guys are named Mike and one is named Brian. I don't catch the girl's name. The soundtrack is a mix of Violent Femmes, Smiths, and Depeche Mode, and the thick scent of clove cigarettes hangs in the air. The room is shadowy, not lit with the usual bright overhead fluorescent lights, which is annoying for me but I guess most sighted people don't like those glaring fixtures, standard in every room in Probus Hall. They must have slung a scarf over it or something.

"Just sit anywhere," one of the Mikes says, which is less helpful than he might think. I keep my grip on Cricket's arm and follow as she sits on what I realize is the edge of someone's bed.

We make awkward small talk about our classes and how many papers we have to write in the next few weeks. More people drift in. Someone hands me a plastic cup filled with something vile, maybe Gatorade and vodka, but I drink it anyway.

Cricket gets in an argument about whether or not practicing yoga is a form of cultural appropriation and post-colonial oppression. She thinks it is. One of the Mikes insists that yoga isn't a real Indian tradition but was made up to con rich white people. I have nothing to say about any of this, so I down another drink. At least this time the mixer tastes like pop.

The conversation wanders around to discussion of a cartoon published in the campus paper last week. Brian says it was homophobic.

"Did you sign the petition to get the paper to publish an apology?" he asks.

"Yes!" says Cricket.

"What about you?" Brian asks. Cricket has to nudge me before I realize he means me.

"I wouldn't know, I can't read the paper," I say.

Cricket takes this as an opportunity to get on her soapbox again about accessibility on campus, which I find embarrassing. Everyone agrees with her in principle, but I can tell they don't want to talk about disability, or even think about it. The conversation quickly goes back to gay rights.

Brian tells a long story about being the first person at his high school to take another guy to the prom. I have to admire him for that. No one tried anything like that at my school. I don't think there were any gay kids at Knob Park High.

"Brian's wearing a t-shirt that says 'No one knows I'm gay,'" Cricket whispers in my ear, giggling. She's been drinking too, judging by her boozy hot breath blowing in my ear and down my neck.

"Really?" I don't get it. Why would someone wear a shirt like that?

But Cricket seems to find this the funniest thing ever. She whispers it a few more times, leaning up against me and laughing hysterically.

"No one knows I'm gay!"

Once she's that close, I take advantage by wrapping my arm around her and pulling her even closer. Her form presses up against mine. She's small and lithe, a narrow waist and small round butt. Suddenly I'm super turned on.

As soon as her laughter calms, I press my face into her wild mass of hair and whisper back, "Hey, wanna get out of here?"

She nods, her face pressed up against mine.

I feel around on the bed until I find my cane, and we stumble out into the hallway, which thankfully is properly lit, because my head is spinning. This time I have my arm around Cricket's shoulders and I don't let go.

We have to go the long way around because someone puked in the stairwell again. The smell is overpowering the moment she opens the door, and I nearly start gagging myself. We stumble backwards, laughing, and head for a different staircase at the opposite end of the hall.

By the time we get back to our hallway, I feel slightly less like the floor is moving under my feet.

"Uh, ok, this is your room…" Cricket says, extricating herself from my arm.

I grin at her. "You wanna come in?" I can hear Nate's voice coming from Carson's room behind us, so I know we'll have the room to ourselves, at least for now.

"Sure…" She doesn't sound sure, but I grin at her even more widely, then clumsily turn to unlock the door. It only takes a few tries before I find the keyhole, scraping the key along the heavy wood, then circling around the stiff metal lock until the key goes in.

I swing open the door with a flourish and gesture for her to sit on the bed. The light is already on, probably because Nate forgot about it. Maybe it would be more romantic without the overhead fluorescent on, but it's the only way I can see her so I don't want to turn it off.

I sit down next to Cricket on the bed, trying not to swing my head around in a weird way to look at her. I can see her knees, with her hands resting on them, then that shining blonde hair on her shoulders. She has a kind of flowery smell clinging to her that has been filling my nose all evening, but I'm only now aware of it.

"Thanks for inviting me to the party," I say, as the silence between us threatens to stretch on too long.

"You're welcome."

"I had a good time."

"Me too."

Ok, now, I think. *Don't miss your chance.* I look at her shoulder, then her chin. I have a good guess for where her mouth is, enough not to crash into her face. Probably. I go in for a kiss.

As I lean in, Cricket leans away, like some kind of dance move she's practiced in advance. I catch myself and pull back right before I topple over into her lap.

"Uh…it's getting late…" she mumbles. "I mean, it's after midnight. I'm feeling really tired. I think I had too much to drink. I don't want to be bothering you. I think I should go. Good night."

Before my foggy brain can catch up to what's happening, she's off the bed and out the door.

I'm still sitting there, dazed, with my mouth hanging open. What the hell just happened?

12

ABBY

I always sit in the second seat of the third row in lit class, so Nick knows where I am. As usual, he shows up about a minute before the lecture begins. I guess he walks a bit slowly, because he has to pay attention. Still, it's impressive that he gets around on his own after only living here since the start of the semester. Allenville isn't that big, but it took me a while to figure out the crisscrossing diagonal streets.

I've been congratulating myself all week for making friends with Cricket after the slam, and not being jealous. *Don't say anything*, I remind myself.

Nick sits down heavily next to me and folds up his cane. He's wearing jeans and a black t-shirt, looking fine as usual.

"Hey." I poke him in the ribs with the eraser end of my pencil as a greeting. "How's it going with Cricket?" Shit! The words just tumbled out.

I expect him to give a lovesick grin, or tell me to mind my own business or something. But instead, he squirms away with a slightly embarrassed grimace.

"That good, huh?"

"I tried to kiss her and she leaned away," he whispers.

At the front of the lecture hall, Roesman shuffles his papers at the lectern.

I whisper back, "Oh, ouch! Shit, I'm sorry. If it makes you feel better, I'm like 80% sure she's a dyke."

"What? For real? What makes you say that?" Nick raises his eyebrows in surprise

"I dunno, she pings my gaydar. The whole crunchy hippie thing she has going on, I guess."

"Now I feel even stupider for thinking she was flirting with me."

"Don't feel dumb. She *was* flirting with you. I saw how she looked at you during the poetry slam."

"Why would she be flirting with me if she's a lesbian?"

"Maybe she's bi like me."

Any longer conversation on this topic stops as Roesman starts lecturing about *Tristram Shandy*.

I slide my eyes over to Nick, trying to gauge his response even while furiously taking the most meticulous, neatly written notes I can manage. This was a calculated reveal. I've been feeling like I should come out to him at some point, but I couldn't find the right moment. If he gets all weird and homophobic, maybe I could get over my stupid, pointless infatuation. On the other hand, it would be a tremendous bummer.

His expression doesn't give me any hint. I have to look back at my notebook before my handwriting devolves into a hopeless scrawl.

The lecture goes on and on about narration and the construction of self. We have another paper due in a few weeks. I think I'm going to write more on blindness in *Jane Eyre* and *Frankenstein*, even though it's risky. I feel so exposed. I really don't want Denise the TA or Roesman to guess my secret. And Nick should be the one writing about it from his personal experience, but it's very clear he doesn't want to. So why not me? I can't think of any other topic that even comes close to interesting me in the same way.

When the lecture concludes, Nick stands up and shakes open his folded cane. It snaps into shape with a series of clicks.

"So?" I hurriedly toss my notebook into my bag before he can leave before me. "What I said earlier, are you ok with it?"

"Oh, you mean you being bi?"

Aha, so he was thinking about it.

"Yeah." I stand up and follow him out of the row of seats.

"I guess so. I mean, why not?"

"So you don't have an issue with gay or bi people?"

"Not really. I never met a gay or bi person before." He takes my elbow as we walk out into the hallway.

"That you know of," I say.

13

NICK

Ok, so I guess Cricket doesn't *like me* like me. At least not in that way. If I'm honest, I'm not heartbroken over her. The humiliation of leaning in to kiss her while she pulled away, though, that stings. So much so that the best strategy is to try to pretend like it never happened.

Cricket also seems to have come to the same conclusion, because the next day she appears out of nowhere next to me in line at lunch in the dining hall, acting overly cheery. So I guess we are both pretending I never tried to kiss her and now we're only friends.

The only one who asks me about it is Abby. Wait, did Abby just tell me she's bi? How did I not know this about her? Now I'm even more sure she doesn't like me in that way, just like Cricket.

Ok, so I've struck out twice now. At least I'm still friends with Abby and Cricket. That's good, right? Maybe I'll meet someone at the party this weekend.

Carson has big plans for going out to a party at a frat nicknamed Triangle which is for engineers. He claims it will be cooler than the one we went to before. I don't know why he thinks a frat full of engineers will be anyone's definition of cool, but whatever. Nate is super into it for some reason.

This weekend is Halloween. It was never a big holiday for us, because even when we were little and could see ok enough in daylight, we were already nightblind, so walking around after dark on our own was a no-go. While our classmates roamed the neighborhood, we usually stayed home together and ate candy, watching *It's the Great Pumpkin Charlie Brown* on TV. Back then we used to sit side by side with our noses nearly touching the screen.

"I don't have to wear a costume, do I?" I ask as we're getting ready for the Triangle party.

"Nah, it's fine," Nate assures me.

I throw on what I'm pretty sure is a black shirt, to get in the mood.

As it turns out, the Triangle party is even more wild than the one we went to before. Those engineer nerds are out of their minds. The house is cramped, people standing shoulder to shoulder, chugging beer from plastic cups, music blasting. Beastie Boys again. Everyone shouts the words together. This time I get into it, for once turning off my brain and jumping along with everyone else. It feels good to let loose.

The music switches to Jane's Addiction and the crowd breaks up, people jostling around at random out onto the porch or up to the second floor.

"Hey, they're jumping from the upstairs window onto the lawn!" Carson shouts excitedly. "Oh my God, these dudes are fucking maniacs! We have to try it!"

"What? No! Are you out of your mind?" I shout back. The ambient noise level is only slightly lower than before.

"It's ok, they put mattresses on the lawn," Carson explains as if this makes it at all safe and not completely insane. "Come on, let's go!"

"No way!"

"Yeah, come on! Don't be such a pussy!" Nate slurs.

Nate and Carson disappear upstairs while I elbow my way through the crowd onto the porch. I'm seriously planning how I'm going to explain to our parents that the child they think of as the smart one has died jumping out of a second story window. But a few minutes later, Nate and Carson come bounding up the stairs to the porch, whooping like morons and pounding me and each other on the back.

They stumble back inside to get more beer. I stay out on the porch, breathing in the cold air to try to lessen the spinning sensation. I lean back against one of the wooden pillars and drain the warm remnants from my cup. The porch is only slightly less crowded than inside, and there are people standing all around me doing the same.

"Heeeeyyyy, nice costume," slurs a dude in front of me.

"Uh, it's not a costume?" Wait, maybe he isn't even talking to me. Sometimes I answer the conversation happening next to me. It's embarrassing.

"Yeah, you're dressed up as a blind man, right? With the white cane and all?"

"No, I really am blind," I say, biting back a ruder reply. I rattle my cane in my hand. I'm holding it extended by my side in a futile effort to avoid bumping into anyone.

"Whoa, no shit!" he exclaims as if it's an earth-shattering revelation. "But you don't look blind."

I wish I had a better answer to this. What I want to say is *fuck you asshole!* But I'm trying not to get in a fight like last time.

"Miiiiiiiike!" shrieks a girl next to the asshole. "What's wrong with you?" She puts a hand on my arm. "Sorry about Mike," she says. "He's a dick."

"Fuck you, Vicky!" Mike replies, but he's sort of half laughing, hopefully more embarrassed than angry. "Sorry, man."

"Whatever, dude," Vicky says. "Why don't you make it up by getting us a refill?" She plucks the empty cup from my hand.

"Sorry about that," she repeats, leaning closer. She seems tall for a girl, maybe the same height as me or even slightly more. "I'm Victoria, but you can call me Vic."

I stick out my hand, and she shakes it firmly. "Hi, I'm Nicolas, but you can call me Nick."

"Ooooh, that's funny!" She giggles drunkenly. "Nick and Vic! I guess we were meant to be."

It's a stupid joke, but somehow I can't stop laughing. Vic tells me she's an engineering major, a sophomore, and she lives in the same dorm as I do. For some reason she also thinks it's super important that I know she's a goth. She describes her outfit in great detail. Her description sounds like word salad to me, but the gist is that it involves a lot of black. She leans against me as she's talking and all I can think about is how I can convince her to come back to the dorm with me.

She still has her hand on my arm, and I hold it, lacing my fingers in hers and stroking her palm. She leans in even further, so I can feel her beery breath on my face as she talks.

"Hey, you're really cute," she says.

"You don't have to sound so surprised."

She laughs some more. "I mean it! You're a hottie."

This has to be a good sign, right? There's no chance this chick is a closeted lesbian.

"Hey, you wanna ditch this lame party and go back to the dorm?" I probably wouldn't have been so bold if I wasn't drinking, but hey, why not?

"Ok, let's go."

I'm amazed that worked.

"Oh wait, I gotta tell my brother I'm leaving." Shit! Now what? This chick is not gonna wait for an hour while I stumble around trying to find Nate.

"Wait here, I'll be right back," I say, sort of pushing against her as if I can stick her in place.

I stagger back into the house. The carpet of the main room is so soaked in beer it squishes slightly under my sneakers. The music has changed to Prince for some reason, and I can hear Carson shouting along the words. I've never been so grateful to hear that asshole's voice. I manage to get his attention and let him know where I'm going.

"That tall chick with the Betty Page cut and the black lipstick?" he asks. "Is that a costume or does she dress like that every day?"

"Just tell Nate I'm going back now and don't come in without knocking."

"Hey, I got you, bro!" Carson punches my shoulder. "He can stay in my room."

When I get back out to the porch, miraculously, Vicky is still there. We walk back to the dorm together, but she doesn't offer her hand or arm, and like an idiot, I don't ask. Instead, she walks near me, nearer than a sighted person normally would, so I'm sort of feeling her with the side of my arm, which is awkward as hell but once we set off this way, I just go along with it. I can't believe I'm about to get lucky with this chick, and I'm afraid that if I make any sudden moves, I'm going to scare her off.

So Vicky and I do this weird side by side walk back to the dorm, then we have to go down three different hallways to find a stairwell that doesn't stink of vomit. It's a relief when we finally make it back to my room.

I snap on the light, hoping our room isn't too much of a disaster. Nate and I try to keep it tidy so we're not tripping over shit all the time, but it's probably been over a week since we did laundry. Maybe two. Does it smell bad? I've heard you can't always notice your own smell. I hope the room doesn't stink.

"Hey, why'd you do that?" Vicky asks as I toss my cane in the closet and pull off my shoes.

"Do what?"

"Turn on the light? I thought you were blind." She's still standing by the door, sounding skittish.

"Oh! Ah, well, yeah, I'm legally blind but I can still see a little."

"But I thought either you can see or you can't."

"No, it doesn't work that way." Why am I having to explain this to her? This isn't the conversation I want to be having right now. "But anyway I turned on the light for you."

"I like it better in the dark." She snaps the light off without even asking. Shit! I was hoping I could get a look at her, or at least parts of her, but apparently not.

We sit down together on the lower bunk. I try not to think about how Cricket was in this exact same spot a week ago. At least this time, when I lean in to kiss Vicky, she kisses me back, running her hands all over my back and pressing up against me, so there's no mistaking that she's into it.

I've never done it before with a girl as tall as I am. I'm used to being the bigger spoon. It's not bad, just different, the way our bodies fit together equally. It would be fine, except she's not very confident in bed. Once we're naked and lying next to each other, she keeps squirming away when I run my fingers over her, even though in the single bed there isn't anywhere to go.

"Are you ok?" I ask finally. It's weird how she keeps kissing me and touching me, but doesn't want me to touch her.

"Yeah, sorry. I've never done it with a blind guy before," she says.

"But you just told me you like to do it in the dark. How is that any different?"

"I guess it isn't…"

"Look, we don't have to do it if you don't want."

"No, I do! I mean, I want to do it." She grabs my cock, which is still hard, because I'm a dude and there's a naked girl in the bed with me. Wait, is she trying to stick it in already? Now I'm the one pulling back.

"Uh, we should use protection, right?" I say. "There's a box of condoms in the drawer of the nightstand."

Sex ed in our high school mainly consisted of one of the male gym teachers shouting at us that having sex was exactly the same as putting a loaded gun to your head and if you don't want to die of AIDS you have to use a condom every time. It made an impression.

I'm surprised to hear her grumble a little about using condoms. Maybe Vicky didn't have the same class at her school. I insist, and she hands me one.

Sex with Vicky is ok. I mean, it's not bad. But it's hard to lose myself in the moment when she's being hot and cold like this.

When we're done, she quickly pulls her clothes on and goes to the bathroom down the hall. When she comes back, she asks if I need her help getting to the men's room. What the hell? I'm too tired to be polite about this shit.

"You know I live here, right?" I mumble with my face in the pillow.

"What?"

"I know where the bathroom is. I use it multiple times every day."

"Oh. I'm just trying to be nice, you know? You don't have to be a jerk."

"Sorry." Why am I the one apologizing? Thankfully, she takes this as her cue to gather up her things and go back to her own room.

I take myself to the bathroom all on my own, then fall into bed, exhausted. I don't even have the energy to find my pajamas, so I strip off my jeans and sleep in my shirt and underwear. Somewhere in the back of my mind as I drift off, I notice that Nate still hasn't come back.

14

ABBY

Halloween used to be my favorite holiday, but this year I'm just not feeling it. I don't bother to make any plans. Nothing seems fun or interesting. Nick has moved on, and I have to let him go. Maybe things didn't work out with him and Cricket, but there will be someone else.

Normally the theater department has a big blowout party on Halloween, but organizing it takes effort, and this year no one stepped up to do it. Wow, we all suck.

Jen sees me moping around the house and declares that we are going out no matter what. We dress all in black for the occasion. Ok, actually I wear all black all the time to hide the fact that I could only bring what I could fit in a suitcase on the plane. I have a fraction of the clothes of the other girls who get driven to campus by their parents with a U-Haul. So I just wear my regular clothes.

We walk across campus to a house party Jen heard about. The night air is clear and chilly, a proper Halloween mood. I start to feel hopeful, but the party is lame and I don't know anyone there. After an hour of awkward, shouted small talk with strangers over top 40s blasting at full volume, we ditch and head out into the night again.

"Sorry," Jen says as we crunch through the fallen leaves at the edge of campus. "Oh, hey, there's Probus Hall. Some kids from my practicum are having a party in their room. Wanna check it out?"

A dorm party sounds even lamer than the house party we just left, but it's not like I have anywhere else to be. And maybe I'll run into Nick.

No! As we walk down the familiar overheated, fluorescent-lit hallways, I remind myself that I'm here for a party with Jen and nothing else. Nick is probably out anyway.

The party is wild. A bunch of freshman dudes have somehow pushed all their furniture into the corridor and covered the ceiling fixture with a big uncut sheet of red lighting gel, probably stolen from a campus theater. "Tainted Love" plays in an endless dance remix. The room is packed with sweaty, drunk people dancing like crazy.

Jen dives in, but I linger at the doorway. Someone hands me a shot of Jaegermeister in what looks like the plastic measuring cup for cold medicine. Ugh, gross. I toss it back anyway.

I catch sight of Jen in a corner of the room cramming her tongue down the throat of some skinny guy with long hair. I assume this is the practicum classmate who invited her to this soiree. I take this as my signal to leave.

I wander away from the party down the hall. I pass by the open door of the RA's room, where he's talking to some irate residents and waffling about whether or not to shut down the party. I love Probus Hall, but nights like this make me grateful I don't live here anymore.

And there I am, on Nick's hallway. Dammit! I didn't mean to be here. It's late, but maybe he's still up. I raise my hand to knock, but before I do, I hear his voice through the door, talking to someone. A girl.

God dammit! What is wrong with me! I knew this was a mistake but I had to step in the shit anyway.

I turn to leave without making a sound. He never has to know I was here. As I turn, I see into the room directly opposite. The door is open a crack, and inside are Nate and Carson, kissing. Probably more than kissing, since their shirts are off.

I take off down the hall, trying to scrub the image from my mind. What the hell did I just see?

I speedwalk to the opposite end of the dorm but by the time I get there, the party has broken up and the RA is goading some very drunk boys into dragging their bedframes out of the hallway back into their room. Jen is nowhere to be seen. I search up and down the halls but I can't find her.

It's past midnight, and I've had enough. Jen can find her own way home.

As I walk out the main entrance, I spot Nate sitting on the steps by the door. For a second I think it's Nick, but as I get closer I can tell it's Nate. I could pass by him and he'd never know, but I don't think I could live with myself if I did that. At least he put his shirt back on.

"Hey Nate, it's Abby." I try to make my voice sound light and casual.

He turns his face up, but his eyes wander around somewhere in the direction of my feet. Unlike Nick, who usually makes eye contact, even if it's after weaving his head around first.

"If you came looking for Nick, you're too late. He's hooking up with some goth chick from the Triangle party." Nate's voice is flat, affectless.

"I didn't come here looking for Nick. For your information, I came to a party with Jen."

"Oh? So where is she?"

"I dunno, with some dude." I pause. "So, you and Carson, huh?"

Nate goes rigid. "I don't know what you're talking about!"

"C'mon man, it's cool! I don't care if you're gay."

"I'm not gay!" He's nearly shouting.

Oh man. I know what I saw. There's only one reason why Nate is here freaking out instead of continuing to make out with Carson. I don't want any part of Nate's gay panic crisis. If I could extract that memory and hand it over to him, I would.

"I promise, I won't tell Nick. Or anyone else." I try to sound reassuring, but Nate gets a wild, frantic look on his face.

"Tell him what!"

"Exactly, dude. There's nothing to tell. And you don't tell Nick I was here looking for him, because I wasn't. I was at a party, ok?"

"Yeah, ok."

I leave Nate there on the steps to the dorm, clenching and unclenching his fists. Dude needs someone to talk to but he clearly doesn't want that person to be me.

As I walk back across the quad, groups of students in costumes that range from half-assed to truly terrible stumble around drunk and shouting.

Fuck Nick. I'm so done with him. I wish I had stayed home.

15

NICK

The next morning, I have a moment of hungover panic when I discover Nate still isn't back. A second later, I'm more concerned with the state of my stomach. I race down the hall to the bathroom, hoping I'll make it in time. I do, just barely.

When I'm finally empty and return to the room, Nate's voice comes from the top bunk.

"Oh, you're back," he says calmly, as if I was the one out all night, not him.

"Where were you?"

"With Carson." I feel like there's something strange in his voice when he says this, but I can't put my finger on it, and he doesn't say anything else. Maybe I'm imagining things.

Or maybe not. Carson doesn't join us for lunch (we slept well past breakfast). And not the next meal, or the next, or the next.

"Where's Carson?" I ask Nate over lunch near the end of the week.

"I dunno."

"Thanks, good talk," I say sarcastically.

When Nate is annoyed or frustrated, he always cracks his knuckles. If it's something small, he does them one at a time, pressing his thumb against each finger in turn. If it's something big, he does all of them at once, pushing his fists together. I hear him doing it now, all the fingers together, *crack crack crack.*

He doesn't ask me about Vicky, and I don't say anything. What would I say, anyway? I wasn't looking for a one-night stand but that's what I got. Hooking up with her was not the fun time I was expecting. She ran off like she couldn't get away from me fast enough.

Now what? Obviously we're not doing this again. But since we live in the same dorm, pretending she doesn't exist would be rude. On the other hand, I can't just smile and wave at her if we pass in the corridor or in the dining hall. I wouldn't even know she was there.

A week goes by, but I don't hear anything from her.

"What's wrong?" Cricket asks. She's been eating meals with me and Nate every day, filling the Carson-shaped hole in our lives.

"Nothing's wrong," I say, shoveling tater tots in my mouth.

"You look like something's wrong," she insists.

"He's broken up over that Goth chick," Nate says. "They hooked up and now she's avoiding him."

God damn it, Nate. How does he know everything going on with me when we never talk anymore and I feel like I don't know anything going on with him?

"She's right over there at the next table," Cricket says. "She's been watching us the whole time. Maybe she's just embarrassed. You should talk to her."

Instead of answering, I push the food around on my plate. Mystery casserole, ugh. I kind of want to know what's up with Vicky, but the middle of the dining hall feels like the wrong place for this conversation. But really, anywhere would be the wrong place. The hallway? The gross stairwells? Our room, with Nate in the top bunk, and Carson and Cricket and whoever else wandering in whenever they feel like it?

Cricket helps me and Nate to bus our trays. I'm holding her elbow as we're leaving, with Nate following behind me, when she suddenly stops, causing us both to collide slightly with her, like a slow-moving car crash.

"Oh hey!" Cricket says in the fakest voice ever. "Vicky! How're you doing!"

"Hey," I mumble.

"So." Vicky sounds awkward as hell. "I guess we need to talk."

Oh man, nothing good ever follows that sentence. I want to jump out the window, or maybe murder Cricket for setting me up like this.

"Ok, see you later!" Cricket leaves with Nate, who says nothing.

Vicky is a black smudge seated at the table in front of me. She stands up, and without a word, grabs my hand and drags me over to a corner by the window. I hate it when people do that, but I'm too nervous to say anything to her. I'm hyper aware of the noise in the dining hall, hundreds of voices, the clink of glasses and cutlery. It smells like bacon grease and sugar cereal. I wish we were at least in the hallway outside but I guess Vicky isn't done with her meal yet. Once you leave, you can't come back in without paying again.

At least by the window there's enough light that I can see her. I realize I'm seeing her face for the first time. Parts of her face, anyway. One blue eye, ringed with a lot of black eyeliner. Greasy dark hair with bangs. An unhappy looking mouth, turned down.

"I'm really sorry." Her words come out in a rush as if she's delivering a rehearsed speech. "You seem like a great guy and you're, like, super hot and all, but I just can't do this. I'm really sorry."

"Do what?" I wasn't aware "this" was anything. Why can't we consider it a one-night stand and leave it at that?

"I can't date a blind guy! It's, like, too much responsibility, y'know?"

"I can take care of myself. I've somehow managed on my own up until this point."

"Oh?" It kills me how she sounds genuinely surprised. "But it's not only that. I'm like, suuuuuuper into movies and TV. Seriously, fandom is my *life*. I don't think I could be with someone who can't go to movies with me."

I consider explaining to her how stupid this statement is, that I go to movies and watch TV all the time, but by this point, I have no interest in dragging the conversation on any longer than absolutely necessary. I want to tell her she's being a dumb bitch, but I was raised to be polite, so I keep my mouth shut.

"I can't take the responsibility," she continues. "I mean, if we dated, I could never break up with you. It wouldn't be fair to you. I'm sorry, I guess I'm too shallow to be with a handicapped person."

"You got that right." I turn away before I can say something much, much worse.

"The door is the other way," she calls after me, because that's how much my life sucks.

When I get back to our room, Cricket is still hanging out with Nate.

"Thanks for nothing," I tell her sourly.

"I'm sorry!" Cricket says, when I recount what happened. "I had no idea. I thought she was into you."

"Wow, you're really terrible at reading people," Nate says.

"That sucks that she laid all that ableist bullshit on you," Cricket continues, ignoring him. "But maybe it could have been a learning opportunity. You could explain how she's wrong to assume that you can't date like a normal person."

"No, fuck that!" I fling myself into my desk chair and turn on my computer. "I never want to speak to her again. Why should I have to talk to her for even one minute?"

"Yeah," Nate says. "It's not his job to educate her."

"But you could be the one to open her mind and make real change in the world." Cricket will not let it go. Typical.

I put on my headphones to listen to the screenreader. "Sorry, I have work to do."

Cricket says she has work too, but instead of leaving to go do it somewhere, anywhere else, she lies down on my bed and pulls out a coursepack. What the hell?

I try to ignore her. Now that we're into November, it's crunch time. I have so many big projects coming up, not the kind of thing you can leave until the last second, and anyway it's not really my style to pull an all-nighter. When you have to listen to every line of text read out loud with a screenreader, even at triple speed or faster, leaving work until the last second isn't an option.

I plunge back into debugging my program for database class. Write a program in C++ to sanitize data and upload in batches. Sounds easy, right? I thought I had it but it just won't run.

SEG FAULT, the tinny voice says in my ear. Over and over until I rip the headphones off again in frustration.

Cricket doesn't get up until Nate goes for an afternoon tutorial. They leave together.

16

ABBY

Despite my resolve to take notes for Nick and nothing else, the next week after Brit lit class I find myself at the café on the corner with him yet again, enjoying myself way too much, helping him rewrite his paper proposal.

TA Denise silently passes back our proposals after class. Mine has a red check mark at the top, which I guess indicates approved. But Denise being a total bitch means I have to step in when she lazily thrusts the paper in Nick's direction without saying anything.

"It says 'revise and resubmit,'" I tell him, because otherwise how would he even know?

His face falls. "Hey, I thought my proposal was pretty good. What the hell?"

He shoves the paper in his backpack and stands up, letting his cane snap open.

"Sorry." I give him my arm as we walk out into the hall. "Denise is the worst." I keep my voice low because the TA is still in the classroom behind us. "Bragging all the time about the Ivy League school where she was an undergrad, and how much better the students are than us. Hey, bitch, you're stuck getting your PhD here with the rest of us plebs."

"And why can't Professor Roesman accept an electronic submission?" Nick complains. "All my other classes let me do all the assignments on the computer. This is the only class where everything has to be on paper."

"I dunno, man, these English profs are luddites."

"I have no idea what they want on this paper. Nate was right, I'm going to tank my GPA in this class."

"What? No way! This class isn't that hard. Come on, I'll help you."

So there I am not only talking to Nick but sitting with him in the same café where I was the third wheel on his sort-of date with Cricket, helping with his paper. I can't let him give up on his grade, not in a class this easy. I try not to wonder who he's seeing now. If he doesn't say anything about her, I'm definitely not going to ask him.

We sit down at a tiny round table by the condensation-streaked window. Moving carefully so as not to knock over our cappuccinos, Nick pulls his proposal out of his backpack and hands it to me.

I glance over the computer-printed page and Denise's illegible scrawl in red pen.

"Here's your problem," I say. "You just repeated back what was in the lecture."

"So? I thought that's what we're supposed to do."

"Nah, they're looking for some original thought."

"Easy for you to say. How can anyone have an original thought about a two hundred year old book that millions of students have already written papers on?"

"It doesn't have to be something no one in the world has ever said before. It just has to be something you think up on your own. And why did you pick *Middlemarch* for your paper? You said it was the most boring book we read all semester. Why not write on *Frankenstein?* You said you liked it the best."

He squirms around in his chair and accidentally knocks his folded-up cane off the edge of the table with his elbow. I pick it up and put it back.

"You know," I say slowly, picking my words carefully, "My paper is expanding my classroom rant on ableism and the metaphor of blindness in *Jane Eyre* and *Frankenstein*. But I feel like you should be the one writing on that, not me."

He gets this funny look on his face like the whole topic makes him uncomfortable.

"No."

"Why not? It's your real life. You need to give your perspective."

"Hell no! I'm not putting my real life into a stupid term paper. You want me to share something that personal with snobby Denise, just so she can tell me it's bad?"

"Fair enough." I don't say that I'm also kind of nervous about this topic being too personal. What if Denise guesses my big secret? But I doubt she would. Most people don't know devotees are even a thing. But Nick on the other hand, he's a different story. I'm longing to tell him and at the same time wishing it wasn't a thing that existed in my mind at all. Why can't I just like him straightforwardly, without this weird thing coming in between us? Or better yet, not like him at all since he's with someone else and we're just friends.

"It's fine for you to write about," Nick continues, "but I'm not touching that topic."

We're both silent for a few minutes as we finish off our coffees. The afternoon sun coming in the window lights up Nick's face and I wonder how much he can see me. Damn, why does he have to be so handsome? He's frowning slightly, like he's thinking hard. This is being friends, I tell myself. Helping out with a paper and nothing more.

The espresso machine behind us hisses loudly.

"Ok!" he says suddenly. "I think *Frankenstein* is actually a secret love story between Victor and the monster. They're totally gay for each other."

"Whoa, I think you're right!"

"Come on, I was kidding."

"No way, if you write it properly, Professor Roesman will eat it up, I promise you."

We go over the novel again, adding up all the evidence. Nick's face lights up with excitement. Talking about this, working it through together is fun.

"Dude, you have to write this paper," I tell him. "This is kind of genius."

Nick flexes his fingers. "Ok, but I can't take notes here. I've gotta get back to my room and type it into my computer before I forget."

I let him take my arm so I can guide him around the tiny round tables in the crowded café. Once we're outside on the corner, I reluctantly shake my arm free.

"Ok, I'm going the other way," I say.

"Yeah, ok." Nick looks disappointed.

"See you next week in class." I wonder for a minute if I should just go with him, but no, the thought of sitting in his dorm room where he's doing it with some other girl is just too much.

"Thanks for the help." He waves uncertainly. The cold air makes his cheeks go pink.

"No prob." I turn and walk in the opposite direction before I lose my resolve.

I cross the quad, heading away from Probus Hall, back to my house. Nick and I spent so long in the café that now the next period classes are ending. Students stream out of the buildings lining the quad, hurrying in every direction.

Out of the corner of my eye, I catch sight of a flash of movement, a white cane sweeping back and forth. My head swivels around almost on its own. That can't be Nick. He's on the other side of campus. Oh right, it's Nate coming out of class with a backpack slung over one shoulder. He walks straight in my direction, striding briskly through the crowd and trusting the other students to get out of his way.

I'm not really excited to have a conversation with Nate, but I feel a moral obligation to say something and not take advantage of the fact that he can't see me.

"Hey Nate, it's Abby."

He stops abruptly, his expression shifting from bemused to annoyed.

"Hello Abby." Nate frowns in my direction.

"What class are you coming from?" Why am I making small talk with Nate? I feel so awkward, but since I started this conversation, I can't just run off.

"Intro to Sociology. It's a gen ed requirement, but it's actually really good, way better than I expected."

"With Professor Ortiz, right?"

Nate nods, his frown lifting.

"I took that my freshman year," I continue. "It was awesome. Have you done the week on disability activism yet?"

"Yeah. I thought I already knew about the ADA being passed a few years ago and all that, but there was a lot more that I hadn't heard about before. Why don't they teach us any of this in high school?"

"You know, if you're interested, there's a whole class on disability studies you can take next semester. I never took it because it clashed with my required practicum. But I've heard it's really good. You should take it."

"Thanks. I think I will." Nate smiles.

"Ok, see you later."

"Wait." Nate holds out a hand uncertainly. "I, um… I don't know what you think you saw in the dorm last weekend…"

I roll my eyes. "Dude, what you do with your buddy is your business, but I promise you, no one cares if you're gay. It's really not a big deal."

"What?" He looks surprised. "No! I was going to tell you, Nick isn't seeing anyone. I know he likes you, and I don't want you to get the wrong idea."

"Oh my God!" What is this, junior high school? I can't believe Nate is gossiping to me about his own brother. And trying to set us up, what the hell! "Ok, I really have to go now," I say.

"Oh, and there's nothing between me and Carson. Nothing!"

"Whatever, dude. See you later!"

17

NICK

I'm deeply asleep, dreaming that I'm trying to hand in my revised proposal for my gay *Frankenstein* paper, but I can't seem to find the front of the lecture hall. I wander around but the desk is always just out of reach. Behind me, someone is pounding on the door to the lecture hall, but class is already over.

"Go away!" I shout.

The pounding gets more insistent.

I roll over with a start, and suddenly realize that was a dream. I already handed in my proposal earlier in the week, and Denise approved it on the spot. But the pounding on the door seems to be real.

"What the hell?"

I wrench the door open. The sound of ringing bells fills the room.

"C'mon, man! Fire alarm!" It's Carson.

"Oh, right." I start pulling on my shoes and coat methodically. At least every two weeks, some drunk idiot decides it would be hilarious to have an unplanned fire drill. If it's a Saturday night, it's almost certainly a false alarm. I'm not in a hurry.

"Hey, where's Nate?" Carson says from inside our room.

"Nate?" I call out, but no one answers.

"He isn't in his bed." The room is so tiny, if Carson can't see him, he's definitely not here.

"He said he was going to study at the library and not to wait up," I recall sleepily.

"Yeah, but it's one AM."

That *is* strange, but there's nothing we can do right now. Carson lets me take his elbow, and we join the line of students trudging from their rooms, downstairs and out into the frigid night.

"Is the fire department here yet?" I ask when we get outside. We don't even bother to cross the street, but just stand around on the sidewalk by the entrance.

"Nah, I don't see them."

Fuck, it's going to be a long wait. We can't go back in until the fire department comes to turn off the alarm.

I'm wondering if I can sit down on the curb when Carson, whose arm I'm still holding, spins around.

"I see Nate! He's right over there!" Carson yanks me along behind him as he takes off.

We walk about halfway down the block, pushing past groups of sleepy dorm residents.

"Hey, asshole!" Carson demands. "Where the hell were you? We were worried about you."

"Oh hey." Nate's voice floats over the crowd, sounding what, embarrassed?

"Hi guys." It's Cricket. What the hell?

"Oh my God, did you guys hook up?" Carson sounds disgusted.

"No!" Cricket shouts.

"Uhhh…" Nate says at the same moment.

"Yes, you did!" Carson says. "Don't lie. What, so you thought you could make up a story about going to the library and no one would ever know? What is wrong with you?"

"So what?" Nate is instantly on the defensive. "We're grownups. We can do what we want."

My stomach drops in the sudden silence. A minute later I realize it's not just my imagination. The fire alarm has turned off.

"I'm going back to bed," I mumble and turn away without waiting for a reply, leaving Nate and Cricket to their walk of shame. I head for the light that I figure must be a door. There are like ten entrances to the dorm, so if I follow the jostling bodies all around me, I can find my way easily enough.

This always happens every time there's a fire alarm in the middle of the night—someone gets caught coming out of their room with a secret hookup, and their friends all laugh at them. I never in a million years thought it would happen with my own brother.

And with Cricket, of all people! It's fucking creepy, man. I mean, we never officially dated or even kissed, but still, she was flirting with me. And now she goes for my twin? What's wrong with her? And how could Nate do that to me?

I fall back into bed but I can't sleep. I spend the whole night tossing and turning angrily. Nate doesn't come back until the morning.

"Hey," he says as he walks in, as if nothing is up.

I don't say anything, which is a shitty thing to do, but I'm beyond mad at him.

"Nick?" I hear him put his cane in the corner and start changing his clothes. He must still be wearing the same outfit from yesterday. Gross.

"Nick, don't be an asshole. I can hear you in the bottom bunk. You're not that stealthy."

"I'm the asshole?" I burst out. "What the fuck do you think you're doing?"

"Taking a shower." He rummages around in the closet, probably getting soap and a towel.

"You know what I mean! How can you get with Cricket after…" I trail off.

"After what?" he sneers. "I'm sorry, did you think she's your property? She's an adult woman, you know. She can do what she wants."

"I never said—! Ugh, why do you have to be this way? Doesn't it bother you that she went from me to you?"

"No. We're different people. Cricket is mature enough to recognize that," Nate says loftily, then departs for the shower, slamming the door behind him.

18

ABBY

I don't know what Nate thought he was trying to accomplish by telling me about Nick, but it's not going to work. Ok, so maybe Nick isn't going out with anyone at the moment, but he surely will soon. It's like girls are throwing themselves at him. I'm not going to be one of them.

I'm eating breakfast by myself one morning when the phone rings. I run into the hallway to pick it up, wishing we had a cordless phone. We just have an old corded one in the hall alcove like it's the 1920s, which is probably when this house was built.

"Hello?"

"Abby! It's Ted. How are you?"

Dammit! I told Jen we should get caller ID but she didn't want to pay extra. I've avoided talking to Ted since he left town.

"I'm fine. How are you?" I keep my voice as neutral as possible, thinking regretfully of my toast going cold on the dining room table.

"It's so good to hear your voice! I'm so glad I finally got hold of you."

"Sorry, I've been busy." This is true, but also he's been leaving me messages on the answering machine that I've been deleting.

He asks about my classes but before I can give much of an answer, he goes on and on about his MFA course, how hard it is, threaded through with humble-brags about how well he's doing in his oh-so-demanding, prestigious program.

Whatever. I consider putting the phone down as he's talking but even *I* am not that rude. Hearing his voice, I can picture his face so clearly. Ted has long brown hair that he wears in a pony tail, and a goatee. When we were together, I thought it made him look so bohemian, like a 1950s beatnik, but now I think it's pretentious and kind of gross.

I cut him off as he's obviously ramping up to another anecdote about his writing workshop. "Hey, that's great, man. I'm happy for you. Really. But I have to ask, why are you calling me?" The NLB got their damn tape recorder back. What does he want?

Ted's voice falters slightly. "I just, well...I miss you, Abs. I've been thinking about it a lot, and I realize I made a mistake breaking up with you. I think we should get back together."

"Seriously?" I hate how hearing his voice makes my heart beat faster, but now I feel my blood pressure shoot up. Is this some kind of joke?

"Yes, seriously. You'll be graduating next semester. Once you're done at Calstock, you can move out to Iowa to be with me."

"Oh, so I should apply for the MFA? What's the deadline?" I don't want to do a graduate degree, but on the other hand, I don't have any other plan.

Ted gives a little snort of laughter. "Oh, there's no way *you're* getting into Iowa."

I'm so stunned by this that I don't even respond.

"You can move out here with me," Ted continues. "I'm sure you could find a job at like, the campus bookstore or something. And it would really help me to have you proofreading my writing like you used to."

"Uh huh." Is that what he thought of me while we were dating? Just free labor? "And what about you know, the devotee thing? Are you ok with it now?"

Ted sighs heavily, making the phone line whistle and crackle. "I wish you were normal. We can try just, like, not talking about it."

Part of me wants to scream at him, slam the phone down, and never speak to him again. But somehow I can't do it. Isn't this what I want? To be with a hot blind guy, but as a regular girl, not as a devotee.

"Well?" he prompts impatiently.

"I don't know."

"Just promise me you'll think about it."

"I'm not promising you anything."

I put the phone down slowly, feeling like my soul is leaving my body. I should have told him off. Hell no am I moving to butt-fuck nowhere to be Ted's personal secretary. Why does he still have this hold on me? I find everything about him annoying, and yet hearing his voice, I'm back in the headspace of last year when he was all I could think about. Get out of my head, dammit!

After lit class, Nick asks me to help him with his gay *Frankenstein* paper, and like a dope I say yes. He's so excited about writing something actually good, and I enjoy working on it with him too much to say no.

Of course we have to go back to his dorm room to read the draft on his computer. The door to his room is locked, which means Nate isn't around, thank goodness. Carson's door is shut too. I try not to think about either of them.

"Fucking Nate, man!" Nick exclaims as he fumbles around with the key.

"What?" I assume Nick means something about the door being locked, or I would have kept my mouth shut.

"He's going out with Cricket." The door swings open and Nick tosses his cane and backpack in the closet.

"Really?" I sidle in behind him. The room is reasonably tidy but with two massive wooden desks and the bunk beds, there isn't room for much else.

"Yeah. There was a fire alarm in the middle of the night and he turned up in her room. Now they're making it 'official.'" He makes air quotes with his fingers.

"That sucks, man! I'm sorry."

He sits in front of his desk and turns backward in the chair, waving me over to Nate's desk chair. "It's weird, right? How she was with me then him? When I tried to talk to him about it, he accused me of being a male chauvinist pig."

"What are they thinking?" I have an idea, but I promised Nate not to say anything.

"He's practically been living in her room for the past two weeks."

"Her roommate doesn't mind?"

"Her roommate moved out after she got diagnosed with something called systemic candida and her naturopath gave her this crazy diet. Said she couldn't eat anything in the dining hall. Now the RA is pretending not to notice a dude sleeping in her room." Nick scratches at the back of the wooden chair with his thumbnail. "I know it shouldn't bother me but it does."

"It *is* weird. You two look almost exactly the same. You even wear matching clothes sometimes."

"That was an accident."

"Whatever, it's weird. I mean Cricket going with both of you, not the way you wear each other's clothes. If I had a twin, I'd wear her clothes too."

Nick laughs, all straight white teeth and that sunny smile.

"I guess you were wrong about Cricket being a lesbian, huh?" he says.

"Guess so."

19

NICK

Abby helps me with my gay *Frankenstein* paper, giving me tips on how to structure it better, and checking it for typos. I actually look forward to working on the paper, because it means I get to spend time with her. I love how excited she gets as we talking through my ideas.

I get a B+. When Denise the TA hands it back to me, she says, "Ok, here you go," in a tone of voice that suggests she's worried that I might argue over my grade and she can't take any more grade-grubbing from us unworthy slackers. I know because she has said that last part out loud a few times during the last tutorial.

The joke's on her because 1. I have no idea what she wrote on my hard copy paper until Abby tells me after class and 2. that grade is way higher than I expected for my ridiculous topic in a class I was sure I would fail. I still give her a bad evaluation though because she needs to knock it off with the Ivy League snobbery.

But I'm so glad I took this class, because otherwise I would never have met Abby. And reading all those books was actually interesting. I get to spend even more time with Abby as we cram for the final. Talking through all her lecture notes with her, I realize this was probably my favorite class. The only problem is now that it's over, when am I going to see her again?

I don't even get to see Abby at the exam, because I take my test at the CSD in a tiny room by myself, where I can use the CCTV to read the questions and type my answers on a computer. A bored work study student watches me.

I try to concentrate on the test but as I'm typing out my answers, I keep hearing Abby's voice in my head. That weekend she spent reading to me was so intense. I'm longing to hear her voice again. I have her phone number, but it would be weird to call her right after the exam, right?

So I wait a few days, trying to play it cool. But when I finally call her, she's literally on the way out the door to the airport. I apologize, she says have a good vacation, and that's it. As I hear her hang up, I kick myself for not getting her parents' number. I miss her already.

The next morning, Dad comes to pick us up. The dorm is already deserted. Carson drove himself to Anterfax a few days ago, and Cricket's parents picked her up yesterday.

If Dad notices any weirdness between me and Nate, he doesn't say anything. He asks how finals went, and we both say good, then the rest of the way back to Chesterford Hills we listen to sports radio.

We have a quiet Christmas, just our parents, me and Nate, our younger sister Emily, and our grandmother. Everyone wants to know all about college, so it's easy to talk a lot about the details of daily life and our classes without having to get into the uncomfortable territory of our social lives. We help Mom prepare the food and clean up. Mostly we spend our time in front of the TV.

It feels strange to be back at home. Every surface, every piece of furniture, even the smells, it's all so familiar, but the house feels quiet and almost empty. I'm so used to being surrounded by other people all the time. It feels weird not to eat off a tray surrounded by noise. I realize I'm also used to being able to walk anywhere I want to go. Now if I even want to go to the store for a bag of chips, I have to ask my parents for a ride.

Emily, who's a sophomore in high school, wants to know every detail about college. She's already planning to go to Calstock State when she graduates.

"So is it like a non-stop sex party in the dorms?" she asks over dinner.

"Emily!" Mom sounds scandalized.

"No, mostly we're just doing homework," Nate replies seriously.

"Oh my God, Nate! I'm rolling my eyes at you so hard right now," Emily sasses him, before turning to me. "What about you, Nick? I bet you're getting with all the girls."

"No! You've been watching too many movies. It's not like that at all."

"Well, have you at least gone to a frat party?"

"Maybe once or twice, but honestly, it was kind of boring. It's hard to get your bearings when it's so dark and noisy and crowded."

"Don't let anyone tell you what you can and can't do," says Grandma sanctimoniously. "You can go to parties if you want to."

"Grandma!" Now Nate is the one sounding shocked.

"What? Your grandfather used to take me out dancing all the time. He was quite the ladies' man." She titters girlishly, which makes all the rest of us cringe so hard.

Our parents take us on the usual round of errands and seeing family friends who exclaim over how grown up we look. I know they mean it as a compliment but hearing that just makes me feel even more like a kid.

On Saturday night, Nate and I are home alone. Emily goes to a friend's house, Mom and Grandma go to Mom's ladies' bowling league, and Dad is next door playing poker with the neighbors. Before he goes, Dad asks if we're sure we don't want him to take us anywhere. No, we're sure. We don't want to be dropped off at the mall like a couple of kids. We've lost touch with our friends from high school, and we never really made any friends at community college.

"Ok, suit yourselves," Dad says as he walks out the side door. "Just holler if you need anything."

We flop down on the sofa in front of the TV in the living room. Nate flips the channels until he finds the one airing back-to-back reruns of *Star Trek: The Next Generation* and *Deep Space Nine*. It's the perfect thing to watch on our own because we've seen it all before, so we know exactly what's happening, and anyway the dialog makes everything so obvious, we don't feel like we're missing anything even without the visuals.

We're halfway through the second episode when the phone rings. I drag myself from the couch to the phone in the kitchen.

"Hello, Bauer residence."

"Um, hello? Is this Nate?" It's a girl's voice.

"No, it's Nick."

"Oh. May I speak to Nate, please?"

It takes me a second to recognize her.

"Cricket?"

I've been avoiding her since she and Nate started going out. It's easy to avoid someone when you have to wait for them to let you know they're around. But hearing her voice on the phone now makes me realize that even though supposedly they're an item, Nate has not spoken to Cricket once since we left the dorm. She's probably busy with her family. Her hometown is Saintwin, which just like Chesterford Hills is a small town only a few hours' drive from Allenville.

"Hey Nick," she says warily. "Is Nate there?"

"Yeah, hold on."

We trade places, me back on the couch, and Nate in the kitchen. I try to concentrate on the TV and not the low murmuring of his voice on the phone. He doesn't say much, though. After a surprisingly short time, he's back on the other end of the couch.

"She broke up with me," he says without emotion during a commercial break.

"What!" I flail around for the remote and try to turn down the volume, but I get it backwards. The sound shoots up to ear-splitting levels before I manage to mute it.

"What are you doing?" he grumbles.

"Don't you want to talk about it?"

"What's to talk about? She said, 'It's not you, it's me.'" Nate grabs the remote from me and turns the sound up. The episode comes back on.

I've heard that when someone says "It's not you, it's me," it's 100% you and they just don't want to tell you, but I don't know if that's true. The whole thing still doesn't make any sense to me.

The episode comes to an end. Nate turns the TV off then cracks his knuckles real loud. Neither of us gets up from the couch.

"I'm sorry you got dumped," I say, trying hard to sound genuinely sympathetic and not like I'm secretly gloating. "That sucks."

"Whatever. Her loss," Nate says stubbornly, but I can tell it's bothering him.

"It's ok to feel bad." Even though I'm selfishly relieved that it didn't work out with them, I'm not proud of being so petty, and I honestly feel bad that Nate is hurting over this.

"But I don't feel bad," he insists. "I like her, but I think she's right, we're better as just friends."

"Ok…" I think back to how I tried to kiss her and she leaned away. Why would she do the same thing again? Except with Nate, I'm pretty sure they had sex, judging by the number of nights he spent sleeping in her room. Not that I'm going to ask.

"I'm sorry," Nate says suddenly.

"Sorry for what?"

He fidgets around on the couch, running his fingers in the grooves of the upholstery, making a buzzing sound.

"I know you were upset that we were dating. I still don't think there was anything wrong with it but I felt bad that you got jealous."

"Dude, I'm not jealous! I only liked her for a minute. But don't you think it's weird that a girl would be with both of us?"

"I guess. It would be different if you had actually dated for a year or something instead of maybe just thought about flirting for a weekend. But I don't want any girl to come between us, ok?"

"Ok, me neither. Thanks."

At that moment, Emily comes home, so that's the end of our conversation. But later, I lie awake in my childhood bedroom, wondering why I still feel so shitty about this. I slightly hate myself for being glad Cricket dumped him, that's one thing. And for another, Nate basically said he's sorry I felt bad, which isn't much of an apology. But mainly, what's bothering me is this huge gulf between us that didn't used to be there.

It's not like we ever spent a lot of time talking about our feelings. We are guys, after all. But somehow it felt like we always thought the same way about everything, so we never needed to say that much. Everything was just understood. That conversation on the couch was awkward as hell, and I still feel like we're not understanding each other at all.

And even more than that, it's like there's a dark cloud over him all the time. He's always been kind of a smartass, but he never used to be so grumpy. He's feeling bad about something, even if he denies it. I chalk it up to getting dumped, and try to leave it at that, because whatever it is, he isn't going to tell me.

And that, I realize, is the worst of it.

20

ABBY

I was hoping to see Nick after exams, but I can't think of a reason to call him that wouldn't be too weird. Even as I'm getting on the plane home, he's still on my mind. I'm sure he's busy having a Norman Rockwell kind of Christmas with his family.

It's always a bummer to go home at this time of year. New York in winter is a slushy, drippy mess. The subway reeks of wet wool and pee. I don't have the lights and presents to look forward to like everyone else, just the crowds and delay at the airport, and the cold gray weather. My family stopped making a big deal of Hannukah after I turned eighteen.

Like always, we go out to eat on Christmas at our favorite Chinese restaurant, where we see half the congregation of my parents' synagogue. Everyone asks what I'm doing after graduation. I smile and say, "Damned if I know," while staring them in the eye, daring them to test me with a follow-up question. No one does.

"Lighten up, will ya?" Dad says as the latest round of alterkakes hurries away from our table. "Nobody likes a sourpuss."

I roll my eyes and help myself to another Peking duck pancake. Mom gives me the side-eye. I'm sure she's going to say *Haven't you had enough?* Or *A minute in your mouth, the rest of your life on your hips.* My grandmother's favorite saying.

But instead she says, "I've been talking to Joanie and she says she can find you a position in the mailroom after you graduate." Joanie is one of the senior editors Mom works with. "I know it's not much but there is room for advancement. Some of the top editors started out in the mailroom."

I doubt that very much, but I don't say so.

"Just promise me you'll consider it," she insists.

Ugh, why is she doing this to me? I feel like I'm being steamrolled. Even though it's a crap position, it's with a major publisher. There are probably three hundred English majors in my graduating class who would give their eyeteeth for this job. How can I turn it down?

"I'll think about it," I mutter. Mom gives a self-satisfied little nod that makes me die inside.

I appreciate that she's trying to help, I really do. But I don't want to be an editor like Mom. I want to do my own thing. I'm just not sure yet what that might be. And I'm not ready to admit that I've gotten through four years of college with nothing to show for it.

In the middle of the week after Christmas and before New Year's, the dead time where nothing happens, Ted calls me.

"Hey, Abs! Merry Christmas." He's sounding very pleased with himself. Once again he goes on and on about how great he's doing in grad school, how much everyone loves the genuine and authentic voice in his writing. I make encouraging noises but in reality I'm not paying attention.

There's something pleasingly hypnotic about the sound of Ted's voice. I keep flashing back to moments when we were together, how much I liked watching him do things. His sensitive fingers. The way he turned his ear towards me when we were talking.

Dammit! I don't want to get back together with Ted. But I can't stop being attracted to him. I feel trapped.

After a solid quarter of an hour of talking about himself, Ted finally asks what I'm up to.

"Nothing much, the usual holiday round," I say.

"No, I mean have you decided what you're doing after graduation yet? You said you'd consider moving out here?"

"I said no such thing. Besides, my mom made me a job offer here."

"Oh come on, you don't want that job. You'd only be doing it to make them happy. You have to live your own life."

He's right. I do want to come back to the city but it has to be on my terms, not hers.

"I didn't say I would take it."

"Of course you won't take it. You're going to move out to Iowa with me. Come on, babe. I miss you so much."

"You broke up with me," I remind him.

"I'm sorry! Jeez, how many times do I have to say it?"

"Ok, gotta go bye!" I put the phone down before I say something I regret.

Dammit, this vacation sucks. I wish I was back at school. I think back to that weekend I spent reading to Nick, with him sitting so close to me, the look of rapt attention on his face. At the time, I was worried I would never get through that damn book, but now I wish I could live inside that moment forever.

21

NICK

Monday after New Year's 1994, Dad drives us to Allenville. I feel guilty saying goodbye to him so fast, when he seems a bit sad that we're leaving, but it's such a relief to be back at Calstock State.

The first thing I do when I get back to the dorm is call Abby. She sounds happy to hear from me. I think. After we each recap our boring trips home, I ask her casually what classes she's taking this semester.

She sees through me instantly. "Almost all my credits are for my senior thesis. Unless you're taking a performance practicum, we won't be in the same class."

"Oh."

"Well actually, I have one more breadth requirement. I'm planning on taking medieval history."

I know nothing at all about medieval history but suddenly it sounds like the most interesting topic I've ever heard of. I have to find a way to get in that class.

Later the same day, Nate and I head over to the Center for Students with Disabilities to register. Every other student registers in person in a ridiculously complicated process, where you get an appointment time to wait in a long line, then give a slip of paper with the classes you want to a middle-aged lady sitting in front of a computer. She types in your choices and tells you the classes you want are all full already and you have to pick something else. At least according to Carson, this is how it goes.

For us, we tell our choices to a random work study student in the CSD and they promise to send us our schedule in a week. I list off a bunch of required classes for my computer science major, plus medieval history. Nate says his choices, including one on disability studies that he says Abby recommended to him. If he knows why I want a random elective so far outside my major, he doesn't say anything.

On Friday afternoon we still haven't heard back from the registrar about our schedule. When I can't stand listening to Nate pace around our tiny room and crack his knuckles any more, we go to the CSD office in person to ask what's going on.

The work study kid at the desk disappears for a long time. Finally some lady comes from a back office to tell us our class schedule. Nate gets the disability studies class, but other than that, neither of us is enrolled in any of the classes we requested. I've been given a random assortment of intro level lectures in math, logic, and even philosophy.

"Excuse me, but this is not acceptable," Nate says evenly.

"These are the only classes available to you. Sorry." She doesn't sound the slightest bit sorry.

"How can that be?" Nate insists. "We were supposed to have priority for enrollment."

"No, that's not the way it works. We processed your request in line with university policies," she says, whatever that means. "The classes you requested were all full. In any case, the counselor assigned to you feels these classes would be a better fit for your abilities."

"What the hell!" I shout. "How am I supposed to graduate on time with this?"

"I can give you a referral to our academic counselor for extending your candidacy."

"No!" I feel something inside me snap. "I don't want a fucking referral! You can't do this to us! I thought this office was here to help us! Why don't you fucking help?" I'm so angry I can barely get the words out.

The more I yell, the quieter she gets. "Maybe we can revisit this issue when you're feeling calmer."

I'm about to yell again when I feel Nate's hand on my arm.

"Excuse us."

He drags me out of the office. I'd like to say I slam the door indignantly but we end up fumbling around and tripping over each other's canes, stumbling outside like a couple of idiots.

"What the hell!" It's not like him to take this kind of thing lying down. "You know we have to graduate on time!"

Tuition at Calstock is shockingly expensive for a state school, and even though we got scholarships, there's a strict cutoff after our senior year. The money came from our local benevolent society, a bunch of old rich dudes who play golf together and sometimes give charity to people they think are the most worthy.

At the banquet dinner where they gave us the scholarship checks, the head of the society clapped each of us on the back and congratulated us.

"You're going to study hard, right, boys?" he wheezed at us, puffing out the odor of stale cigarettes and whisky. "No smoking pot or cultural Marxism, right?"

I nodded, having no idea what he was talking about.

"And none of this endless deferring graduation, neither," he went on. "Why, my own son tried to spend ten years in college, but after year six, I cut him off! Yer finished, I said!"

Then his wife hustled us off to be photographed for the local paper. In the car on the way home, Dad said don't sweat it, the son in question was probably trying to avoid being drafted in Vietnam but we didn't have to worry about that.

"The scholarship," I remind Nate. "We can't take extra time, even if it's not our fault."

What I don't say is even aside from the scholarship, I really want that medieval history class. If I'm not in a class with Abby this semester, I might never see her again. Studying with her was the highlight of every week, and I can't imagine a semester without her.

"Yeah, yeah, the scholarship, I know," Nate says. "But that was only an admin person. She can't do anything to change it. We have to take this to the top."

When we get back to the dorm, Nate marches off to Cricket's room to tell her the whole story. It must be a slow news day at the student paper, because in the big Sunday edition, the headline is "Accessibility Woes Continue for Visually Impaired Students."

This time, there isn't any nonsense about how inspirational or pathetic we are. Cricket just lays out the facts about how we won't graduate on time. There's a long quote from Nate, saying we should be able to choose our own classes like everyone else and not have them assigned to us.

The article also includes quotes from CSD employees. I don't know how he did it, but somehow Nate found the name of the student worker who wrote down our requests on the paper slips, and Cricket gets an interview with him, too. He explains that all the slips from students using the CSD were left in a file until Thursday afternoon, then everyone was allocated whatever classes were still open. Cricket shows him the CSD brochure that mentions priority registration, but he shrugs and says that's what he was told to do. Apparently they always do it this way.

"Damn, girl! You totally stuck it to them!" Carson says admiringly after he reads us Cricket's article over lunch.

"Well, we'll see if it does any good," Cricket says.

We only have until the end of the first week of the semester to drop or add classes. Nate is prepared to camp out at the registrar's office until they give in.

But to my surprise, first thing Monday morning, we get a phone call from the Vice Dean of Students who apologizes for the situation and promises there will be an overhaul of registration policies at the CSD.

"I'm sorry about this semester, though," she says. "It does seem like most of the classes you chose are full, and I can't force the instructors to overload. But there's typically some movement in the first week. I recommend you go to the classes you want on the first day and submit add requests. You can do that directly at the Office of the Registrar, no need to go through the CSD."

"Thank you," Nate says. He was the one to pick up the phone, and I'm left listening in with my ear pressed to the other side of the receiver. "But if you're going to change the system, we shouldn't have to go through the CSD at all next semester. We should register directly, like everyone else."

The Vice Dean gives a heavy sigh. "This system was put in place to help students like you, who have difficulty reading the course guide and filling out the paperwork."

"So make the course guide and forms available in an accessible format," Nate replies. "I have the right to choose my own classes, not to be told by someone else what's best for me."

I'm impressed by how much he's talking back to her. I probably would have been too embarrassed to do more than mumble thank you.

"Yes, well, we'll be reviewing our policies." She sounds eager to get off the phone. "Are you ok with getting to the Registrar's Office? Do you need any help with that?"

"No, I don't need help. If I can manage to untangle this mess, I can also handle normal registration on my own," Nate snaps.

I resist the urge to poke him in the ribs and tell him to take it easy. He's talking to a dean. She could just as easily tell us to suck it up, nothing can be done. She didn't have to call us at all.

"We'll look into it," she says frostily, and signs off.

22

ABBY

The first week of the semester, I'm greeted by Nick's face staring up at me from a thousand copies of the school paper. I've been longing to see him again and now suddenly he's everywhere.

In the photo, Nick is standing next to Nate in front of the CSD office. Nate is frowning, face pointing down and away, but Nick is smirking right into the camera. Like he's got one over on them. Which I guess he does, because the article nails the CSD. It's by that hippie chick, Nate's beard. I have to admit, she did a good job.

After reading the article, I'm not expecting to see Nick at the first lecture for medieval history, but there he is. I spot him in the hallway, struggling through the crowd, looking a bit lost. I call out and his head jerks up.

"Hey," he says all casual-like as I push my elbow into his hand.

"Hey, dork." I guide him down the corridor to the lecture hall. "What're you doing here? I thought you had to take Philosophy for Mechanical Engineers. It was in all the papers. You're famous."

"Don't remind me! It's been a huge pain in the ass."

"Whatever. No one's writing front page articles about *my* class schedule."

"Please, I wish I could be anonymous like you."

As we angle into the narrow seats, I clasp my chest and fall back. "Me? Anonymous? Take it back! I'm a star, baby!" I say in my best Ethel Merman voice.

Nick laughs as he sits down next to me, his face lighting up with a broad grin that makes my heart sing. I quickly look away, bending over to get my notebook and pen from my bag.

"Does Cricket's editor know she pitched a front-page article about her boyfriend? Man, the student paper will print anything."

"Nah, they broke up back in December."

Interesting, but I'm not touching that mess. I change the subject quickly.

"Sorry they screwed up your classes. So you managed to get the ones you wanted?"

"Yeah, lucky for me, Prof Agarwal totally saved me. He saw the article and said he's trying to make sure all CS majors graduate on time. He let me into his class and convinced the profs in the other two classes I need to overload."

"Oh, awesome."

"That just leaves this one." He stretches back in the hard plastic chair like he's settling in, getting comfy.

"Wait, you're not enrolled?"

Nick shakes his head. Just then, the professor turns on the microphone and introduces herself as Professor Gilbert.

I squirm around in my seat, not sure how to feel about this. I was surprised when Nick called me last week. I assumed we would drift apart, like so many former friends once the semester ended. If I hadn't told him about this class, I would probably never see him again. And he still might not get in. What would be less bad, to drift apart or end up in another Ted situation?

I squirm around in my chair, trying not to think of what Nick might say if he knew I'm a devotee. Don't, I tell myself. Focus on taking notes.

The lecture is surprisingly good. Professor Gilbert is as nerdy and exacting as you might expect, but she still drops in little jokes and sarcastic comments here and there. Nick seems into it, laughing along and sitting forward like he's caught up in what she's saying. My heart starts racing just seeing that smile. Danger! Danger!

After class, I guide him down to the front of the room and listen as student after student begs Professor Gilbert to be let in. She has the same message for all of them, no matter their circumstances.

"Look, if it was only the lecture, I'd let you all in. But there isn't room in the tutorials, and I only have one TA."

She directs everyone to put their name on the waiting list, written down by the TA, whose name is Scott.

"First come, first served," he says.

"Who knew you had such a love of history," I say to Nick as we part ways outside. He gives me such a grin, I feel undone. This sucks. I have to do something to put some distance between us before we both fall into something we regret.

23

NICK

I'm sure there's no chance I'll get that history class with Abby, but I guess a bunch of other students drop because by the end of the first week I'm enrolled. I can hardly believe my luck.

It's not just me wanting to be with Abby. The class is actually fascinating. I never thought the lives of English peasants or wars of succession would be interesting, but here we are. Professor Gilbert has this kind of sardonic, deadpan style of delivery while she's relaying the most outrageous stories of corrupt popes and backstabbing royals and whatnot. It's hilarious.

I think Abby is enjoying the class too because she giggles to herself as she takes notes. After each class, we walk together over to the CSD office where she drops off her notes, then we go for a coffee at the café down the street. Mostly we talk about the lecture, or sci fi and fantasy books and movies we like. It feels good, just hanging out like this.

Nate isn't so lucky. Only one of the psych classes he wanted is open. For the other three, he picks some sociology lectures instead, but he doesn't seem to mind. He says these are more interesting anyway.

A few weeks into the semester, the temperature plunges and the snow falls constantly. The public schools all close, but the university stays open.

"Man, walking to class is going to suuuuuuuck," Carson moans over breakfast.

"Suck it up, candy ass!" Nate says, but in a teasing way, and they both laugh.

Whatever was eating at Carson seems to have disappeared over break. Since we came back, all four of us have been hanging around together like best friends.

"Why won't they cancel classes?" Cricket frets. "Walking across the quad is a health hazard. Instant frostbite. The weather report said to stay indoors."

"I heard that ten years ago, some prick in the law school sued the university for tuition for a snow closure, and now the school won't ever close no matter what," Carson says.

"Sounds like bullshit to me," Nate says. "Everyone lives within walking distance, so why should they close? You're all a bunch of wimps."

"I heard that if you can find your way through the steam tunnels, you can walk to every building on campus without going outside," I say.

Nate scoffs. "Please, you can barely find your way above ground, never mind in the steam tunnels."

"Yeah, I heard some kids went into the steam tunnels to party and got trapped and died down there. Their bodies were never found," Carson says ominously, like he's telling a ghost story at summer camp.

"There's no way that's even remotely true!" Cricket exclaims in exasperation. "It would have been in all the papers, and don't you think their parents would have sued the school?"

"The time is nine-thirty AM." I hear the tinny robot voice of Nate's talking digital wristwatch.

"Gotta go," Nate says, standing up, and the rest of us follow.

"Will you be ok with the snow?" Cricket asks us as she leads us to the tray carts. "Do you want a hand?"

"Nah, it's fine," Nate says. I can't ask for help after that.

Navigating through the snow is a challenge, since all the echoes are deadened and the landmarks on the sidewalk I'm used to finding with my cane are buried. But if I leave at the right moment, I'll be part of a big crowd heading from the dorm at the same time, and they make so much noise, I can follow along well enough.

Getting home is a little trickier, since there isn't the same big group to follow, but at least by afternoon, the snow has been tramped down more. Somehow, I manage.

The snow continues off and on for weeks, and I get used to finding my way by searching for the piled up snow along the sidewalk instead of the grass. It's always a little nerve-wracking to stick the tip of my cane in a snowbank, because of the possibility it might get stuck or break, but if I don't poke it too hard it's usually ok. I feel like I spend all my time wrapped up in a heavy parka and huge boots, freezing my ass off as I'm walking across campus painfully slowly, then sweaty in the hot classrooms.

That's just when I have to go out, though. In the evenings and weekends, when we stay in the dorm, Nate and I wear shorts and t-shirts because our room is so ridiculously overheated. We even stuff a towel in front of the radiator and open the window, and it's still hot. Everyone's room is like this. Cricket writes an article about how energy waste on campus is contributing to global warming.

At the café with Abby after class, the tile floor is slick with melted snow tracked in by everyone's boots, and the air is humid with the steam from the espresso machine and the smell of wet wool. My face slowly unfreezes as I sip cappuccino from a thick ceramic mug.

Abby has decided that instead of doing one big performance at the end of the semester, she's going to do a series of what she calls "installations" every week.

"Everyone always does some one-man show at the end of the semester, you know?" she says, and I nod as if I do know. "It's just a lot of pretentious monologuing," she continues, and adds with a sneer, "Risk-free theater."

When I laugh, she gets defensive. "What's so funny?"

"Sorry! You say that all the time, but how can theater be risky? The audience is only sitting in a seat. Are they going to be attacked by pirates or what?"

"Maybe! The whole point of live theater is that anything can happen. The audience should feel challenged. Everyone is too complacent."

"I though the point was to be entertained."

"You're so bourgeois," she says, but with a note in her voice that's making fun of herself for saying this as much as she is teasing me.

Abby's first performance or "installation" is at nine AM on a Sunday, which is the only time she could book the theater space. Actually it isn't one of the regular theaters on campus. It's just a lecture hall, but she says it has a proper stage.

When I first show up, I'm half afraid I've got the wrong room because it feels so empty, but the other classrooms were locked so this must be it. A few minutes later, I hear several more people come in and sit down.

Abby comes out onto the stage and thanks everyone for coming, then launches into her performance. For her first show, she's decided that she's going to repeat the same words over and over again, she says to get people to think about the meaninglessness of language or something like that.

"Circle!" she shouts. "Circle! Siiiirrrrrcullllllll!"

She goes on and on like this for a solid hour. It's a performance I can only describe as punishing, for the audience as much as for her. The words she chooses are a random collection of nouns: toy, house, motorboat, lunchbox. If there's any reason behind the words she chooses, I can't figure it out.

It's a little like the Meat Poet, but not as funny. Something's lacking. I wish I could tell her exactly what's missing, help her make it better. Maybe she should try throwing processed meat products at the audience.

As the hour wears on and Abby's voice starts to get hoarse, I'm reminded of how she read to me last semester. Now that was a performance. Luckily all my textbooks came in on tape or disk this time so she doesn't have to do that again, but hearing her on stage makes me miss that strange weekend we shared.

By the time she finishes, Abby has nearly lost her voice. She thanks us all for coming, and there's some ragged applause, so at least I know

I'm not the only one in the audience, but there can't be more than a handful of people in the lecture hall.

I walk down the stairs until I find the edge of the stage with the tip of my cane. I can hear her thanking various friends for coming, and talking to someone named Catherine about a video recording. I stand by the stage awkwardly, waiting for her to notice me.

"Nick! Wow, you didn't have to come!" Abby rasps from up on the stage.

"Oh, well, it was, um, great. Very risky," I say, which makes all the friends around her burst into laughter. Wait, was that the wrong thing to say? I thought that's what she wanted. Now I feel dumb.

"Thank you," Abby says seriously.

I plunge on with what I had planned to say, even though I'm already dying of embarrassment, and I can feel my ears getting hot. "Yeah, congratulations. So, um, do you want to go out to get, like, a coffee or something? To celebrate?" My original plan had been to ask her out for a drink but that was before I found out the performance would be at nine AM.

"Oh," she says, her voice sounding funny "I have plans with Catherine already."

"Ooo, Catherine," says one of the girls standing next to her. "You mean a hot date with Catherine." All the friends laugh but Abby doesn't deny it. My stomach drops. A date? But I thought we were getting closer. Disappointment crashes over me.

"It's really nice of you to come. I appreciate it. I'll see you in class, ok?" Abby says.

"Oh, yeah, sure! See you then!" I say cheerily, trying not to seem crushed. I overcompensate by grinning like an idiot and giving her a thumbs up before stumbling back up the stairs. A thumbs up, so stupid. Sheesh, what is wrong with me? She must think I'm a total idiot.

24

ABBY

I feel bad seeing how disappointed Nick looks when I tell him about Catherine. I thought he understood we were being platonic friends. Ok, I guess I have been seeing him every week and hanging out a little after class. If I'm honest, getting closer like this makes me nervous. I keep hearing Ted's voice in my head saying I like him for the wrong reasons. Besides, he hasn't hesitated to get with other girls. Why shouldn't I?

I fidget through a lecture on Charlemagne, with Nick sitting beside me, his face unreadable. Is he angry? Does he want someone else to take his notes?

But no, after class he asks me to get coffee with him again.

"Sorry about the other day," I say as we sip macchiatos.

I know he wants to ask me about Catherine, but I can't bring myself to tell him. I really do like her. Actually, I've had a low-key crush on her since freshman year, but she was always in a relationship with someone else, until recently. She's French Canadian, with the cutest accent. A vocal performance major with long, luxurious hair and a dreamy expression, like a Pre-Raphaelite painting come to life. I asked her out and she said yes.

I can't say any of that, so instead I fill the space with chatter about my senior thesis.

"So get this, Howard said there's no way he's sitting through a hundred performances instead of just one." Howard is the name of my thesis supervisor. Nick was surprised the first time I called a prof by his first name, but that's how it is in the theater department.

"And anyway, it's not a hundred performances," I continue. "It's only going to be like five or six. But he still said no way. So now I have to videotape each one and give him the tapes, which he says he'll watch at the end of the semester. Can you believe that? Such bullshit!"

Nick nods sympathetically.

"Anyway, the theater department gave me a video camera to use, and Catherine said she would record me, which is totally saving my ass."

"I understand," he says. "You owe her."

"Well…" Ok, now or never. I'm not keeping secrets from him. "About that…it's not only that." I push myself to say the words out loud. "I have to tell you. We're dating."

"So it's true, what your friend said?" He frowns at me.

"Hey!" I was feeling bad for hurting him but that look on his face puts me on the defensive. Does he think I'll wait around while he sleeps with every girl in Probus Hall? "Don't get all jealous with me, Nick! I have a life, you know!"

"Well, yeah, of course." He moves his head around in that weird way that I know means he's trying to see me, one bit at a time. Watching him do that triggers my devotee feelings, to my shame.

"Stop it."

"Ok, I'm sorry!" He stops moving his head and looks contrite. "We don't have to be friends if you don't want."

"It's not so easy being your friend."

Nick's mouth gapes open but he doesn't say anything.

"You don't get to be jealous of me going out with someone else, when you've done the same thing. I'm going out with Catherine and don't you dare say anything about it."

"Ok." He tries to take a sip of coffee but realizes he's already drained the cup.

It's better this way, I tell myself. So why do I feel so terrible?

25

NICK

"Nick!"

Cricket's voice cuts through the white noise around me. I jump.

"What?"

We're all eating dinner in the dining hall together as usual. Dinner is some sort of noodle casserole. I've been picking at it, spacing out while the others talk.

"I said are you ok?" she repeats. "You haven't said a word since we sat down."

"Girl trouble," Carson says. I can hear the smirk in his voice.

"Shut up, asshole."

"How is Abby these days?" Nate asks in exactly the same tone as Carson.

I had decided not to say anything, but before I realize what I'm doing, I blurt out, "She's started dating some French Canadian chick named Catherine!"

"Whoa, no way!" Carson hoots. "Sounds like the start of a porno."

"She's videoing Abby's senior thesis performances."

"Oh my God, it *is* a porno! Please tell me she's filming a naked pillow fight."

Nate snorts, but Cricket is indignant.

"Women don't...get together just to play out some sexist male fantasy. That's such bullshit!"

"Sorry man," Nate says to me, ignoring her. "Guess she was never into dudes after all."

"Who knew she's a lesbo," says Carson.

"She told me she's bi."

"Well anyway, it was very brave of her to come out to you like that," Cricket says seriously.

Was it? Abby always seems so confident about everything she does. I can't imagine she's scared of anything.

The next few weeks, Abby continues with her "installations," which are all at odd times and in random places around campus. I go to all of them. We're friends, after all. Friends show up for each other. I don't want her to think I was only being nice in hopes of getting some.

One busy morning, she stands in the archway between two engineering buildings and puts on her makeup in public, as students stream by on their way to class. I stand on the opposite side, listening to the voices bounce all around the stone and brick walls. No one seems to notice her. I keep hoping she'll crack the code on this performance art thing, do something she feels proud of. But so far she's just getting frustrated.

"Shit! That was a total bust!" Abby says after Catherine turns off the video camera. "I don't think anyone realized that it was a commentary on the performative nature of daily life."

"Yeah, you just looked like a sorority girl who's running late to class." Catherine puts the camera away in its huge plastic briefcase.

I'm trying to be friendly to Catherine to prove to Abby (and to myself) that I'm not jealous. It's not going great. Catherine never speaks more than a few words to me.

"Maybe you should have worn a costume, so people would get that it's a performance," I say, crossing the walkway carefully, trying not to bump into anyone.

"What do you think I'm wearing! I borrowed a ball gown from the costume shop." Abby's angry voice echoes in the stone archway.

"Oh, sorry, I didn't notice." I mean, I saw that she was wearing some sort of long dress, but I didn't get the details. It's dark under the arch and I can't see much, even though it's a bright sunny day. The snow has mostly melted but the air is still cold.

"All right, fine. Next time will be better," she promises.

I hope she's right. I hate how hard she's being on herself. I wish there was more I could do to help, but all I can do is show up.

Next time is in the theater again. She borrows a bunch of clothing from the costume shop and hangs it around the stage (so she tells me in advance, I can't see the stage) and does an hourlong improvised religious ceremony. She's basically worshipping the clothing. Even I get the meaning of this one.

Abby's performance is weird and more than a little boring but I think more about what Nate and Carson and Cricket said. It's incredibly brave of Abby to get up there and perform like that. It's not that she doesn't care what people think of her. From what she's said to me, I know she cares a lot. But it's like she has this idea of how the world should be and she wants to share it in hopes that people will get it.

Judging by the applause at the end, there are only a few people in the audience, probably other students majoring in theater. Or theatre. I clap as loud as I can, to make it sound like a bigger audience. I want her to know there are people who appreciate what she's doing.

"Hey Nick, we need to talk." Cricket shows up in my dorm room late on a Thursday evening.

Nate is out somewhere, so it's just me. Something sounds weird, anxious in her voice, and instantly my heart rate goes up. Stupid. I feel like we're having "the talk" but we're not even dating. There's something different about her, but I can't quite put my finger on it.

I say yes, but instead of talking, she wants to go for a walk in the Kagishkaw Botanic Garden. That's this huge park right next to campus.

We hike across the quad and down the main street. I hang onto her elbow praying I won't embarrass myself by tripping over the sidewalk as she takes off at her usual speedy pace. The fresh air feels good for a change. As we enter the park, the air has a mossy, damp, grassy smell. The days have been getting warmer, the first spring thaw, even if the nights are still cold.

For a while, the only sound is our feet on the path and our breathing. Cricket sets a punishing pace. I pick up my feet extra high with each step to make sure I don't trip, even though I probably look like a dork.

"It's dark," Cricket says when we're well into the trees, slowing down at last.

"Yeah." I try not to sound out of breath. Man, I need to exercise more.

"So, um, you can't see anything, huh?"

"No." Shit! This is getting more ominous. What the hell, Cricket? But she sounds more nervous than anything.

She slows to a stop and scuffs her feet on the ground. "Did you see me at all before we left, in the light?"

"I dunno, a little I guess. Why?" I drop my hold on her elbow.

I can hear her rustling and fidgeting around. "Oh, nothing. I just…I just got a haircut, that's all. Did you see it?"

"Oh, yeah, sure," I lie. I guess I did see her general shape. Maybe that's what was different, no cloud of long yellow hair around her shoulders, but I wouldn't have noticed if she didn't say anything.

"It's like this now." She grabs my hand and brings it to the back of her head. I hate when people do that, but I don't say so. She rubs my hand along the back of her head, and I feel that yes, she has short hair now, short on the sides, almost like a guy but not quite.

"Nice haircut." I try to sound sincere and not like I'm wondering why the hell she had to bring me all the way out here only to tell me that. And why cut it all off anyway? I thought it looked good long. What I could see of it, anyway.

Cricket drops my hand and starts shifting around again. "Thanks." There's a long pause. "So I decided it's time to be a lesbian."

The way she says it is so strange I almost laugh. What does she mean "It's time?" Did she set an alarm clock or something? But catch myself just in time. "Oh, ok. Um, good?"

"Yeah?"

What am I supposed to say? It's not like she needs my permission. "I'm not homophobic," I clarify. "It's ok with me."

"Even though we…?"

"Yeah, that was kinda weird."

"I'm sorry!" she bursts out. "I've been a mess. I don't know what I was thinking. I guess, I thought I could be straight if I met the right guy. And you're, well, you're really cute in a clean-cut white boy kind of way."

"Me and Nate," I say before I can stop myself.

"I'm sorry!" she says again. "Like I said, I was a mess. I didn't mean to hurt you. Nate was so understanding, and we both, I mean he…" she trails off.

"He what?"

"Never mind. You should talk to him yourself."

"Did you already tell him about you being a, um, a lesbian?"

"Yeah, I talked to him this afternoon, and he said I should tell you myself. So that's why I'm telling you now."

"Ok. Thanks for telling me." Even to my own ears my voice is flat and awkward. Abby was right about her, I realize. But I don't say that.

"Are you sure? You're not angry?" She still sounds anxious.

"No, why should I be?"

"I didn't mean to lead you on or anything. I just…I was kind of in a panic all last semester, trying to fix myself. I thought I could make it all turn out right if I tried hard enough."

"Well, I do feel kinda dumb for not figuring it out sooner."

"Don't be. It took me until now to figure it out too." There's another long silence, them she says in a choked voice, "I'm sorry I screwed everything up. I really do like you and Nate, I mean as friends. But I understand if you don't want to be friends after all this."

On an impulse, I reach out, and she's right there. I give her a big hug, which is not like me. Our family isn't that touchy-feely. But it feels right in the moment. She slumps against me and squeezes me back.

"I'm not mad, I promise," I say, my chin resting against the top of her head. "I still want to be your friend. I'm sure Nate said the same thing."

She nods, her head moving against my chest. "Yeah, he did." She gives a little hiccup, and I think she might be crying. "Thanks. You guys are the best. You have no idea how much this means to me."

When I get back to the dorm room, Nate is there.

"Did she tell you?" he asks.

"Yeah, she did." I kick off my sneakers and put my cane and jacket in the closet.

"And?"

I lay down on the bed. Nate is in the bunk above me. "And what?"

"You're not still mad at her?"

"Of course not. I mean, I was mad before that she jerked me around, but after hearing how upset she was, I couldn't bring that all up again. I just wish she had told me sooner."

"She told us when she was ready."

"So did you guess? I mean before, when you two were together?"

"No, I had no idea." His voice is flat. I don't believe him.

26

ABBY

"Where is Catherine?" I'm trying not to panic.

"I'm sure she'll be here," Nick says, based on nothing.

My installations have not been going as well as I hoped. But I'm not going to be discouraged. I just have to try even harder on the next one.

I call this installation "Halloween in April." It's an interactive performance where I pass out candy and see how people respond. Will they accept the offered treat out of season? Their reaction will be a commentary on interbeing in the candy-based economy of holiday gift exchanges.

"What, like reverse trick-or-treating?" Nick asks when I describe it to him.

"No, it's more like a critique of the postmodern condition..." I can see that I've lost him already. "Ok, fine, yes! It's reverse trick-or-treat. But I don't want to schlep all over Frat Row. Who knows if people will even be home? I'm going to do it in Probus Hall. It'll be less walking and there are always people hanging around."

So that's why I'm standing in at the main entrance to the dorm in a pointy hat, a long black dress, and a green witch mask, holding a pillowcase full of candy. I have the video camera in its clunky gray plastic briefcase, and I need Catherine to film me so Howard can see my performance.

But Catherine is nowhere to be seen.

"Do you want to use the phone in my room to call her?" Nick suggests when we've waited half an hour.

"No! Fuck her! If she's going to be all flaky, canceling dates, not showing up, then the hell with her!"

Nick shuffles his feet awkwardly. "Uh, sorry. Maybe you can do this a different day?"

"No! I'm here now, and I have other shit to do. I've already spent too much time on this project, and this candy was super expensive. Do you have any idea how much Halloween candy costs? And there wasn't much to choose from."

"Yeah, I guess it's the off season."

"Well, I'm still doing it. You're going to have to hold the camera."

"Me?!"

Nick looks incredulous but I'm sure he can do it if he sets his mind to it. I put the plastic briefcase on the floor.

"I'll get everything set up and start recording. All you have to do is point it in my direction."

"You do realize I suck at pointing things in a specific direction, right?"

"Whatever, it'll be fine. The hallways are all brightly lit, and you can see this giant pointy hat, right?"

"Sort of."

"Well, I'll be talking the whole time anyway, so just follow my voice."

"Ok, I'll try. But I'm not responsible for you getting a failing grade."

"Dude, you suck at this!" Carson says, laughing. "I can see your cane in the bottom of the frame."

We're all sitting on Carson's bed because he's the only one with a TV and VCR, watching the fifteen minutes or so of footage Nick managed to get before we gave up.

"We could try again," Nick offers. "I'll be more careful this time."

"No, it's ok," I say. "Really, don't worry about it. The video is plenty long enough."

"Does he look horrible?" Nate asks from the other side of the bed, sounding delighted.

"Oh yeah, he's gonna have a shiner," Carson confirms. "Hey, pass some of that candy over here."

"Do you need an ice pack?" Cricket asks.

"No, I'm fine," Nick says.

He started off so well, following me down the hallway, but I guess it was a mistake for him to hold the camera right up to his face and try to look through the eyepiece. As I walked down the hall, I went through a set of double doors that are usually both open, but for some reason today one was closed and Nick walked right into it.

I feel terrible. This is all my fault. Nick insists that it's nothing but I feel so, so guilty. I should never have pushed him to do it.

"This video is hilarious," Carson says, rewinding it to the beginning again, and narrating the whole thing for Nate. "He's shaking the camera all around like a drunk crazy person. Ok, now I can see the edge of Abby's black dress in the top corner of the frame. Mostly I'm seeing Nick's sneakers and him waving his cane around. Oh wait, now Abby's knocking on someone's door. Stop walking, Nick! Ok, he stopped but he's holding the camera crooked and I can't see Abby's face, just her shoulders and arms."

On the video, we faintly hear my voice offering some dorm residents Halloween candy. Two girls politely turn me down and one dude says yes. But the camera is still aimed at my shoulder so you can't see their faces.

"Ok, here we go!" Carson hoots, as Nate cackles beside him. "Walking down the hall. Slow down! Aaaand, boom, right into the door!"

The video shakes around wildly as Nick curses, then the screen goes black.

"Ok, that's enough." I pop the tape out. But no one gets up. They just lounge on Carson's bed, eating my Halloween candy.

"It's a good thing you didn't go to my room," Cricket says. "My new roommate is Wiccan, and she would have given you an earful about cultural appropriation and perpetuating harmful stereotypes."

"Aw, that would have been awesome!" For the first time I think maybe this performance can be salvaged. "I kinda wish I got that on tape. Maybe I'll go try your room later."

"I'm sorry but I'm not available to be your cameraman," Nate says. We all laugh, even me.

"I'll do it," Cricket says, to my surprise.

"Ok boys, the Halloween party's over." I sweep the remaining candy along with the empty wrappers into my pillowcase in a jumble. Carson gripes about chocolate on his bedspread.

"You don't have to do this," I say to Cricket as we walk down the hall to her room.

"It's fine. I want to help. Anyway, I feel like I owe you," Cricket's voice goes quieter, her tone suddenly more serious. "It's because of you that I had the courage to come out."

"Me? What did I do?" I barely know this chick.

"Oh you know...you're dating a girl like it's nothing, like you don't care what people might say. And everyone was like, it's no big deal. So I thought, what am I so scared of? Why am I tying myself in knots trying to force myself to be with a guy, when I can just be like you and go for what I really want?"

If only she knew. What I really want is so much more complicated.

"Also I was so jealous that you got to be with a girl and I haven't yet."

I give a snort. "Yeah, well, I think I've just had the pleasure of being dumped by a girl."

"No, don't say that!" Cricket's sweet round face crinkles with concern. "I'm sure it was only miscommunication. C'mon, let's see if my roommate is in."

She unlocks her door, but the room is empty. Who knows where the Wiccan roomie is and when she'll be back.

"Thanks anyway, but I gotta go return this camera." I hold up the gray plastic case apologetically.

"Sorry your performance didn't work out. Come back anytime if you want."

I've already given up on this particular installation idea, but I don't get into that with Cricket. I only smile and nod.

"Oh, and y'know, we're all going camping in a few weeks. You should come along."

When I tell her I've never been camping before, her eyes get huge and incredulous, but I just shrug. I'm a city girl. My parents' idea of roughing it is a hotel without room service. Cricket goes on and on about how much I'll love it. I'm pretty sure I'm a charity case to her but I let her talk me into it. Why not. It's not like I have anything else going on in my social life.

When I get home, I'm almost afraid to even look at the answering machine, but there are no messages. The red zero glows in the dim hall. I try calling Catherine, but she doesn't pick up.

I call her again the next day, just to be sure, but still no answer. Ok, I can take a hint. I didn't say anything to Cricket, but I know this isn't a misunderstanding.

In our last conversation, I told Catherine about me being a devotee. I was trying to be open and honest with her, and she threw it back in my face, called me a sexual predator. I tried to stick up for myself but I felt defensive and she wasn't listening. She told me I need therapy.

Haha, joke's on her. As if I haven't been seeing a therapist since I was twelve years old. It's like my birthright. My family goes to therapy more often than synagogue.

I tried to explain being a devotee to her as just another kind of attraction, a normal variation in desire, like how my therapist talked about it with me. But it's so hard to even get started when there is literally nothing written about it. No book or coming out story or even case study. It's too rare. My therapist said she suspects it's actually more common but most women don't talk about it. They just become nurses. That's not me, though. I'm not the nurse type.

Catherine put on her shoes and walked out the door before we could get into any of this. She didn't seem upset, so I thought we could talk more after my installation, but I guess not.

Well if she's going to be a cowardly asshole about it, fuck her. I won't call her again.

27

NICK

The bruise on my face fades a lot quicker than my embarrassment at walking into a door like an idiot. I wanted to help Abby with her senior thesis and I couldn't even do that. And did she and Catherine really break up? I want to ask her about it but I can't think of a non-creepy way to bring it up.

I'm walking back from Object Oriented Design class. This class has been kicking my butt, but I think I'm finally getting the hang of how to make a bajillion tiny programs to work together as one big program. Prof Choi told me I'm improving, so that's good, right?

The weather is nice, so I take off my jacket, holding it on one hand and swinging my cane in the other. Spring in the Midwest is usually just another word for winter, but on clear days the sun can almost fool you into thinking it's warm.

I'm enjoying the bright sunshine and trying not to crash into anyone as students cross the quad in random directions, when I'm brought up short by someone yelling my name.

"NIIIIICK!" It's Carson.

I pause. "Over here!" he shouts somewhere on my left.

I carefully pick my way through the crowd in the direction of his voice. Apparently there are a lot of other students sitting in the big grassy area of the quad, under the trees, because I whack a few of them with my cane. Carson comes running up to me.

"This way! Nate and I are sunbathing."

I try and fail to come up with a mental image of this scene.

"Wanna hand?" Carson offers me his elbow and leads me in a zigzag over the grass, around other students.

"Hey," I say, so Nate knows I'm here. "Are you really sunbathing?"

"Oh yeah," Nate says. "Carson here has taken off his shirt and everything. Showing off his six pack."

They both laugh, which I take to mean that he's kidding. Maybe? I drop my hand from Carson's elbow hurriedly, just in case.

"What are you doing?" I ask.

"Shh, we're listening to Preacher Mike," Nate says.

From what I've heard from the other students, Preacher Mike is a regular, not only at Calstock but at other universities all over the tri-state area. Ever since the snow melted, he's been out on the quad almost every afternoon, shouting some bullshit about hellfire and the dangers of communism or whatever. I've been trying to block him out.

"Why are you listening to this asshole?" I don't have anything against religion but hate speech is just wrong.

"It's hilarious," Nate says. "He's going on and on about the Children of Sodom and the evils of homo-SEX-ualiteee."

"Apparently the gays are going to make it illegal for any professor to say 'God' or 'Jesus' on campus," Carson adds, snickering.

"Lucky for us Preacher Mike is here to save us from the gay brainwashing," Nate says, and they laugh.

It's far too nice a day to be listening to angry ranting. I just want to sit in the sun.

"Shove over," I say to Nate, prodding slightly at his butt with the tip of my cane, like a lever.

As we're settling ourselves in, Preacher Mike notices us, because of course he does. Whenever Nate and I are together in public we're always the center of attention.

"My children!" Preacher Mike booms. Earlier, his voice was coming at us from a high angle, I assume because he was standing on one of the cement benches that line the quad, as he always does. But now his voice is closer. I'm really hoping he doesn't come over to us.

"My sons! You are in darkness, but there is light ahead!"

I want to crawl away, but Nate is just getting started.

"What light?" he calls out. "Lo, God has smote me!"

"That doesn't sound right," Carson says. "I think it's 'smitten.'"

"Smited!" Nate calls out.

"The Lord is with you!" Preacher Mike intones.

"No!" Nate shouts. "For the sin of masturbation, God has struck me blind!"

The whole crowd erupts in laughter.

"Your mother always warned you that if you touch yourself, you'll go blind. Well, it's true!"

People laugh even louder.

"Watch out or it will happen to you, too!"

Evidently Preacher Mike chooses to ignore us, because when I hear his voice again, it's much further away. He goes right on ranting about how Marxism is a tool of Satan, as if nothing happened.

I heave a sigh of relief. "Can't a guy just enjoy the first warm afternoon in months?"

"Oh, I'm enjoying it a lot," Nate says.

"Yeah," Carson adds. "We can't let this shithead think it's ok to say things like that."

"Whatever." I don't agree with Preacher Mike's homophobia but I also don't want to argue. It doesn't have anything to do with me. I lean back in the sunshine and do my best to ignore everything around me.

Nate prods me in the shoulder. "Hey, where's Abby?"

"I dunno. History class isn't until tomorrow."

"Jeez, what are you waiting for? Ask her out already!"

"Yeah, this campus is full of gorgeous lesbians. Ask her out now before another one swoops in and carries her off," Carson says.

I sit up again. "Hey, none of your business! Anyway I can't just ask her out. If Abby decides she's a lesbian, I have to respect that."

Carson groans as if he can't believe how stupid I'm being. "I know you feel like you got burned before, but trust me, Abby ain't Cricket. She said she's bi, right? She's definitely into you. Watching you two pine after each other, I'm embarrassed for both of you."

"But I don't want to ruin our friendship."

Nate gives a strangled kind of laugh. "Trust me, you won't."

"What if I make things awkward and she still has to be my note taker?"

"So get a new note taker!" Carson says.

But Nate doesn't say anything to that, I notice. He gets it. Having a disability means we have to be careful with people who help us, not take them for granted or ask too much. So maybe Abby and I will only be friends, nothing more. That would be ok, right?

28

ABBY

"Spring BREAAAAKKK!"

Carson bangs open Nick and Nate's door, bellowing like a deranged gorilla. Of course those two idiots are still asleep even though it's nearly noon.

I showed up over an hour ago at Cricket's room like she asked, and helped her pack up for our camping trip. She very kindly lends me a sleeping bag and a bunch of other things because all I have is a backpack with some clothes and a toothbrush. Then we go looking for the guys but only Carson is ready to go.

"Get up, assholes!" Carson shouts. "We're leaving in ten!"

"I'll be ready in five," Nate says from the top bunk and rolls over.

"It's break. I should be able to sleep in if I want to," Nick complains. He sits up, looking groggy, with his hair going every which way.

Cricket and I hover behind Carson, blocking the hallway with all our stuff. It hardly matters since the dorm is mostly empty already. Other, cooler people are flying to Florida for spring break, but we're only going as far as the nearest state park.

I try not to notice that Nick's only wearing a t-shirt and boxers. How does he look so adorable first thing in the morning? With a groan, he staggers out of bed and over to the closet with his arms outstretched.

Needless to say, we don't leave in five or ten or anything like it. Carson decides he wants to eat lunch in the dining hall, while Nate takes a leisurely shower. Nick turns on every light in his room including a flashlight, searching for things then throwing them into a duffel bag. I offer to help but he says he can do it, so I sit on the bed next to Cricket.

Watching him groping around in the closet, occasionally putting a shirt or something right up to his face, is seriously triggering my devotee feelings. I love seeing how he does ordinary things, how he moves through the world differently, how he manages so well even though he can't see. My whole body is tingling, right down to the soles of my feet. It's literally killing me. I try to keep an expression of bored indifference on my face, like Cricket. If Nick knew I was feeling this way, he would never speak to me again. Stop it, I tell myself. Just stop it. At least he put on some damn pants.

I finally ran into Catherine the other day as I was at the theater department main office, booking space for my next installation. We passed in the hall and I could tell she was trying to pretend she hadn't seen me.

"Hey, what's up," I said, daring her to ignore me. "How ya doin'?"

"Fine." She glanced at me for a second then slid her eyes away and hurried down the hall.

I wish she had come out and said she's dumping me because she thinks I'm a sick pervert. Nothing she says could be more cruel than the script I make up in my head, what I imagine she's thinking about me. At least she could do me the favor of ending with a big screaming argument. But like my housemate Jennifer says, there's no good way to get dumped. It sucks no matter how it happens.

I try not to think about Catherine. But watching Nick just makes it worse. Does she think I want him to be helpless and dependent? Because that's not it at all. I want to tell her it's the opposite—I'm sitting here getting turned on watching how competent he is, how he doesn't need my help. But it's still the fact of his blindness that's sexy to me, so I guess nothing can make that ok in her mind.

And then there's Nate. I mean, objectively he's handsome too. The way he does things, how different he is from Nick, it's also interesting but not in the same way. I don't feel the same magnetic attraction to him, and not just because I know he's gay, even if he hasn't come out yet. And not just because he's Nick's brother and it's weird to go after both of them. I have to agree with Nick, it was slightly uncomfortable that Cricket went from one to the other but she was in the throes of her own gay panic, so I can cut her some slack on that.

Some people assume that I would go after anyone with a disability. Jen still points out every elderly person in a wheelchair we see at the supermarket and waggles her eyebrows at me suggestively. It's so insulting. Just because I'm attracted to one feature doesn't mean I would go for every person with that one feature, what the hell? Besides, attraction is more than physical, there has to be some emotional connection as well.

So no, I only like Nate as a friend, and if I weren't a devotee, no one would even question me for being into one twin and not the other.

I wish you were normal. I'm still having an imaginary debate in my mind with Ted, and despite my best arguments, he always wins with that one line. I consider bailing on this whole poorly-planned trip, but just when I've made up my mind to take my backpack and walk home, Carson reappears and starts carrying all the bags downstairs.

We all pile into Carson's ratty old Honda Civic. Nate rides shotgun, arguing with Carson about the radio, switching at random between college rock and sports shouting. Nick takes the middle seat in back, between me and Cricket. We have to stop for gas and snacks, so by the time we hit the highway it's already late afternoon.

As we leave Allenville behind, passing by endless corn fields, I put thoughts of Catherine and Ted out of my mind, and my mood starts to lift. Cricket and Nick play punch buggy, and I join in. He makes us laugh, pretending to see cars that aren't there, while we pummel each other. "I'm Too Sexy" comes on the radio, and we all sing along. I start to feel glad I came on this trip after all.

But then Carson says "uh oh" and as it turns out he doesn't know the route as well as he thought. Cricket and I wrestle over the map, with Nick getting in the way. Carson curses and tells us to turn off the overhead light because by now the sun has gone down. It's a good thing we got lots of snacks at the gas station, since we're too lost and distracted to stop for dinner.

After a long stretch of shouting and backtracking, we finally pull into Big Squirrel Lick State Park. But instead of getting out, we drive through parking lot after lot without stopping. Each one has a huge sign posted saying "No camping."

"Shit!" Carson whips the car around each lot, tires squealing.

After over an hour of this, he finally finds the camping area. I stumble out of the car, dizzy and nauseated from eating Skittles and Combos for dinner. Carson and Cricket spring off to the campsites, but a few minutes later they're back.

"All the spots are taken," Cricket reports.

"Fuck!" Carson shouts. "How was I supposed to know you need a reservation?"

The campsites were not at all what I was expecting. I thought we were going to the woods. But this place looks like a giant parking lot with electrical plugs. There are rows upon rows of RVs lined up right next to each other. Why would anyone drive all the way to the great outdoors to spend a week living in a parking lot with hundreds of other people practically on top of each other? Goyim are so weird.

"I thought camping was sleeping in a tent in the middle of nowhere," I say.

"That was my plan," Carson growls through gritted teeth.

Cricket wanders off again, and I see her talking to a tall guy with a grey mullet and pot belly, while the rest of us wait awkwardly by the car. A few minutes later she jogs back.

"That guy over there says if we drive down that road there all the way to the end we'll come to a hilly area where we can camp and the rangers never go check." Cricket points toward the dark end of the daytime-only parking area.

"What kind of guy?" Nate asks suspiciously. "Are we talking dirty hippy or potential serial killer?"

"Why not both?" I say, laughing.

"So we'll be camping illegally," Carson says flatly.

"You got a better idea?" Cricket asks.

"Nope. Just so we're clear that's what we're doing."

"Fuck it, let's just go." I'm tired of standing around.

We pile back into the car and drive down a bumpy unpaved road until Carson pulls slowly into another parking area.

"That's it, end of the line," he says grimly as he cuts the engine.

I help get our bags from the trunk. As soon as all the interior car lights switch off, we're plunged into darkness more profound than anything I have ever experienced before. It's almost shocking how totally dark it is.

Cricket and Carson scout ahead for a likely spot to set up our tents. I follow behind with Nick and Nate each with a hand on my shoulders, although honestly they probably would be better off on their own. I stumble over the uneven ground as much or more than they do.

"Sorry, this is the best I can do in the dark," Cricket says as we reach the spot she has picked out. The ground is noticeably sloped, rough with tree roots and rocks, and wet with dew. "I don't think we can set up a campfire. The rangers might notice."

"Also we don't have any firewood," Carson says. "Fine, let's just set up the tents and go to sleep. It's almost midnight. We can figure out something in the morning."

Cricket brought two tents, a little one and a big one, but setting them up in the dark is a challenge. She and Carson start arguing almost immediately, their flashlights strobing as they swing them around, trying to hold the light with one hand and set up the tent with the other.

The plan is for Nick and Nate to share the smaller tent, and the rest of us in the bigger one. I thought Nate and Carson would share a tent, but apparently not. Maybe they're not together anymore?

Even by flashlight, I can see the looks Carson gives Nate. He still likes the guy, whether they're together or not. Carson is a handsome dude. A little too muscly for my taste. But the way he looks at Nate is so obvious. If Nate could look back, would they be exchanging smoldering gazes? I want to shake Nate, tell him to get his head out of his ass.

But I promised him I wouldn't say anything, and besides, I doubt he would welcome any advice from me.

"Here, Nate, can you hold this for me?" Carson asks, but instead Nate switches the flashlight off and throws it to the grass.

"If you're really worried about the rangers, you should turn off the flashlights," Nate says in his bossiest voice. "Here, give me that tent pole." He sets about lecturing everyone on how they rely on their eyes too much and they need to trust their fingers instead. He clearly loves ordering everyone around. I can't help but notice Nick sighing in irritation every time Nate gives a command. God, these two.

Nate tells me to clear a flat space on the ground to set the tent on. I feel around in the dark, brushing away twigs and stones. Is this what it's like for them? Of course not, and not just because they can both see light, and Nick a bit more than that. They have training and practice, and I don't. Being in the unaccustomed dark gives me a strange, unreal sensation.

Thinking of Nick's sensitive fingers feeling around is so freaking sexy. I love that we're both doing the same thing for a moment. I get so turned on wondering how he perceives this experience, if it's the same or different from me. But like always my attraction to him is tinged with guilt, knowing that he wouldn't like it if he knew what I was thinking.

But it's Nate I really worry about finding me out. He would never have turned out that flashlight if he knew I'm a devotee, or encouraged me to pretend to be blind like him. Not that I want to be blind myself. Argh, why does this all have to be so complicated?

29

NICK

I honestly didn't think Abby would come along on this trip. She keeps saying she doesn't know anything about camping, but she's been surprisingly relaxed about all the screw-ups so far. I hope she's having a good time, because I'm enjoying just having her here with us. Like, a lot. Every time she puts her hand on my arm I get this little shock. I want to put my arms around her, but not in front of everyone.

Even though it's late and we're all exhausted, there's still a lot of messing around instead of going right to sleep. We take forever to find the sleeping bags, sort out all the crap we brought along, scout out a tree to discreetly pee behind, then Carson breaks out a case of beer. Where did he even get that from? We're all bumbling around in the dark, getting tangled up in the tents, tripping over tree roots. For once I'm not the only one. After one or two disgusting warm beers, we're all laughing like idiots.

We're still sitting around outside the bigger tent when Abby announces that she's ready for sleep. But first she has to brush her teeth. I'm not sure why she can't skip a night like the rest of us but she seems intent on this one thing, only she can't find a bottle of water or her toothpaste.

"There's some in our tent," I offer. "Hold on, I'll get it for you."

"No, I can get it," she says, elbowing me out of the way as I'm trying to crawl inside the tiny tent, so we both end up in a heap on the ground.

Honestly, I wasn't planning to just tackle her. I was hoping to be a little more smooth. Maybe it's the beer, although I'm only moderately buzzed, or maybe it's the slight feeling of unreality after how ridiculous this whole evening has been, but the next thing I know, we're wrestling together on the floor of the tent. The sleeping bags and thin foam mats only slightly cushion the uneven, rocky ground and tree roots underneath, but I hardly notice. All I know is that she's round and warm pressed up against me, and I've never felt so good.

We don't speak, but her hot breath blows in my ear and I squeeze her even tighter. She's wearing a fleece sweater that makes her even more warm and soft. Our bodies fit together naturally. There's nowhere else I want to be ever.

She pulls up my sweatshirt and I stifle a groan at the sensation of her cool, smooth fingertips trailing over my chest. Her breathing gets faster but I can tell she's also trying to keep quiet. We're both aware that the others are just on the other side of a sheet of polyester that does nothing to insulate the sound. I can hear them joking around and laughing, and pray that they're too distracted to notice us.

I reach under her shirt and unhook her bra. She gives a little sigh as it comes open and that sound almost kills me, the way her voice is husky but small, making herself vulnerable to me. My heart is racing because I realize this is what I want more than anything, but I'm also worried that she might not feel the same way. Things between us are complicated. I don't want to ruin the moment but I want to be sure.

I'm about to open my mouth and say something awkward and stupid, but she saves me by lunging forward right at that moment and kissing me hard. She kind of misses at first before locking into the right position, and I realize that right now in the tent, we're both equally in the dark.

I've dated girls before, not counting my one-night stand with Vicky. Two girls, in my senior year of high school, but only for a few months, one after the other. They were both ok but kind of shy and quiet. At the time I thought the sex was good but it was nothing like this.

Abby is wild, yanking off my shirt and clawing at my back, not enough to hurt, but scratching in a way that sends sparks shooting up and down my spine. I run my hands all over her, taking in her luscious form. She's small and round and curvy in all the right places. Within a minute she's pulled off her sweater and shirt, and bra. Then she's pressing herself up against me again, like she can't get close enough. How did I get so lucky?

Still trying to keep quiet, I pull open the button of her jeans, and she wriggles out of them. She does the same for me. I flip around and plant my face between her legs, delighted at the way she trembles and shakes in an effort not to make noise. She's hot and slick and my tongue goes around and around. I want to make her lose her mind, and I feel like I'm succeeding.

I'm kind of hovering over her, leaning down, and the next thing I know, she's grabbed my cock in her hands. I feel like I'm going to lose it right there. For a second, the thought flashes through my mind that Nate will never forgive me if I come all over his sleeping bag. Which one is his? I have no idea. I push the thought aside. I try to hang on longer, while I push Abby over the edge. She arches her back, her legs straight and taut, her breath catching in her throat.

A second later, she shifts her grip on my cock, cupping my balls with one hand, and that's it, I'm obliterated, exploding in a flash of light.

We fall asleep curled up together in a tangle of clothes, sleeping bags and camping gear. It's blissful, drifting off with her in my arms, breathing in the smell of her.

In the morning, we're both stiff and sore from sleeping on the uneven ground. My back is seizing up and my hips feel bruised from the tree roots poking up against the base of the tent.

Abby unzips the tent flap with a groan. A murky gray light fills my remaining vision.

If Nate has a problem with our unplanned sleeping arrangements, he doesn't say anything. Maybe if we could see each other, he would raise an eyebrow at me or roll his eyes. But as it is, we all just creep about silently as we pack up.

Luckily, the rangers never catch us, and we manage to drive to one of the legal campsites early enough in the morning to snag an open spot, maybe a cancellation or someone leaving early. Carson and Nate drive out to the nearest store outside the park and pick up more food, while the rest of us set up the tents. Or rather, Cricket sets up the tents while Abby watches and I putter around, mostly failing to be useful.

I can't stop thinking about last night. Does this mean I have a chance with her? Does she want to go out with me, or was she just feeling horny? But I can't talk to her with Cricket around. To be honest, I'm scared to say anything at all to Abby. She acts normal, joking around with Cricket, so that must mean she's not consumed with remorse, right?

The rest of the day is everything we were hoping for. The weather is mild and sunny, and we spend the day hanging out and relaxing. Nate brought along a soccer ball with a bell in it, and we all kick it around a field for a while. After lunch of peanut butter sandwiches, Cricket leads us on a hike for a few hours. For dinner we set up a real campfire and have hot dogs and smores. Abby calls it all "disgustingly wholesome."

Somehow in reshuffling everything at the new campsite, Nate's things get put into the bigger tent and Abby wriggles into the smaller tent with me without asking.

Finding her in my arms a second night in a row feels almost too good to be true. But I notice she's avoided being alone with me all day.

"You don't have to sleep here if you don't want to." I hope she can't feel how much my heart is hammering as I say it.

"I know."

"I mean, I won't be offended if you'd rather be in the other tent."

"Don't you want me to be here?"

"Yes, yes of course! I mean, I…" Why is it so hard to say these things I've spent so much time thinking about? What if I ruin our friendship? Or say something stupid and screw it all up? "I really like you," I whisper.

"I like you too." She hugs me tight, and I hug her back. We're lying on a tangle of sleeping bags, pillows, and clothes, but I don't care. No matter what happens, it will be worth it for this moment right now.

30

ABBY

Reader, I shagged him.

I swear, I didn't go on this camping trip intending to hook up with Nick. But every time I see him smile, that big open grin, I get a little jolt. Then after a few warm beers, the little jolts turned into a lightning bolt and before I knew it we were rolling around in the tent. I certainly didn't intend to do it with Nick while his brother and friends listened in from a few feet away, but I didn't not do that either.

But our trip only lasts two days. By the second morning, it's raining, a steady drizzle that never lets up. Cricket says she doesn't mind, she wants to go for a hike anyway. In the afternoon, the rain turns to a downpour and we give up. We drive back to campus, arriving late at night, and that's the end of spring break.

It's so hard to come back from that to everyday campus life. Carson drops me off at home and Nick goes back to the dorm. I have a ton of work to do on my senior thesis but I can't stop thinking about him. I'm brimming with the desire that I've been trying to repress since I met him. My entire body is humming with electricity.

I try to sit down on my bed with a notebook to plan my next installation, but it's like my brain is on two tracks, one for schoolwork and one for Nick. I've got a constant loop running with images of him: the way he feels around with his hands, the way he moves his head. The way he always seems so happy to see me. How much fun we had joking around on the trip. His goddamn smile that kills me every time.

If I date Nick for real, I'll have to tell him I'm a devotee. And that he's not my first blind guy. Even thinking about that conversation makes my heart speed up with anxiety.

But maybe I'm jumping the gun. We hooked up over one weekend. It's not that serious. I don't need to tell him yet.

The next history lecture is on illuminated manuscripts, which to be honest is one of the least interesting topics of the semester. Nick shows up a few minutes late, so I don't even get to talk to him before class starts.

"Hey," I whisper as he slides into his usual seat, so he knows I'm there.

"Hey," he whispers back. "I missed you." He puts his hand on my knee and I feel a spark shoot through me.

"Me too."

"Quiet please!" The TA Scott turns around and glares at us as Professor Gilbert goes on and on about those freaking illuminated manuscripts. He's kind of a dick.

"Let's hang out this weekend," Nick whispers.

"I can't. I have to prepare for my last thesis performance."

"Then how about tonight?"

"Ok, I'll come by after dinner."

"Ms. Adelstein!" Scott hisses. "Please be quiet!"

I spend the rest of the lecture, and then the rest of the day, waffling over whether or not to go on this date with Nick. If it even is a date, who knows. He said "hang out" not "go out," right? Maybe this is just a friends-with-benefits kind of situation. If it's not serious, then I don't have to tell him. Keep it casual.

After dinner (leftover Chinese takeout, the only thing in the fridge), my legs carry me across campus to Probus Hall of their own volition. It's like gravity drawing me to him, and I can't resist.

As I walk up the sidewalk, in the twilight gloom I can see someone sitting on the steps to the main entrance. I get closer, and yep, it's him. I wonder how long he's been waiting for me.

"Hey, handsome."

Nick jumps up when he hears my voice. "Hey, gorgeous." He pulls his cane out of his back pocket and lets it fall open.

I take his hand. Like really hold his hand in mine, not just letting him put his hand on my elbow. It feels good, but suddenly I'm a little shy.

"So…what's the plan?"

Nick shrugs. "I dunno. Nate is studying in our room."

"We could take a walk." That's what I always used to do when I didn't want to be in my dorm room or spend money at a café.

Nick nods and we set off toward Kagishkaw Botanic Garden.

The air feels crisp, cold but in a good way. It rained earlier but now it's clear, as if everything has been scrubbed clean. As we enter the park, the air suddenly turns colder and the noise of the cars falls away. I breathe deeply, taking in the smell of the damp grass.

It feels good to be walking in unison, our feet hitting the dirt track at the same time. There's a full moon, and the grass and trees are silvery and bright.

Nick picks up his feet high with each step, so as not to trip over any tree roots or loose gravel.

We come to a rise where we stop, the night air blowing chilly all around us. There are trees all around, but at the top of the rise is a clearing, the green grass shining in the moonlight against the dark night sky. It's beautiful. I feel like I did on the camping trip, like we're outside the bounds of everyday life, and whatever happens here is in a separate world. So why not go for what I really want?

Nick stands next to me with a look of anticipation. God, he's so hot. I want to rip his clothes off right here. Or something to let him know how I'm feeling. And if this thing between us isn't going to last, I might as well enjoy it while I can.

I grab his hands and put them on my breasts. I'm wearing a sweater, a shirt, and a bra, but still. His eyes go wide with surprise and he gives a nervous little laugh but I keep holding his hands against me, until he squeezes me back.

"Was I too bold?" My voice is a hoarse whisper.

"No, I like it." Now he's got his arms around me. I look up at him, his face glowing in the moonlight. His eyes are closed.

I surge upwards in his arms and kiss him hard.

I've heard of fireworks at a kiss but I always figured that was a stupid cliché, an exaggeration. But I swear, in that moment, in my mind I'm seeing sparks, brilliant points of light exploding all around us. I don't know how long we stand there, pressed together, locked in this incredible exchange of energy that seems to grow and grow.

I want this to last forever, but at the same time, the frustration is almost unbearable. I want to be lying naked in bed with him, not standing here, in public and exposed. I rock my hips against him but he pushes me away slightly with a little groan.

"You're killing me," he whispers.

"Too much?"

"I'll never live it down if I have to walk back across town with stained pants."

I laugh. "Want to come back to my place?"

"Yes."

We don't talk much, except for some nervous, conspiratorial giggles, as we walk back out of the park as fast as we can.

The botanic garden is in between the dorm and my house, so it's not long before I'm leading Nick up the stairs to the porch and unlocking the front door.

"Helloooo?" I call out just in case, but no one answers, thank goodness. "Guess Jen is out." I lead him to the staircase directly across from the front door. "No need to feel shy."

We go up the stairs and down the hall to the left to my bedroom, then we're kicking off our shoes and he's falling on top of me in the bed. Good thing I cleared off all the dirty laundry earlier.

I can hardly believe Nick is here, for real, in my own bed. We grapple and roll around, and it feels so good, like we fit together perfectly.

He pulls off my sweater and in a few minutes we've both stripped naked. I've left the light on so I can see him. He has a light sprinkling of freckles across his shoulders that I never noticed before.

"You ready?" I whisper in his ear. I'm pressed up against him and his cock is jumping up against me so I don't really need to ask out loud but I feel the need to say something. This is always an awkward moment but I'm not doing it without protection.

"What?" Nick slides his eyes back and forth, searching for me.

I smile and sit up. "Hold on, I've got condoms and lube in the drawer. You want to do it, right?"

Nick chokes out a strangled yes.

"Safety first." I push a condom into his hand.

He carefully feels the sharp flat edges of the square pack. He fumbles around for a while ripping it open, then when he tries to slide it on, something goes wrong. He's still hard, but the condom won't unroll more than an inch or two. With a sigh of frustration he pulls it off and tries again but it still doesn't go on.

"What the hell?"

I take the condom from his fingers and toss it on the floor. "I think it was upside-down. Don't worry about it. It happens sometimes." I take out a new one, pull it out of the package, and check that it's facing the right way up before handing it to him. "Here, try this."

This time he slides it on with no problem.

Then we're right back to the same wild energy. I'm pulsing and vibrating, sparks shooting off in all directions. We're coming at the same time, and it's hotter than any devotee fantasy I've had up to now.

Tell him, a voice whispers in my ear as I stare into his face, looking relaxed and happy. But the thought of saying anything that might ruin the moment stops me. I imagine him frowning, looking disgusted with me, and I lose my nerve. Why can't I just enjoy this moment with him, just as we are?

31

NICK

"Wow." I lay next to Abby, both of us still panting.

"Yeah." She hands me some tissues for the condom. "That was amazing."

I kind of want to ask her if it's always like that, if it's normal for her. Because sex with Abby is more than amazing. It's better than anything I've experienced. I'd like to think other girls were into me, but being with them was nothing like this. Was I just missing out before? But I don't want to hear about sex she had before now, so I don't say anything.

We lay there together, blissfully drifting off to sleep. I'm already starting to dream when I hear a click. Did she just turn the light off?

Instantly, I'm wide awake. "What time is it?"

"I dunno, late. You can stay over if you want," she murmurs sleepily.

"No! I didn't tell Nate where I am. I didn't even tell him I was going out after dinner."

"Oh shit!" She clicks the light back on and I can hear her shuffling around, getting dressed. "It's one AM. Do you want to call, or go back?"

I grope around the bed, searching for my underwear and shirt. "If he's gone to sleep and I call and wake him up, he'll be pissed. I should go, sorry. I have class tomorrow morning anyway."

"I'm sorry! I didn't think about it. I can walk with you if you want."

"No, I wouldn't make you do that. Besides, it's not safe for you to walk back home by yourself." I struggle back into my jeans, hopping around to pull them up.

Abby calls a taxi, and the dispatcher promises to send one right away. We go downstairs to wait in the living room, so we can see/hear it pull up in front. The minutes tick by painfully slowly as we sit silently on the couch. Shit! If I could see, it would have been no big deal to walk home, even if I had never been here before. I hate that I've ruined the mood. Abby doesn't say anything. Is she having second thoughts about being with a guy who can't even get home on his own?

The taxi finally arrives after nearly an hour. All that for a drive that takes less than ten minutes.

I tiptoe into our room, trying to be quiet in case Nate is asleep, but I shouldn't have bothered. The second the door closes behind me, his angry voice is coming from the top bunk.

"Where the fuck were you?"

"I'm sorry! I went out for a walk with Abby and I guess I lost track of time."

Nate gives a grunt and I hear him roll over. I start getting ready for bed as fast as I can, pulling off my clothes and brushing my teeth at the little sink in the corner. I feel like shit, for making Nate worried, for leaving Abby and making her wait for the taxi.

The little hard plastic cup slips out of my fingers and clatters around the sink. The wood frame of the bunk bed creaks as Nate rolls over again.

"I thought maybe you were hit by a car," he says tonelessly.

"I'm sorry!" I say again, hating the whiny note in my voice. What else can I say?

"I was going to call the police to look for you but Carson said to wait until morning. He said you were probably getting lucky with Abby. That's it, wasn't it?"

"Yeah," I whisper, crawling into the lower bunk.

"Hope it was worth it," he says, and rolls over one more time. A few minutes later, I hear him snoring softly.

The next day, I apologize a few more times but we don't talk about it. That's the way it is with us now, I guess.

Abby phones in the morning to make sure I got home ok. I apologize to her too, but she insists it's no big deal.

"Freaking small town with no proper taxi service," is all she says. "Next time I'll show you the way, then you can walk on your own and not have to rely on the world's slowest taxi. I swear, it's like there's only one cab for this entire town."

Next time. My mood lifts immediately. She wants to see me again.

"Or I can tell Nate I'll be out overnight. I mean, if it's ok with you…"

"Of course it's ok, ya dope! How about on Friday?"

Hell yeah on Friday. This time I remember to tell Nate I'll be staying over.

"Have fun," is all he says.

Abby meets me at the dorm after dinner, and we walk across campus together. This time I try to pay attention to the route so I can do it on my own, but it's hard to concentrate on memorizing the turns and landmarks when she's right there beside me, my hand on her elbow, brushing up against her.

"Is Nate ok?" she asks as we cross the main quad in front of the library.

"Eh, I guess so. He's still being a little weird, but I think he's just jealous that I'm with a hot girl."

Abby pokes me in the ribs and laughs.

"What?" I say. "It's true. You're smokin' hot."

We've reached the other end of the quad and I pause to get oriented at the corner before we cross a busy street, still trying to map out the route in my head.

"I mean, he might have a chance to meet girls if he ever did more than homework and play video games with Carson." I say.

"Yeah, whatever." She jostles me playfully.

When we get to Abby's house, she introduces me to her housemate. Jen shakes my hand and says hello awkwardly, as she's on her way out.

"What's up with her?" I ask Abby as we go upstairs to her room.

"Who cares." Abby gives me a little shove towards the bed.

She doesn't have to tell me twice. Nothing else matters as I yank off my shirt and tumble on the bed with her. The second time is just as amazing as the first.

We're lying next to each other, all relaxed and happy, when she asks me The Question. She kind of squirms around, running her nails gently over my bare arms, giving me a tingly sensation, but I can tell she's working up to something.

"What?"

She squirms some more, then blurts it out. "What's it like being blind?"

I get some variation of this question from almost everyone I meet, and I don't mean only close friends. People waiting in line at the grocery store, on the bus, in a restaurant, even just passing on the street, everyone feels entitled to ask me. I usually blow them off.

With Abby, I don't mind that she asks me, but I still don't have that much to say.

"My life would be so much easier if I could drive a car." I know this isn't the angsty, poetic answer people are looking for, but it's the truth.

"No, I mean what does it feel like," she says.

"I dunno, I try not to fixate on it, you know?"

"Yeah, I get it. Sorry I asked."

"No, it's ok. Sometimes it's so embarrassing, like I'm bumbling around underwater and everyone else is swimming by me. I feel like such an idiot when I can't find the right button on the elevator fast enough, or when I lose something that's right in front of my face. But then other times, like when I find my way across campus without stumbling or getting turned around, it feels so awesome. Like I just did this amazing thing, but no one else appreciates it."

"I appreciate it," she says softly. "I think you're awesome."

"Thanks." I give her a squeeze, just a little, but inside I'm swelling up with happiness. I've never said these things to anyone else. Knowing that she gets it just melts me.

"Do you mind if I ask more?"

"Sure, go ahead."

"You could see when you were a kid, right? When did it start...?"

"My vision was always kinda weak, even when I was little. I couldn't see anything at night, depth perception was bad, things were always blurry. Nate was even worse. He couldn't see colors well either."

"So do you remember what things look like?"

"Yeah, more or less, and I can remember getting around easier, but there was never a time when I could see everything clearly."

"So you knew...?"

"That I was going blind? Oh yeah, I can't remember not knowing. Our grandfather had RP too. It's genetic but it's x-linked, so it skips generations. My mom doesn't have it but she passed it on to us. If I have kids, they won't have it but they could give it to my grandkids. Anyway my mom grew up with her dad being mostly blind. He died before we were born, but my mom recognized the signs when we were little and had us tested right away."

"Wow, you're lucky."

"I guess. Nate idolizes our grandfather but it feels weird to me since we never met him. Nate's always telling me I'm doing it wrong."

"Doing what wrong?"

"Everything. Being blind."

"How can you do blindness wrong?"

I shift around uncomfortably, stretching out and putting my arms behind my head. Maybe I shouldn't have brought this up. "So you know Nate's a total and I'm still a partial, right? But I'll probably be a total eventually. Nate's always telling me I need to stop relying on the tiny bit of vision I have left, that I need to stop thinking and moving like a sighted person, and embrace what he calls 'deep blind.' Like getting better at Braille, using echolocation like he does, better cane skills, blah blah blah, all that."

"Nate really does have an ego bigger than God, huh?"

I give a sharp laugh in spite of myself.

"Sorry!" Abby says. "I didn't mean to be insulting. I mean, he is your brother. But just because he's always like 'my way or fuck you' doesn't mean he's always right."

I sigh and kick my legs. This is the uncomfortable part. "Yeah, but the thing is, Nate *is* always right. Maybe I'm the jerk."

Abby tries to snuggle up to me. "You're definitely not a jerk. And trust me, Nate isn't always right about everything."

"Thanks, but what if I'm just being contrary? Think about it. We're identical twins, mono/mono with the same DNA. So basically we have the same body. I can't say 'You don't know what it's like' because he knows exactly what it's like. We both have the same experience. And even when I think I'm so sure about something, it always turns out that he's right in the end."

"Oh, I don't know about that. You need to give yourself more credit."

"Thanks." I say that to put an end to this whole conversation which is making me feel strange and unbalanced. I like that I can talk about these things with Abby, that there's someone besides Nate who I can share it with. But something about the way she talks about it goes in a direction I'm not expecting, and I can't figure out why. I fall into a restless sleep.

32

ABBY

I'm half excited and half freaking out over getting serious with Nick. When am I going to tell him? But I don't have time to think about that now, because I've got to put together my thesis, not just the performance itself, but the essay and documentation, all the other parts that Howard expects to see.

Honestly, the installations haven't been going great. I get these ideas in my head that seem edgy and cool, but then when I do them it doesn't translate and I don't know why. I feel like I'm on stage shouting into the void and no one's getting it. Hey, that's another idea.

My final performance is at ten AM on a Saturday because that's the only time I can use the stage. I bribe Jen into helping with lights, curtains, and video recording by paying for all our groceries for the month. She needs the tech credits anyway.

I walk out on the darkened stage wearing a floor-length flowy white dress that I borrowed from the costume shop. I hope that it looks ethereal and cool to the audience. In actuality the dress is made of polyester and reeks of sweat.

As I come out on stage, my heart sinks to see how few people are in the audience. But I catch sight of Nick in the front row. He's the only one who has been there for me, every single time. And not only showing up, but asking me about my ideas, and genuinely interested in what I'm trying to do. That's more than I can say about anyone else I know, including Howard, my so-called advisor.

Jen turns up the spotlight on me.

"Ladies and gentlemen, thank you for attending this, the final performance of 'Senior Thesis Re/Flex,'" I intone in my loudest, most confident stage voice.

I let my mind go blank as I pace around in a circle, letting whatever weird mumbling, humming, groaning noises I can make flow out of me. I'm really going for it, challenging the audience to keep up with me. The noises get louder and louder, until I'm screaming, then I run as fast as I can at the proscenium arch, which is a solid, immovable pillar because this is a lecture hall, not a real theater.

I'm gratified to hear an audible gasp from the audience as I collide with the wall and bounce back slightly. Take that, normies!

I run at the arch on the other side and do the same thing again, then again and again, running back and forth and hitting the wall on either side. It hurts like hell, but that's what art is all about, right? I do this long past what might be thought of as a reasonable repetition, giving the audience time to marinate in the deep concept. At least that's my intention.

Then I walk calmly back to center stage, bow deeply, and thank everyone for coming. The applause is depressingly sparse and hesitant.

I try to block out the sound of polite, I-don't-get-it clapping. The only person whose opinion matters is Howard, and he isn't even here. I give him the VHS tape the next week. He takes it with a resigned sigh. He's a short guy with a big bushy mustache like it's still the 1970s.

"Here's the last one!" I say with forced cheer, as if I can persuade him by example to be excited about my project.

"This performance art shit is harder than it looks, huh?" Howard tosses the tape on his messy desk.

"You said you want us to take risks." I force myself not to break eye contact with him, even though I'm dying inside.

"There's risks and there's risks." He leans back in his desk chair. "The only thing that never changes is the avant-garde. And you're no Maria Abramovic."

"Ok, thanks!" I run out of his office before I humiliate myself by bursting into tears in front of him.

No, I save my big dramatic theater kid meltdown for my bedroom at home. I crank up the volume on the tape deck and play The Smiths "How Soon Is Now?" over and over while I lie on the bed, staring at the ceiling. Tears slip out of the corners of my eyes, into my hair, onto the bedspread.

I run through an endless loop of what I wish I had said to Howard. Like maybe if he had given me any actual direction or advising, I would have done better. But no, he told all of us that he didn't even believe in teaching acting at university, that if we were serious actors we would already be cast in real productions and not hanging around for a useless certificate.

Serves me right for coming to this crappy school anyway. Even the professors don't think my degree will be worth a damn.

When I told my high school friends I was going to a big state school in the Midwest, they were shocked. Why would I leave New York? Everyone knows the best performing arts schools are in the East. But haha, I applied to all of them and Calstock is the only place I got in, my backup school.

Morrisey's voice crackles out of my cheap speakers, crooning words that feel like they're about me. I just want to be loved like everyone else. Why is that so hard? Now here I am at the end of four years of college, with no job, no prospects, and hiding who I really am from the person who matters most to me. No wonder Howard panned my work. Performance is supposed to be about authenticity, but I'm too scared to be real with Nick. God, I suck.

I get my grade at the end of the week. I can't bear to see Jen's pitying look, so instead of telling her, the first person I tell is Nick.

"I got a B+!" I wail into the phone.

"But that's a good grade?" His voice is tinny in my ear.

"No! For a normal class it's an ok grade but that's not how it works for the senior thesis. An A+ means 'I'm writing your MFA recommendation letter now.' An A means 'Ok, well done, not bad.' And A- means 'Mediocre, but you tried, so I will take pity on you.' No one ever gets below A- on the senior thesis. No one!"

"But a B+ isn't that bad," he insists.

"Yes it is! Anything in the B range is basically saying, 'Your art is bad and you should feel bad.'" I can't help it, my voice cracks and the tears start flowing. "I really tried!" I sob. "I mean, I really, really tried. I wanted to show them all something new and daring, but in the end it was worse that the most worn-out Shakespeare monolog. I know he gave that bitch Karen Roche an A for her Desdemona. Why do I even bother when everyone just wants the same thing over and over?"

"I think you were so brave and cool."

"For real?"

"Yeah! Anyone can memorize a script. But it's hard to think up something totally new. I think you were so brave to put yourself out there and go for it."

I take a deep, shuddering breath.

"Aw, you're the best." I say goodbye and set down the phone.

Nick is sweet to try to cheer me up, but I feel like a directionless, talentless loser. I'm about to graduate. There's nothing I love more than theater, but apparently I suck at it. Now what? At least I have a hot boyfriend. But he only likes me because he doesn't really know me.

33

NICK

The next few weeks are like heaven. Ok, a weird sort of heaven with shared showers and toilets, bumbling around the dining hall, and a lot of homework. But none of that matters. All I can think about is Abby.

I'm filled with this hum of excitement all the time. I can hardly even sleep. I keep hearing her voice, feeling her hands on me, how she feels under my fingers. In class, I sit next to her, listening more to the scratch of her pen than to the lectures.

I write two short papers for my history class which Abby helps me proofread, and I get B+ each time. I think that's a good grade, no matter what she says. I know she's hurting over her senior thesis. I try to help her, but I don't know what to say to make her feel better.

Between all my schoolwork and her feeling so bummed about her project, we never manage to have a relationship talk. Like where this is all heading, if we're seriously dating or just friends with benefits. I mean, I know for sure I want to be with her, but does she feel the same way?

And then the semester is all over and I have to go back home for summer break, so I can't be with her at all for three months. It feels like forever. I want to go to Abby's graduation ceremony to cheer her on but it's scheduled for a Monday afternoon and we all have to move out of the dorm the Friday before. Nate thinks this is due to collusion between the university and the local hotels to increase profits. Maybe. The hotels triple their rates for graduation weekend.

With our parents coming to take us back home and the rush of moving out, I can't find time to see Abby before her graduation. It's just as well, since her parents are coming from New York and it would be awkward. I don't know if she would introduce me as her boyfriend, or just a friend, or what. It still feels too early for meeting parents.

Dad and Mom both drive up from Chesterford Hills, and within an hour we've cleaned out our room and loaded up the car. It's all finished much faster than I expected and my parents are eager to be back home for lunch. I don't want to be teased by Nate or my parents or anyone else about Abby so in the end I don't say anything about going to meet her.

We bump into Cricket in the hallway as we're taking the last load down to the car. She gives us all big hugs and makes us promise to keep in touch.

"Keep in touch how?" says Nate. "Send a carrier pigeon to the forest?"

Cricket is spending the summer as a counselor at a Girl Scouts camp again.

"I meant when we all come back next semester," she says.

"We should all get a house together." It's Carson. Has he been here the whole time?

"Yeah, that's the plan," Nate says. Wait, what? There's a plan? Before I can say anything, he continues, "Cricket, you should join us too. The more people, the cheaper the rent will be. What do you say?"

"Yeah, sounds great! Let's do it!"

"Ok, I'll scout around and let you know what I find," Carson says. He's taking summer classes so he can graduate one year early. Because he's enrolled for summer semester, he can stay in the dorm, unlike the rest of us.

"All right, so it's a plan. Keep us updated," Nate says.

As we pile into the car, I feel like I'm going back to being a kid again. I didn't even get to say goodbye to Abby like I wanted to, because I'm on my parents' schedule, not my own. Like I'm in high school still.

Dad curses as he takes a wrong turn down one of the many one-way streets around campus.

"That Oriental boy seems very nice." Mom turns around to face me and Nate in the back seat.

"Mom!" I hate how whiny my voice sounds but I can't let her comment slide.

"What? What did I say?" she protests.

"Say 'Asian American' not 'Oriental,'" I tell her.

Nate starts cracking his knuckles.

"So you're all going to live together next school year?" Dad asks, changing the subject.

"Yes," Nate says firmly.

There's a moment of silence. Are Mom and Dad exchanging a look? For a minute I'm worried my parents might say something like *Do you think that's wise?* or *Wouldn't it be easier to stay in the dorm now that you know your way around? We can request the same room again.* But they don't.

"Sounds like fun," Mom says.

"Since when did we decide we're living off campus?" I say, again sounding like a whiny kid. Shit! Five minutes in the car with my parents and I'm already regressing.

"We talked about it a lot," Nate says. "In the dining hall, in the lounge, more than once. You were there. You were too busy thinking about Abby to pay attention."

"Oooh, a girl? Who is she?" Mom asks.

"Are we going to get to meet this Abby?" Dad adds.

I briefly consider opening the car door and throwing myself to the sidewalk. It doesn't feel like we're on the freeway yet. I might only be maimed instead of mercifully killed.

"She doesn't have a car," I say dully as if that explains everything. Doesn't it, though?

Abby will be spending the summer (and I hope all next year) in Allenville, working in a bookstore. But even though Chesterford Hills is only a few hours away, she doesn't have a car and obviously I can't drive either. Also her new work schedule is pretty brutal, especially compared to a student lifestyle, so she can't get away that easily. I'm counting the days until summer break is over. The one thing that makes leaving Allenville bearable is the thought that it's only three months.

"It's only June but September can't come fast enough." I'm sprawled out on Nate's bed on the morning after we get home from school. He's sitting at his desk listening to the screenreader babble away at top speed. Nate and Dad keep discussing ways to make a Braille display with moveable pins for the computer but so far it's all just talk. I ignore whatever Nate is reading and wonder if it's too soon to call Abby. Would she be happy to hear from me or would it be weird? I've been home fewer than twenty-four hours.

I roll over with an impatient groan. "Just a long boring summer with nothing to do, huh?"

I'm not expecting an answer. I didn't even think Nate was listening to me. But to my surprise, he switches off the screenreader and his chair squeaks as he shifts around.

"Actually, I'm not going to be here."

"What?" I sit up. Why is my heart pounding suddenly?

"There's this summer camp in Wisconsin for kids with disabilities. I'm going to be a counselor there for two months. Mom is driving me out there the day after tomorrow."

I sit there on the bed with my mouth hanging open, stunned. Nate has a plan for the summer? Since when?

"W-why didn't you tell me?" I stammer finally.

"I'm telling you now."

"I can't believe you waited until the last second to tell me!"

"What difference would it make? Do you want to be a counselor too?"

"No…" Of course I don't, and he knows it.

"We don't have to always do everything together." I'm shocked at the note of anger in his voice. His chair squeaks more loudly as he settles himself in front of the computer again and turns the screenreader back on. I hear the loud pop of his knuckles.

I get up and go back to my room, trailing the back of my hand along the wall as I walk. I feel like my whole world has shaken. I sit on the edge of my bed, arguing with him silently in my head. Of course we don't have to do everything together, duh! Does he really think I'm so clingy that he has to sneak off without telling me? I've got my own life that has nothing to do with him. Who does he think he is, anyway?

But a tiny thought keeps bubbling up: *what am I going to do?*

At dinner, Emily has a million questions for Nate about his summer camp job, questions I never asked. Nate explains about the disability studies class he took and how Professor Klein, a woman with rheumatoid arthritis, changed his thinking about everything and made him understand what he calls "ableism" and "systems of oppression and marginalization." Suddenly, all the ways people talk about us, try to manage us and box us in, it all made sense.

"I thought it was just me," he says. "But it's them, their problem. I've got to do something about it, and that starts with kids, helping them to open their minds too." His professor put him in touch with the camp and they hired him.

How come I never heard him talk this way at school? Or wait, maybe I did. Now that I think about it, Nate and Cricket have been talking about all this disability rights stuff a lot. I always sort of tuned it out. I mean, I agree with them but I've had bigger things on my mind.

You were too busy thinking about Abby to pay attention.

Shit! This gap between us, is it my fault? The thought is so upsetting I can't say a word. Nate chatters on to our sister and parents about how important this camp is, but all I can think about is how he sounds like a stranger to me.

On Monday morning, Mom and Nate pack up the car again. It's a six hour drive, but they both seem cheerful and excited about it. Mom is taking the trip as an excuse to visit her sister. She'll be gone all week.

Nate explains over breakfast that flying would take even longer because there are no direct flights from anywhere near our little town. He would have to change planes three times.

"Stupid hub system," he grouses.

"That's the Midwest for ya," Dad says. "We love driving! Six hours is nothing."

I see a vague shadow of Dad giving Mom a kiss on the cheek, then laying a hand on Nate's shoulder. "I'm proud of you, son. I know you'll be a great counselor."

Dad dashes off to work, and a few minutes later Nate and Mom leave.

"Be good," she says as she hugs me goodbye.

Be good? That's the kind of thing she used to say before leaving us with a babysitter when we were little kids.

An hour later, Emily's friend comes to pick her up. Apparently she got herself a job as a lifeguard at the local public pool, along with a few of her friends.

And that's it, suddenly I'm alone in the big echoing empty house. I sit at the kitchen table drinking the gross weak coffee Mom makes, listening to the clocks ticking away in the dining room. Dad collects grandfather clocks. There are five or six lined up around the walls of the dining room. They all chime slightly apart, which drives me crazy. Sitting here, listening to the endless ticking, I feel like my life is slowly slipping away.

What the hell am I doing? Is this going to be my future after I graduate? I only have one more year and so far I have no idea what will happen next. I've been so focused on the day to day, trying to get all my schoolwork done and get decent grades. But everyone else around me is also doing more than that. I suddenly realize that if I keep on like this, I'm going to end up back here, living in my parents' house and collecting SSI checks for the rest of my life. Nate calls it blind money, as in money we get from the government just for being blind.

I think of Abby. I want to call her but she's probably at her graduation ceremony right at this moment. If I have to move back home after graduation, I'll never see her again.

I set down the coffee cup decisively. That's it, I have to find a job. I run my hands lightly over the table until I find the newspaper Dad read over breakfast. In the utility drawer in the kitchen is a dome magnifier the size of the palm of my hand. Good ol' Mom, always keeping our things in the same place.

I take the paper and the magnifier up to my bedroom and sit down at my desk, where I have a big ring light. With the super bright light on, it's not hard to find the classified pages. The grid pattern contrasts with the columns and photos on all the other pages. But actually reading the classifieds is something else again.

The tiny letters bubble up as I slide the glass dome over the page. Why is the print so freaking small? At the CSD on campus there's a closed circuit TV where I can slide in a book and it puts the text on the screen. I can make each letter as big as the screen. I used it a lot this past year, even though I had to coordinate getting there when the office was open. But it's too expensive to buy myself one.

Cursing, I put my good eye right up to the dome. I can just about make out the letters but it's slow going. I used this dome magnifier all the time in high school. Shit, my sight has really gone since then. It's not a gradual loss, a little more each day. No, I'll go along for months or even years at more or less the same level, then one day it's worse, but sometimes it takes me a while to notice that it's real, and not only a bad day or me being clumsy or a room that's too dark.

I try not to think about it too hard. I mean, Nate's there already. If he can manage, so can I. It's frustrating and sometimes scary but mostly it's just a fact I have to either accept or drive myself crazy resisting. Nate said never give up, so that's what I've been doing, just pushing on as best I can. Except that now he's off doing his own thing and I have to figure out the next step myself.

I waste the whole day with that damn newspaper, but the only result is a splitting headache and a stiff neck. There's not a single job I can imagine even applying for without being laughed out of the room. There are tons of fast food and retail jobs but even if I put Braille labels on the cash register, how would I handle the money? I've heard that in other countries, the bills are different sizes and have tactile markers on them, but no, here in the US we're in love with our greenbacks that all look and feel exactly the same. I always check each bill I have with a magnifier and fold them according to the pattern we learned at O&M training. Whenever I pay for something I try to use exact change as much as possible because I'm always paranoid I'll get handed a one and be told it's a five or ten.

The biggest category of job is food service. Haha, no way. I can just imagine myself as a waiter, tripping with a huge tray, food flying everywhere. Cook, no way. Who in their right mind would give me a knife?

There are a whole lot of random sales or assistant jobs that all end with "Must have own car." Nope.

The other jobs are various kinds of secretarial or receptionist work, heavy on filing, bookkeeping and paperwork. Under the ADA, I could ask an employer to buy a me a closed circuit TV magnifier or computer with text to speech. But the problem is even with those accommodations, I'm painfully slow at reading text. Case in point, this newspaper.

I finally give up and collapse in front of the TV until Dad comes home. Emily calls to say she's eating dinner with her friends.

When Dad asks me what I did all day, I truthfully tell him, "Nothing."

"That's fine, you just relax," he says as we eat bologna sandwiches on paper plates.

I make a pained face.

"It'll be good for you boys to spend a little time apart," Dad says after a minute.

"What does that mean?"

"Nothing. Just don't be mad at Nate for going off on his own."

"I'm not mad." There it is, that whiny child voice again. What is wrong with me?

34

ABBY

Once again, the semester ends in a rush and I don't get to see Nick before he leaves for summer break. My parents fly out for graduation, but I can't enjoy any of it. I don't feel like I've accomplished anything, and I can't even spend time with Nick while my parents are in town. When am I going to be in charge of my own life?

In a panic that my parents might force me to take that job and move back in with them, I fill out an application at Dark Island Books, the most popular used bookstore in Allenville. Against my own expectation, I get hired.

But I should have known from the name. The Dark Island is some kind of hellish waking nightmare. The customers are all entitled jerks. Either they think I'm a moron for not knowing some incredibly obscure title they pulled out of their ass, or they say "I'm looking for this one book with a green cover, do you have it?"

The owner of Dark Island Books is a Vietnam vet with untreated mental illness who occasionally screams at customers if he doesn't like how they are browsing or if they put a book in the shelf sideways. He regularly buys boxes of books that were obviously stolen from the Borders up the street. We peons in his employ pretend not to notice him peeling off the stickers. We are also not allowed to alter his bizarro shelving system which is based on what he imagines to be the cost and marketability of the books, not on anything one might recognize such as topic or author name.

The other employees are Jesse and Tanya. Jesse is a tall guy with a long black ponytail, also a recent grad like me. He's ok, even if he did think that books by Levi-Strauss should be categorized under fashion. Tanya is an aspiring sci fi novelist who suffers from severe social anxiety. She's figured out a system of interacting with customers while avoiding speaking or looking at them as much as possible. At first I found it weird but soon I am actively emulating her. And not only at work either, but also at home.

Jen moves out to California to start an MFA in theater arts. I try to find a new housemate, but Allenville empties out over the summer. The landlord gives me until the end of June to sign a new lease, but when I can't find anyone, I have to move out.

I can't afford a place on my own within walking distance of the tiny Allenville city center where the bookstore is. I take my chances with the housing bulletin board in the student union, and take the first, cheapest room I find.

Maybe I should have been more choosy. I end up in a falling-apart student slum with three slobs, two guys and a girl, who party all night every night. They're taking summer classes and sleeping late, repeating courses they failed the first time around. I'm the only one who has to get up early for work. And I work on the weekends, when they really cut loose with the binge drinking and loud music.

I invest in ear plugs and try to meditate my way to sleep. I grew up in Manhattan, I remind myself. I can sleep through any noise. But traffic sounds and occasional street yelling is not the same as Red Hot Chili Peppers at top volume on a permanent loop.

They're polite enough but I can tell my housemates think I'm weird for wearing all black instead of Calstock t-shirts and for not caring about the football team. Whatever, normies.

I go through the motions every day trying not to think too deeply about anything, like what the hell I'm doing with my life.

Howard comes in to Dark Island Books. I have to endure the humiliation of making change for my former advisor, showing him exactly what I'm doing with my college degree. He smiles blandly at me from behind his giant gross mustache.

Whatever, dude. As bad as it feels to be seen by him in my crappy service job, it's also strangely liberating. He bought a used copy of the latest Stephen King tome. I no longer have to care what he thinks of me. He was a terrible advisor who gave me no direction at all, and he has terrible taste in books. As he walks out the door, I try to forget him.

Think about Nick instead, I tell myself. Thinking of him gives me a warm glow and makes it easier to tune out the long slow days and uncomfortable nights. I can picture his face so clearly, the way his smile lights up the whole room. I miss talking with him about books, sharing notes, just hanging out. Allenville is empty without him here. Sitting behind the cash register in the bookstore, I feel like time is standing still.

When I get home, I give in and call Nick at his parents' house. A girl picks up on the first ring, Nick's little sister.

"Nii-iick, it's your giiiirl-frieeeend." I can hear her shouting.

"Shut up!" Nick's voice is faint in the distance, then a click as he picks up. "Hey." It's so good to hear him on the other end of the line, a tiny drop of normalcy.

"Just a minute." I can hear breathing on the line. "Emily! Hang up the phone!"

"Whatever. Your conversations are so boring anyway."

I wait until I hear Emily hang up the downstairs phone. "Wow, your sister is a brat."

"She's just jealous. She thinks she's grown up and ready for college already."

I ask delicately how he's doing.

Nick sighs. "This fucking sucks!"

"I know, being at home always makes me feel like a kid."

"It's not just that! Everyone else has a job, even Nate. What if I never find any kind of work I can do?"

The note of panic in his voice makes my heart ache.

"I'm sure you'll find something," I say, based on nothing.

"Not necessarily. Did you know that 80% of people with disabilities are unemployed or underemployed? Nate told me that. I think he heard it in his disability studies class."

I did know that. Ted worried about that all the time too. He dealt with it by being a huge asshole, always pushing himself to be the biggest dick in the room. It's how he got into that fancy writing program. Nate is kinda doing the same thing, but Nick isn't like that. It's one of the things I like about him.

"You still have time." I try to sound encouraging.

"Not really. I only have one more year until graduation. I can't get a bookstore job like you and hang around Allenville figuring things out. I've got to start planning from now."

"Ok, so start. What do you need to do to get the job you want?"

There's a long silence on the other end, and I'm worried I might be butting in to something that isn't my business.

But when he speaks again, Nick sounds fired up. "Yeah! I'm going to make a plan."

35

NICK

Abby's right, I realize. I've been thinking about this all wrong. Not just the classified ad job search—it's clear that I'm spinning my wheels on that, pretending like I'm doing something. No, it's more than that. My whole reading strategy is the problem.

In high school, it was easy to magnify words enough that reading print was still pretty fast, good enough to get my assignments done. But now there's a reason why I feel like I'm barely keeping my head above water with my classes while Nate is confidently sailing through, and that reason is Braille. Not every text is available on tape, and about half of the books I get through the CSD are read by student volunteers who honestly do a pretty bad job. But if a book isn't on tape, I've been relying on reading magnified print and I have to admit that even with the giant TV output it's really slow. Decoding one letter at a time is not going to work, and the problem is only going to get worse for me.

I've got to learn Grade 2 Braille. I know I could have gotten Braille textbooks from the CSD this past year because they offered to order them. They also have a Braille printer that will convert word processing documents, including transcripts of notes from class, assignments, or anything else. That's what Nate uses.

Ok, so Grade 2 Braille sounds great in theory—a way to make reading faster and more efficient through abbreviations. In reality, it's a pain in my ass, because there are hundreds of random letter combinations and at least half of them frankly make no sense at all. The thought of having to memorize this whole janky non-system is intimidating.

But if I spend the summer studying hard, I should be able to learn it. If I can be faster and more confident with reading, maybe an employer will be more likely to see me as an educated adult and not a charity case. Who knows. But at least it's something meaningful to do all summer instead of sitting around.

I call the Lighthouse for the Blind in Dunkerton where I did my O&M training. They're happy to match me with a tutor for regular lessons, but I have to go there. Great. I was hoping to present my plan to my parents as a done deal, but instead I have to ask my mother to drive me like a child.

Of course she says yes, in fact both my parents are super supportive of my plan and go on and on about how great it is, to an embarrassing degree. I hate that I have to make my mother drive an hour and a half twice a week, but what else can I do? There's no public transportation out here, not even taxis. Making the switch from print to Braille is a pain in the ass but doable. But dammit nothing makes me feel more disabled than not driving a car.

The first time we drive out to Dunkerton I'm afraid Mom is going to take advantage of the fact that I'm trapped in the car to have a feelings talk. To my great relief, she asks if I have any books on tape I want to listen to on the way. Why yes, yes I do. I get them for free from the National Library for the Blind, and I've already ordered a ton to stave off boredom at home. She doesn't even object when I pick out some pulpy dumb sci fi and pop it in the cassette player.

The Dunkerton Lighthouse for the Blind matches me with a Braille tutor named Vince, an older dude who tells me he's been a total his whole life. I feel a little better that we're on the same team. I don't want to learn Braille from a sighted person. Vince doesn't hassle me about letting so many years go by between learning Grade 1 and trying for Grade 2.

"I know it's a pain in the ass," he says as we sit down on hard plastic chairs at a long metal table.

"My thoughts exactly." I like this guy already.

"Yeah, but getting good at Grade 2 will make your life much easier, believe me," Vince says.

"Bring it on!"

He pushes a huge binder across the table. Inside are thick embossed pages with lists of abbreviations to memorize and lines of practice sentences.

"I'll have you speed reading in no time," he promises.

It feels good to have a routine and a goal. As Vince promises, little by little, I start to get better. When I'm not studying or helping around the house, I sometimes go to the pool with Emily for a swim.

"I'm getting a tan and a six-pack," I boast to Abby on the phone.

"I believe one of those things may be true."

"Hey! You'll be stunned when you see me again."

She laughs. Man, I can't get enough of hearing her voice. I feel a little flush of happiness that I can make her laugh like that.

"How's it going with you?" I ask. I'm worried about her working for an asshole and living with assholes.

"Ok. I mastered the skill of throwing the change back at the customers so it doesn't fall off the edge of the counter and so far this week only one creepy guy told me to smile. Last week it was five."

"What about your housemates?"

"There was actually one night this week that they didn't have a party so maybe they're finally slowing down."

I feel an ache in my chest when I think of her holed up in her bedroom by herself. I wish I was there with her, not stuck here in my childhood bedroom.

"Just two more months." I try to sound hopeful to cheer her up.

"Yay."

To change the subject, I tell her about my Braille class. It's cool how she always wants to hear every detail.

"You're doing good," she says. "Don't give up."

"Yeah, you too."

I want to talk longer, to have her in my ear. But Dad went on a whole rant about the phone bill. He won't come out and say no phone until I get a job because he knows I can't find a job. But that just makes it worse. I reluctantly hang up.

I can't even send Abby an email because the house she's living in doesn't have internet. I replay the sound of her voice in my head over and over.

You're doing good. Don't give up.

I dream about Abby. In my dreams, sometimes I can still see more. Not in a normal way, but in mixed up random images half-remembered from when I was younger. In this dream, Abby is floating in the air, or maybe in the blue ocean, with her springy dark curls fanned all around her head like a halo. She's wearing a glittering, flowing blue dress, and her arms and legs are flung out to the sides. Her smile is beautiful, peaceful. I stare into her face, taking it all in. It feels so natural, so loving, to stare at her like that.

This isn't something I can usually do.

The thought pops into my head so suddenly that it wakes me up, as if I was underwater and a hand pulls me up above the surface.

When I wake up, I realize I've never really seen her face like that, not her whole face all at once. I can see parts through the pinholes, her brown eyes one at a time, her red lips, the way her mouth looks when she smiles. But they're all separate fragments. I feel a stab of frustration deep in my guts. I'll never really see her, and maybe eventually I won't even see those few puzzle pieces.

For that matter, I can't see my own face either. My mental image of myself is from when I was a kid. Do I still look the same? I've gotten taller, my face got more square, I grew a beard (that I shave off, but still).

I roll over in bed, the image of Abby still shining bright in my mind. I try to hold onto it but it's more of a warm, glowing feeling than a clear photo. The more I try to remember her face, the more blurred the memory of the dream becomes. My body remembers though. The soft skin of her cheek under my fingers, her lips as we kiss, the scent of her as I bury my face against her, the sound of her loud, brassy laughter. Is this what Nate means by deep blind, not caring if I can see her face or not? But looking at her, it still feels like something I should be able to do, if only I could pull back the gauzy haze, make the little fragments come into focus together.

I'm suddenly hit with a wave of desire and longing so intense it's like a physical ache, wanting to be with her, to lie next to her. This summer can't be over fast enough.

36

ABBY

I miss Nick so much. It's like a stone in my chest, a weight I'm carrying around every day. I want to call Nick on the phone every day, twice a day, but that would be weird. I try to limit myself to once a week. Also those local long distance calls are freaking expensive. Why does it cost more to call Chesterford Hills than to call my parents in Manhattan?

I give in and call Nick in the middle of the week.

"Nate came back from camp," he says, his voice tinny and distorted on through the phone.

"Oh yeah? How is he?"

"I dunno, Emily said he got tan and fit, but he's still being kind of a dick. I think he wishes he was back at camp. He keeps going on and on about it, how he taught the kids to use echolocation."

"Oh, that's so cool! I didn't know he could do that. Can you?"

"Nah, that shit is hard. I couldn't get the hang of it."

I love talking about this stuff with Nick, even though I keep reminding myself to dial it back, not to seem too interested. He'll think I'm weird, or even worse, guess my secret. But I can't help myself.

"So how's the Braille class going?"

"I finished already. They gave me a certificate and everything."

"Wow, that's great! I'm so proud of you."

"Yeah." I can practically hear him blushing over the phone. "Feels good. Like I really accomplished something, you know?"

"You're fluent now?"

"Sure am. I found the first *Dune* book in Nate's room, and some old copies of *Omni* magazine, loans from the NLB he forgot to send back. It's great to actually read again."

We talk more about what he's been reading, what to pick up next, what I've been reading in the bookstore. It's almost as good as those long afternoons in the café after class.

There's a long pause on the line. I'm sure that Nick is going to say it's time to hang up, but then he says in a rush, "Nate and Carson and Cricket are all going to live together in a house next semester. Wanna live with us?"

"I…" I honestly have no answer for this.

Nick blusters on before I can say anything more. "The more people we have, the cheaper the rent will be. And I hate to think of you living with those assholes. Come on, why not?"

Why not? Because I still have no idea where this relationship is going, and the closer we get, the more I see blaring red lights flashing danger, danger, danger. I can't bear to get closer to him, only for him to reject me because I'm a devotee. My little heart could not handle that again. The thought of telling him is terrifying, but the idea of living together while keeping this secret is equally bad.

And that's not even considering his mess of a brother. I really, truly do not want to live with a closet case and his secret boyfriend, or ex-boyfriend, or whatever is going on between Nate and Carson. Living together with a couple is weird enough, never mind trying to keep it hidden from everyone else. Before I could even consider this, I'd have to talk to Nate about it, let him know that this situation is untenable. But I can't initiate a conversation without giving away why I want to talk to Nate, and I promised I wouldn't do that.

The silence stretches on as I debate all this internally.

"It's ok if you don't want to…." Nick sounds crushed.

Shit! Now he thinks that I don't like him.

"No, I mean yes. I mean, ok, I want to." I try to sound more sure than I feel.

"Ok! Yes! Great!" Nick also sounds unsure, falsely cheery. "I'll tell Carson to find a rental with five bedrooms. And if he can't, he and Nate can always share a bedroom, ha ha."

For a second, I wonder if Nick knows about them, but then I realize he's making the typical straight boy gay panic joke. Oh lord, what am I getting myself into?

37

NICK

"Hey dudes! Home sweet home, huh?" Carson bellows at us from the doorway.

I follow the sound of Nate's footsteps up a set of broken, uneven cement steps, then up an alarmingly creaky set of wooden steps to the porch. Our new shared rental is on Micsawbee Ave, one of the main streets in Allenville.

I can hear Carson thumping Nate on the back.

"Dude! Good thing you can't see it. Sorry, I did the best I could on short notice, but hey, at least I found a place with five bedrooms."

"Good to see you again too, jerkwad." Nate's voice sounds funny but I don't have time to wonder about it. Our Dad comes huffing up the stairs behind us carrying a box of our clothes. He drove us here in a rented U-Haul.

"So this is what my $400 a month is paying for?" Dad says in his jokey voice. "Times two?"

"We can help carry the boxes, Dad," Nate says.

"Nah, I got it. I'll just leave everything in the living room. You boys go in and get the layout."

We follow Carson inside to a surprisingly large and bright living room, with big bay windows letting in enough sunlight that I can make out white walls, hardwood floors, a pile of cardboard boxes. And standing next to the boxes, a slim girl with blonde hair.

"At least it's close to campus," she says.

"Cricket!" I give her a big hug, surprised at the rush of affection at seeing her again. "I'm really glad you wanted to live with us."

"Aw, you're sweet." She gives me a squeeze then lets go. "Is Abby joining us too?"

"Uh...yeah...I mean, yes!" The truth is Abby seemed a little luke-warm on the idea but I'm sure she'll change her mind once she actually sees it. Hopefully. Is it really as bad as Carson said?

Cricket and Carson take me and Nate on a tour of the house. Beyond the living room is a big dining room with bay windows on one side. Cricket already moved in a nice table and chairs set, a loan from her grandmother. The kitchen has an electric stove, to my relief. A gas flame always makes me nervous. Washer and dryer in the basement.

Upstairs there's a big hexagonal landing with four bedrooms on each side and the bathroom opposite the stairs. Then in the attic, one more smaller bedroom. Carson and Cricket have already decided that I get the biggest bedroom to the left of the stairs, Nate gets the second biggest next to mine, Abby and Cricket will be across from us, and Carson will be upstairs.

"That doesn't seem fair," I say to Carson. "You're the one who found the house. You should have the biggest bedroom. I can take the attic."

"Nah, dude! It's all good. I want you guys to be comfortable. It's really fine. Besides, I already put all my shit up there."

It's surprisingly considerate of Carson to do that. I always thought of him as a self-absorbed gym rat but I guess he has his nice side.

Dad carries our metal bed frames and mattresses upstairs, then says bye. I'm not really paying attention. Abby promised to come over in the afternoon when she gets off work.

I'm dying to see her again. As the time gets closer, I feel even more intensely the need to put my arms around her, to feel her solid and real, not only a voice on the phone. And also that lingering doubt that maybe she doesn't want to live with me?

I'm hanging my clothes in the tiny closet when I hear Cricket call from downstairs. "Nick, Abby's here!"

I spring down the stairs, barely catching myself from slipping on the hardwood and landing on my ass like an idiot. The staircase is right by the front door and as I reach the bottom step, there she is, launching herself at me so I stagger back slightly. Her frizzy hair tickles my nose and fills me with the scent of her, all warm skin and sunshine like a summer day. I squeeze her back intensely.

"Miss me?" I mumble into her hair.

"Yeah, a little." I can hear the smile in her voice.

My heart racing, I show her around the downstairs.

"Whatta dump," she declares.

"Really? I think it's kinda nice."

"Nah, I'm teasing you. It's nice and big, airy. The paint is peeling and the floor is all scratched up though."

"I couldn't tell."

"Anyway it's nicer than where I'm living now. If this place is a dump, that one is a flophouse, and the rent is higher too."

Feeling more confident now, I take her upstairs and show her my room, then gesture to the one across the landing.

"That's your room, if you..." I choke slightly on the words, "If you want it."

The springs on my metal bedframe squeak as she plops down. I sit next to her, my heart hammering wildly again.

"You know I want to live with you, right?"

No, I didn't know that for certain until I hear her say it.

"But?"

"But it's weird! Are we going to be housemates or boyfriend and girlfriend? Share a bedroom like a couple or separate rooms like platonic friends?"

"I don't know, whatever you want! I didn't want to pressure you."

"I want to be with you but normally I'd say it's way too early for us to move in together."

"So that's why you can have your own bedroom. I know it's early but I hate to think of you living in that shitty house with those assholes. I wanted to help you."

"I appreciate that, I really do, but I also don't want my lack of options push me to move in with you too fast. It wouldn't be good for us."

My heart sinks. I never thought of any of that. "I just want to be with you," I say, trying hard not to sound too pathetic, but it's the truth.

"I want to be with you too."

She sinks into my arms and more than anything I want to kiss her but I'm still trying to show her that the next move is up to her so I don't.

Abby puts her head on my shoulder. "Ok then, you have to help me take all my crap out of the back of Carson's car and carry it upstairs."

I sit up straight in surprise. "What! Are you playing with me? Why're you pretending like you haven't made up your mind?"

"I'm not playing. I'm serious when I say it's too early for us to move in together. But I'm not staying in that crap hole one minute longer than I have to. Also the landlord told us he's selling the house and everyone has to move out by the end of the month."

"Why didn't you tell me? I wanted to help you. I didn't mean for you to feel trapped."

Abby leans over and kisses me, a deep, loving kiss. God, I've missed her.

"I don't feel trapped," she says, and I can hear the grin in her voice. "There's nothing I want more than to live with you, your identical twin brother, his meathead boyfriend, and your lesbian ex-girlfriend."

"That's not—" I can't even finish the sentence. How did my life get so complicated?

38

ABBY

I didn't mean to say "boyfriend" about Carson and Nate, I swear. As soon as the word slips out I clap my mouth shut, but Nick seems to take it as a joke. I feel a flash of annoyance at Nate for this whole stupid situation. I've got to find a way to talk to him in private.

I mean all the things I say to Nick, about how it's too soon, but even though it's the truth, I know there are other reasons I'm not telling him. But what the hell, I can't resist him. Seeing him again after so long, when he smiles and puts his arms around me, I just melt. My attraction to him is like gravity, and I sink into him. I try not to think about all the ways this could possibly go wrong.

At least I have my own bedroom. So we're dating, but sleeping in separate beds, which feels a little weird. I've never lived with a boyfriend before. When I was dating Ted, I was living with Jen and he was in a dorm. This isn't how I pictured an adult relationship, living together in a big house with a bunch of other people.

The house is not as bad as my place over the summer, but it's not in great condition, and it has some weird features. The kitchen has two sinks, one in the pantry. The basement has a showerhead in the corner, randomly coming out of the wall. There's a bathroom with a bathtub directly off the dining room. Not to mention the normal bathroom on the second floor, and a jury-rigged one built from particleboard on the third floor. All this so the landlord can claim it's a four bath house and charge more. The entire upstairs is covered in the nastiest, industrial-grade wall-to-wall carpet, from the bedrooms right out to the hall. I wouldn't be surprised if the landlord got it used from a dog kennel or something.

In the living room is a bricked-up unusable fireplace and an enormous, hideous couch. Apparently the landlord offered to take to the dump if we paid him $50 but Carson told him to leave it. Carson says this like he scored some great deal. I hate it. The couch is upholstered in orange and blue plaid. It looks like it belonged to a woman who killed her husband with a bowling ball in the 1970s.

And the lights flicker. It's intermittent enough that I wonder at first if it's my imagination. I try to ignore it.

By the time we finish moving our boxes into our bedrooms, it's evening. We all flop down in the living room, on the hideous couch and other random pieces of furniture that should probably also be taken to the dump.

"I'm hungry," Carson announces. "What're we having for dinner?"

"Uh…" Cricket, Carson, and I stare at each other. Nate sprawls on the couch with his head back and eyes closed, like he's asleep. Typical, to be so checked out. I haven't been able to get him alone yet. Next to him, Nick rubs his hands on his thighs, his gaze wandering around uncertainly.

"So none of us knows how to cook?" Nick asks.

"Don't worry, I have a rice cooker," Carson says, as if he has solved our problem.

Silence again.

"What about Nick and Nate? You guys know how to cook, right?" I ask.

"We did a cooking course during O&M training in high school," Nick says, "but since then I haven't made anything more complicated than a sandwich."

"Can anyone cook who won't burn down the house?" Carson asks, glaring at Nate who is still pretending to be asleep.

"What about you, Abby?" Nick suggests.

"I'm not going to be the personal chef for four slackers. You assholes are on your own."

"Yeah, domestic labor is a tool of patriarchal oppression," Cricket chimes in.

So we order pizza for the first night, then afterwards make a trip to Meijer to pick up stuff we need for the house, and also maybe some food we might try to cook later. It's midnight by the time we leave for the store, all of us crammed into Carson's crappy little Honda Civic. Every time he drives over a pothole, the impact jolts right up my spine. There are a lot of potholes.

I don't get the appeal of Meijer. It's just a big box store, a giant supermarket and home goods store mashed together. But the others are ridiculously excited to go. I gather from what they all say as we're driving over that in high school, hanging out late at night at Meijer was the main social activity in all these little towns, since it's the only place open twenty-four hours. Cricket and Carson are enjoying reliving their high school days. But for Nick and Nate, it's a chance to be included in something they always missed out on. They were never invited and of course they couldn't drive themselves.

In the store, I push one of the oversized carts with Nick and Nate hanging off either side. I love doing this kind of thing, guiding them, and being careful to do it right. I don't even care that people in the store stare at us. Screw them. I live in a house with two blind guys, and it's totally normal that we're buying groceries. If I had gone to high school with them I would have invited them along to hang out. It makes me sad to think there wasn't even one person in their high school who would do that.

While the three of us make slow progress up and down the aisles, Carson and Cricket run ahead, grabbing random junk off the shelves. I try to keep us on track by steering towards the housewares aisle, keeping up a steady narration of what I see on the shelves that we actually need.

"I'm getting this pack of dishes cuz it's really cheap. And a set of glasses, too. I'm not drinking out of red Solo cups every day. Oh my God, put that child to bed! It's almost one AM!"

"What?" Nick snaps his head up, finally paying attention.

"There's a family with a little kid at the end of the aisle, probably around three years old. He's wearing pajamas, but still! What is wrong with people?"

Carson comes bounding back towards us.

"Hey dudes, check it out!" He shakes a metal spray canister that rattles.

"You know we can't see whatever you've got there, asshole." Nate sounds tired.

"Silly string!" Carson shouts gleefully.

"Are you a child?" Nate says. "Don't waste money on that crap."

"Aw, he looks so disappointed!" I say. "You just know he wanted to pretend to shoot it out his nose. I'm sorry sweetie, but that joke is lost on these two. You need to up your game."

"It *is* mostly a visual gag," Nick says. "It makes a weird noise and smells bad, that's about it."

"Yeah, and it's totally toxic." Cricket comes up behind us. "Are you really going to destroy the environment all for a two second joke?"

"Aw, you guys are no fun." Carson shoves the can back on a random shelf.

There's another argument in the food aisles as we debate whether to buy communal or individual groceries, in the end coming to a poorly-defined compromise. Carson picks out a carton of instant ramen packs, a ten pound bag of rice, and a container of soy sauce the size of a gasoline can. Cricket adds a pile of aspirational vegetables.

At the last minute I throw in two jumbo packs of sliced bread and a family-size tub of peanut butter. I realize suddenly that I'm the only one here who has experience balancing housework, cooking, and studying. These assholes all are used to having everything done for them in the dorm. Peanut butter sandwiches for every meal it is, then. At least that way there's less chance of someone burning the house down.

It's past three AM by the time I go to sleep on my futon on the floor of my new bedroom. As I drift off, I realize I still haven't talked to Nate.

39

NICK

I've been so excited about Abby agreeing to move in that I didn't fully realize that we still haven't actually signed the lease or handed over our checks. The morning after we move in, as Cricket is struggling to work the coffee maker, Carson casually wanders to the living room and announces that Dwight the landlord just pulled up to the curb.

"Can I ask him what dog kennel he bought the upstairs carpet from?" Abby asks.

"No, shut up." Carson seems uncharacteristically touchy. "It wasn't easy to get him to agree to let us move in before meeting all of us, and we haven't officially signed the lease yet. Let's not fuck it up, ok?"

Wait, we could all be kicked out? I thought this was a done deal. What if he refuses to rent to us? Just when I had persuaded Abby to be with me, now we might have to live apart after all?

"Ask him to fix the flickering lights," Cricket calls from the kitchen. This is accompanied by the sputtering of water vaporizing rapidly and the wafting smell of burnt coffee.

"Yeah, and note down the peeling paint so we don't get charged later," Abby adds.

"Can we get him to fix the faucets too?" I ask. "The water comes out funny and splashes everywhere."

Abby gives a short laugh. "Sweetheart, that ain't a repair issue. The previous tenants took the screens out to use in their bongs. There isn't a house in all of Allenville that still has screens on the taps. If it bothers you, we can buy some at Meijer."

"Oh." I feel like a rube, but at least I didn't embarrass myself in front of the landlord, who I'm now concerned we have to impress.

A car door slams and Dwight comes ambling up the porch steps. He must be a big dude, judging by how much the stairs creak under his weight.

Standing awkwardly in the living room, we all shake his hand and say our names. I get a general sense that he's tall, with grayish hair and meaty hands. He speaks slowly with a kind of windbag delivery that reminds me of my high school gym teacher.

I can tell instantly that Nate and I make him nervous. He does that stammering, overcompensating with polite platitudes thing that only happens when people are freaked out but trying to hide it.

"Two of you! Oh! Well! Good for you, heh heh…"

I stare at him silently, fixing the top left corner of his face in a pinhole, not making it easy for him.

Dwight turns to Carson. "You didn't tell me…"

"Tell you what?" Carson asks, playing dumb.

"This isn't going to be a liability issue, is it?"

"I'm sorry, is there any provision in the Allenville housing code that prevents you from renting to persons with disabilities?" Nate cuts in. "Or is it the opposite? Maybe we should look it up."

"Now, now, I ain't prejudiced!" Dwight puts his hands up defensively. "I used to be a high school social studies teacher, you know."

I don't see what that has to do with anything, but I smile inwardly. I had him pegged, almost.

We hand over our checks, including one each from me and Nate that's twice as large and printed with plasticky tactile ink so we can feel the lines and sign our names in the right place. When Dad got us set up with our own bank accounts last year, I thought it was kind of dumb, but now I'm glad I have it.

Dwight is silent for a moment when he sees our weird checks, but then just says, "Ohhhhkaaaaay," really slowly, like he's not sure this is real money.

Maybe because he's trying to prove to us that he isn't a jerk, or because he doesn't want to be sued, Dwight makes some awkward small talk as he collects our checks, asking our majors and hometowns. Or maybe he's making sure we're not drug dealers or anything.

"So Carlton," Dwight drawls, "where are *you* from?"

"It's Carson, and I'm from Anterfax." That's another small town a few hours away. It's basically the same as Chesterford Hills, or Saintwin, where Cricket is from.

"No, where are you *from?*"

I hear a tiny intake of breath from Carson as he hesitates for a moment before answering, and in that second, I can sense how fed up he is with this stupid question. It's the same way I feel when people say to me that I don't look blind, or make a crack about Daredevil.

Before Carson can answer, Nate breaks in, "He just said he's from Anterfax." But if Nate was trying to shame Dwight, he fails entirely.

"No, where are you *from?*" Dwight insists. "Like, originally?"

Nate is about to get into it, I can tell, probably to start a lecture on why Dwight never asked any of the rest of us because we all look white and doesn't he realize how racist it is to grill the Asian guy on his family background, but Carson cuts him off.

"My parents are from Taiwan," Carson says with a defeated sigh. He's right, we shouldn't be picking fights with our new landlord.

"Oh, very nice!" Dwight exclaims like a collector spotting a rare species. "Tokyo, right?"

"No, Tokyo is in Japan," Carson says tightly. "We're from Taipei."

"That's what I just said!"

"Um, can I ask about the flickering lights?" Cricket sounds desperate to change the subject.

We all troop down the rickety basement steps, where Dwight lectures us about not stacking boxes under the stairs, glances at the fuse box and says he doesn't see anything wrong.

"But the lights in the whole house flicker constantly," Cricket insists.

"I'm not sure this is an electrical issue," Dwight says.

"Yeah, maybe we need an exorcism," Abby mutters from where she's lurking behind me on the stairs. When we were unpacking, she noticed a Ouija board wedged in a far corner of the basement, behind the furnace, and we all had a good laugh imagining the previous tenants freaking themselves out so much that they had to hide it.

"What's that noise over there?" Nate asks loudly.

"Holy shit!" Dwight exclaims.

I assume Nate just pointed to something. There's more exclamations and swearing, then a lot of shuffling around and creaking of what sounds like a ladder.

"What is it?" I ask Abby impatiently.

"I don't know, but there's some kind of wire in the ceiling and it's arcing. There's sparks flying off it. How did no one notice it before? Damn, this really could start a fire."

Dwight messes around and curses a lot more before he gives up on fixing whatever the problem is.

"Sorry kids," he says, sounding not at all sorry. "I gotta cut the breaker until I can get an electrician out here to fix it. Just use flashlights and don't open the fridge for now."

"What the fuck!" Carson shouts as we listen to Dwight's car driving away.

"So we paid him money while he insulted you guys then turned off the power." Cricket's discouraged voice comes from a corner of the couch.

"It's not all bad," Abby says. "You should've seen his face when he realized the blind guy pointed out the electrical problem he missed. It was almost worth it."

I don't even care how much of an asshole Dwight is, or that we'll have to have pizza for dinner again and cold showers. Now it's official,

Abby is living with me. That's worth whatever minor bullshit I have to endure.

After we get settled in and the power is finally turned back on, we have to register for classes. It's too bad I can't share another class with Abby, but living together is better than meeting once a week in a lecture.

I'm hoping registration will go better than last time. Calstock State University has finally decided to enter the modern era this semester by having us register on the phone rather than having to stand in line clutching a piece of paper. But actually the only thing that changed is where we have to wait, on the phone at home, versus in a hallway at the Office of the Registrar. The end result is still the same, reciting the classes we want to take to a lady who types our choices into a computer then tells us the class is already full and we have to choose something else. At least Nate and I can register directly now instead of going through the CSD.

Because we updated our new address too late with the university, the letters with our registration time slot and code are sent to our parents. We play an elaborate game of telephone as I get the digits from Dad, Abby writes them down, then reads them back to me as I call for my turn. But I'm lucky this time. I get into all my advanced classes in my major and I don't have any more breadth requirements like last year.

I hand the phone to Nate for his turn, but things don't go as well for him. I hear a long argument I can't quite piece together. He ends the call by slamming the receiver down.

"This is bullshit!" He cracks his knuckles super loud.

"What's going on?" I ask.

"I told you they wouldn't let you change your major in your senior year," Carson says.

"Why do you want to change your major?" I ask. This is the first I've heard of it.

"I've decided sociology is more meaningful to me than psychology," Nate says loftily. "If I change majors, I can specialize in disability studies. And I can do it too, if they would only let me overload two extra classes."

"Two classes? You're out of your mind!" I can barely keep up with the normal course load, given how much slower I am with reading or listening to recordings, and having to get all my materials and notes through the CSD.

"Thanks for the support, asshole. They let Carson overload two classes."

Carson is trying to graduate in three years to save money. It's rough, but I've met some students who pulled it off.

"Yeah, I just registered and no one said anything. Why won't they let you do it?" Carson says.

"It's the fucking CSD! They put a lock on my registration, and I can't overload. I'm going over there right now to yell at them."

"Congratulations on sticking it to the man," Cricket says to Nate over dinner.

Carson taught us to make instant ramen tastier and more nutritious by adding some chopped vegetables and cracking in an egg so it all cooks together. This has become our main dinner dish. He makes fun of us for eating it with a fork instead of chopsticks, but I can't figure out how to use the damn things without sending food flying everywhere.

"Yeah, it was awesome," Carson says around a mouthful of ramen noodles. "He made a big speech about how the CSD is there to serve his needs and not to 'impede his educational progress'."

"It's bullshit that I have to start every semester by threatening to sue them under the ADA," Nate grumbles. "I've had it with their incompetence and paternalism."

"Are you sure you can manage that much work?" I don't even think about it, the question just slips out.

"Don't you fucking start with me, Nick!"

I've gotten used to Nate's perpetually grumpy mood, but the sudden anger in his voice shocks me. What's gotten into him?

We all finish dinner in silence.

40

ABBY

Since the semester started, everyone else has fallen into a routine of classes and homework. It feels weird not to be doing the same. But being around Nick all the time is amazing, even better than I thought it would be. So far I've managed to ignore the devotee thing. Life together just feels so easy and right.

But Nate, well, that's another story.

I'm sitting at the dining room table, eating breakfast and listening to *Morning Edition* on the radio, bracing myself for yet another day at Dark Island Books. I crunch my toast, delaying having to leave for work as long as possible.

Cricket is across from me at the table, reading the student paper and drinking coffee.

Nick stumbles downstairs, still in the sweatpants and t-shirt he slept in. Even with his hair sticking up he looks gorgeous. As I sip my coffee, I entertain a languid fantasy of pulling off that shirt, running my hand along his chest, down past his waist…

From where I'm sitting, I can see straight into the kitchen. I watch him feel around in the cupboard for a bowl, then in the next cupboard over for the cereal. He shakes the box then squints at the front, but apparently he still can't be sure if it's the Rice Krispies he bought last week because he sticks his fingers in the bag before nodding to himself and pouring some into the bowl.

I love seeing how he does everyday things like this. *He would hate you if he knew how you were watching*, a voice that won't shut up whispers in my head. But what am I supposed to do, avert my eyes? That would be worse.

Nick moves on to the drawer, feeling around in the utensil slot for one of the few remaining clean spoons. Then he takes the mostly empty milk carton from the fridge and pours nearly all of it in the bowl. Damn, we need to have Carson drive us out to Meijer again. And we need to wash the dishes.

I watch as Nick puts the remaining few drops of milk back in the fridge and carefully carries his bowl to the table. The milk in his bowl comes very close to slopping over the edge.

"Shoulda poured the milk at the table," he mutters as he sits down.

"Oh, I thought you wanted a challenge first thing in the morning," I say.

He smiles at me. I want to reach across the table and kiss him.

Nate and Carson roll in, also still in their pajamas, and go to get their breakfast.

"OW!"

There's a crash from the kitchen, then Nate bellows, "What the fuck!"

A cabinet door slams shut. Nate comes stomping back into the dining room.

"We need to have a house meeting NOW." He collides with the table then pounds on it with his fist, making all the dishes jump.

"Are you ok?" I ask.

"What happened?" Cricket says at the same time. She's sitting with her back to the kitchen and didn't see.

"I fucking walked right into the cabinet door that some idiot left open!"

"Yeah, there's a big red mark on your cheek. Want an ice pack?" Carson says.

Nate ignores him. "We're having a house meeting right now! This house is a pigsty and I'm not putting up with it another day. We need to establish some rules about living with a blind person. No leaving your crap all over the floor. I don't know who set out those little rugs everywhere, but I keep tripping over them. No shifting things around in the fridge or cabinets. Unless you want to spend hours putting Braille labels on every little thing, just leave it in the same spot. No leaving your dirty clothes and towels all over the bathroom and your dirty dishes all over the kitchen. And no leaving the fucking cabinet doors open!" He punctuates this speech with another fist bang on the table.

"I'm sorry!" Cricket says in an anguished voice. "The little rugs I got from my grandmother. I thought they looked nice."

"It's a hazard."

"You're right," Cricket whispers. "I'll get rid of them."

"Hey, you don't have to make her cry over this," I say. "I'm sorry I moved the groceries around and you ate the wrong cereal by accident yesterday. I don't mind making labels for the cereal boxes, if you want."

Nate ignores me too. "Who left the cabinet door open?"

Silence around the table.

"Well?"

The silence stretches on tensely, as if he's conducting a police investigation.

I glance over at Nick, but he's grinning like he has no idea what's going on. Oh my God, he doesn't know.

"It was Nick," I say softly.

"What! No, I didn't!"

"I saw you. You got some cereal, then left the box on the counter and the door open and came and sat down. A minute later, Nate walked into it."

Nick's eyebrows go up in surprise, and his mouth opens and closes a few times before he says, "Sorry."

But he says it in that not-sorry voice that implies Nate's making a big deal out of nothing.

"You of all people should know better!" Nate's voice is still at top volume.

"Oh yeah?" Nick stands up. "Who left a coffee cup on the floor next to the couch? Oh right, that was you! *I* was the one who had to clean it up after I kicked it over. And don't lecture me about washing dishes. How come I can't ever find a clean spoon? It's because you're dumping all your dirty dishes in the pantry sink then forgetting about them. So don't come at me with your stupid rules you don't even follow yourself!"

"What the fuck is wrong with you!"

"No, what the fuck is wrong with you!"

Cricket and Carson both look appalled but none of us dare to interfere.

Nick stomps upstairs, leaving his half-eaten cereal to get soggy. Nate gets himself coffee from the kitchen, then sits down at the table, his expression carefully blank, as if he's too good for this argument.

Cricket says a hasty goodbye and leaves for class. Carson goes upstairs to take a shower.

Now, I think.

I glance at my watch. I have fifteen minutes before I need to leave for work if I don't want to be late. There's never going to be a better time to talk to him.

I take a deep breath, my heart racing. Why is this so difficult? "Nate."

He lifts his head up and blinks a few times, his gaze hovering somewhere around the tabletop.

"You know, it makes everyone super uncomfortable when you two argue like that."

He scowls in my general direction. "It's not *my* fault he's such a dumbass."

"That's not what this is about and you know it. You've got to tell him."

His face returns to that studied blankness. "Tell him what?"

"Oh my God! You're fucking killing me with this bullshit!" I sweep up my breakfast dishes and dump them in the overflowing kitchen sink with a clatter. Nate remains sitting at the table.

I return to the dining room, standing by the table. "I can hear Carson sneaking into your room at night. You're not that subtle."

Nate goes red but still doesn't say anything.

"It's not fair to Nick that you're keeping this from him. And it's not fair to the rest of us that you're dragging us all in the closet with you. Just tell him already."

"Shut up! It's none of your business. You don't know what you're talking about." The words spill out of him in a defensive rush.

"Whatever, dude. But you can't keep this secret forever."

Nate sets his jaw like that's exactly what he intends to do.

"And what about you?" he says. "When are you going to tell him what's up with you?"

I'm so stunned all I can do is stare at him. Finally after too long, I say, "I have to go to work."

I grab my purse and rush out the door. What does Nate mean by that? This is my greatest fear, that someone would guess that I'm a devotee. But unlike being gay, hardly anyone knows that my particular attraction is even a thing. There's no way he knows, I tell myself. He must be talking about something else.

41

NICK

Living in this falling-apart house almost feels like a family. A strange, rambling, messy family. Except that I'm still avoiding the one person who actually is family. Nate and I basically just exist around each other, which isn't that hard considering that he's always studying or going to the gym.

The only times we're together is when the whole house watches reruns of *Star Trek: The Next Generation*, no matter how bad or stupid the episode is. But even then Nate and I don't talk to each other directly. Mostly everyone just cracks jokes and competes to see who can guess which episode it is the fastest. Abby is the champ, at thirty seconds into the cold open.

Back in high school, I had a few friends, but not people I just hung around with all the time like this. Most of the other kids found reasons not to get close to us, and a few called us names. Junior year I took a swing at a guy who called us the retard twins. I didn't even connect but I got in so much trouble for that. We were never invited to parties or to hang out at Meijer or the mall. But I never felt too lonely because I always had Nate.

"Just hang on," he used to say every time we were left out of something. "College will be better."

Onasca Community College wasn't better though. No one was rude like in high school, but most of the other students had full time jobs and families. There were no parties or hangouts at all. I didn't make friends with a single person there.

I love living with my friends. I just wish I knew how to get along with Nate, to be close like we used to.

I try not to think about Nate. It's not that hard when things are going so well with Abby. Knowing she'll be home every evening, waking up with her right there, it's the best feeling. I even order some books she recommended from the NLB and read them in Braille, and that's on top of my textbooks. I can't believe I waited this long to start using Braille. Why did I wait? Was it laziness? Or was it because Braille is Nate's thing? It feels good to read on my own and discuss it with Abby.

We each have our own bedroom, but a few nights a week we sleep in the same bed. Neither of our beds is ideal, to be honest. My bed is a narrow single with a metal frame that squeaks, announcing to the whole house every time we have sex. Although the house is noisy all the time. Even in the middle of the night, I hear creaks, groans, weird thumping. Every time I mention it, Abby repeats the joke about the Ouija board in the basement meaning the house is haunted.

Abby's bed is a double futon she laid right on the floor. On the plus side, no noise. But on the minus side, it feels like sleeping on a slab of wood. It's killing my back. So we trade back and forth. The sex is still amazing.

We haven't argued or gotten on each other's nerves, like she was worried about. She seems ok on the surface, but since graduation, it's like she has a dark cloud hanging over her. I know she's still upset about her senior thesis, but I don't know what to say to her to help her feel better about it.

"Shit!"

I'm about to walk out the door to my Monday morning class when I'm stopped by the sound of Abby shrieking in the kitchen. Without thinking, I drop my backpack by the door and race back through the living room and dining room, as fast as I dare without risking tripping over anything. In spite of Nate's outburst, the house seems to stay only moderately cleaned up, and Cricket never did get rid of those little rugs.

"What is it?" I call out as soon as I reach the kitchen doorway. Something about Abby's voice sets off alarm bells in my head.

"I set the stove on fire!" Her voice has a panicky edge I've never heard from her before.

"You what?"

"The burner! There was food stuck to it, and now it's on fire! What do I do?"

Now I'm panicking too. Cricket already left for class. Nate and Carson are still asleep, probably. I haven't heard them since I got up and I don't want to waste time looking for them upstairs. It's just me and Abby.

I have no idea what to do either.

"Put a lid on it," I blurt out, some tiny bit of knowledge popping up from who knows where.

I hear a clang.

"Do we have a fire extinguisher?" I ask.

"I don't know. I think I saw one in the basement. But it sprays chemicals, right? What if it breaks the stove? Dwight will kill us! We'll never get our security deposit back."

We certainly won't get that deposit back if the whole house burns down, but I don't say that out loud. Instead I ask if the fire is out yet.

Abby checks under the pot lid and yelps. "No! It's worse than ever! The whole underside of the burner and the stove top is open. Air is still getting in from the bottom. There's no way to smother it with a lid."

My nose fills with the acrid smoke, making my heart race even faster. I hate feeling so useless. If the whole house burns down, could I save her? Or would she have to be the one to save me? I try to shove that thought out of my mind. Suddenly I have a flash of inspiration.

"You could smother it with salt."

"What salt? All we have is this one little shaker."

"Ok, how about flour, then?"

Abby doesn't even hesitate. The flames must be getting bigger. I hear her rummage around in the cabinet by the stove then rip open the paper bag of flour.

As she dumps the entire bag of flour onto the stove, some of it ignites into a mini fireball. Even I can see the flash. She screams again.

I'm halfway to the phone to call 911, but a second later she says, "It's out."

"Oh my God, I'm sorry!" I feel like even more of an idiot. "I kinda forgot that flour is flammable."

"It's ok, there was enough that it smothered the fire around the burner. Luckily it was only some of the dust that burned."

"And lucky it didn't spread to the cabinets. Are there scorch marks?"

"No, it all looks ok." Abby pauses for a second, then launches herself into my arms, sobbing. "What is wrong with me! I'm such a fucking idiot!"

"No, you're not."

"Yes, I suck! It's all my fault! I was heating up some cream of mushroom soup last night and it boiled over onto the burner but I didn't bother to clean it up. Like an idiot I went to make myself an egg for breakfast and all the caked-on soup from last night started burning. What kind of moron does that?"

I rub her back reassuringly. "Carson burned a pop tart in the toaster last week. I can still smell it."

But she's not listening to me.

"What am I even doing with my life? I feel like I'm failing at everything! The only thing I ever wanted to do was theater, but apparently I suck at that. Now I'm using my fancy degree to sell way too detailed books of military history to creepy assholes who tell me to smile more, and serving as unpaid therapist to my boss who should be on lithium and not in charge of other human beings. Fuck!"

I squeeze her harder. "You don't fail at everything."

"Yes, I do! I can't even be trusted to prepare my own food without burning the house down." She pulls away from me and I hear a clanking sound as she rattles a utensil or something around the scorched coil.

"And how am I ever going to clean this up? There's carbonized soup stuck to the entire burner and a huge pile of flour inside the stove."

"I'll help you," I offer impulsively, even though I have no idea what to do.

"No, don't you have class? Just go, I'll be fine." But even as she says it, she dissolves into tears and I hug her again.

"It's ok," I say, kissing the top of her head. "I can skip one day. My note taker is a guy taking the class for credit, so I'll get the notes anyway. We'll figure this out together."

So that's what we do. We poke ineffectually at the burner with butter knives until Abby finally realizes we can detach the entire coil and open the top of the stove. I scrape the charred bits off the burner over the trash can while she scoops out singed flour. Nate and Carson come down for breakfast, and I can tell they're set to give Abby a ribbing over this but I warn them off with a few choice words. They seem to get it, because they grab some cereal and retreat to the dining room without saying anything.

Cleanup takes us a long time, but finally we manage to get all the char off the coil of the electric burner, scrub the pan that goes under the burner, and remove all the flour from the underneath of the stove top. As we're finishing up, it occurs to me that Abby still hasn't even had breakfast.

I tell her I'm taking her out to eat. She resists at first, but I insist and pretty soon we're walking across campus together to Red Hots for a gourmet brunch of fancy hot dogs and waffle-cut fries. The weather has turned colder, but in a nice way, pleasantly cool, not yet unbearably frigid. The air smells clean and crisp, and the leaves crunch under our feet. We walk along together, me with my hand in the crook of Abby's elbow, my cane in my back pocket.

It's nice, walking with her like this. She strides along at exactly the right speed, not too fast or too slow, and our gait feels perfectly matched, our feet hitting the pavement and bouncing back up together. I trust her enough not to use my cane, knowing she'll warn me if the pavement is uneven or people have left their trash bins in the middle of the sidewalk. It's a bright sunny day and it feels good to be outside. I squeeze her arm.

"What?" she asks.

"Nothing. I'm just happy to be with you." She turns her head, and for a second I'm looking in the right spot to see her smile at me. I've never been so happy or relieved to see her smile. "You don't fail at everything," I say. "I think you're amazing."

She sighs. "Thank you."

"I'm sorry your job sucks so hard. You've got to find something else."

"I know. I'm thinking about it. But I still don't know what I want to do." She pauses while we cross a busy street, then asks, "What about you? Have you thought about what you're going to do after you graduate?"

I don't say anything. Like the sun going behind a cloud, my happy warm feelings are replaced with the icy fingers of dread around my throat. I've been concentrating on getting through this semester with good grades, but every so often the fear from summer break, of being unemployable, useless, living off blind money forever, that fear surfaces again, and intensifies each time. What am I going to do?

42

ABBY

"I have theater tickets!" Nick greets me when I come home from work. He's nearly jumping with excitement, brandishing two long rectangular printed tickets.

I toss my purse and coat on the ugly plaid couch. Nick is so cute when he gets excited like this. I haven't been to any shows since I graduated, not even open mics with the Meat Poet. Nick keeps asking if I want to go, and I keep coming up with excuses not to. But if he has actual tickets to something, I can't exactly say no.

"Thanks. Where did you get them?" I walk into the kitchen to make myself a late dinner.

"When I stopped by the CSD to pick up my class notes, Mrs. Palmer the admin lady asked if I want free theater tickets," he says, following me. "She said Allenville Community Theater gave them a whole bunch so I said ok. Then she said 'Here you go, honey.' Ugh, when are middle-aged ladies are going to stop treating me like a child? Is it never? I feel like the answer will be never."

"That sucks, sorry." I take some leftover rice out of the rice cooker and throw it in a frying pan with a few veggies and crack an egg over the top, another Carson recipe.

"So do you want to go with me?"

"Sure," I say without reflection, because I'm still cooking.

But when I sit down with my plate of fried rice and Nick hands me the tickets, I notice something.

"This is for kids!"

"What? Really?" Nick clearly had no idea.

"Yeah, it's an afterschool program for elementary school kids where they write their own plays and perform them. Who would want to see this besides their own parents?"

"Oh. I guess that's why they're giving the tickets away."

"Yeah, maybe even their own parents don't want to go."

"Never mind then. Sorry." Nick puts his hand out to take them back, looking deeply embarrassed.

I immediately regret my words. I didn't mean to criticize him, and I'm touched that he wants to go to the theater with me, no matter what kind of show.

"No, let's go," I say. "It might be weird."

Weird is not the word. The show is in the same theater on campus where I did the final installation of my senior thesis. I thought I could never set foot in there again but somehow these kids make me forget the humiliation of that performance. The show the kids put on is not a play, but more like a series of short, surreal moments, interspersed with songs that they wrote themselves. There are about twenty kids and three adults who are also on stage with them. One girl tells a long story about a ladybug who makes friends with a spoon and they go off on adventures together. A boy does ballet on the moon. A song about why you shouldn't keep a monkey as a pet. It's not for the reasons you might think—what if it did better than you in school?

The show is a forty minute barrage of loud, energetic nonsense. When it's over, I turn to Nick and say with absolute sincerity, "Wow. That is the most amazing thing I have ever seen. Thank you so much."

Nick gives the happiest grin and I squeeze his hand.

"You should volunteer with them," Nick says as we're walking home. "Didn't it say on the program that they're always looking for more volunteers?"

"Oh, I don't know. What do I know about kids?"

"Just call them and ask."

When we get home, Nick puts the program on the refrigerator door, held in place with a magnet shaped like a piece of sushi. But I can't quite bring myself to call. And besides, I'm very busy at the bookstore. More than once I catch Nick squinting at the program, his nose nearly touching the paper, when he thinks no one is watching.

A week goes by.

"Hey, who drank all the milk?" I say as I attempt to fix myself breakfast. "Come on, is it too much to ask for one decent cup of coffee before I have to face another day of work?"

"Sorry!" Cricket calls from the dining room. "Aren't you lactose intolerant?"

"Whatever! Soymilk in coffee is gross."

"I'll buy more later." I can hear Cricket crunching cereal from here. I'm sure she was the one who finished the milk and left the empty plastic jug on the counter.

"Oh hey, look at this!" Nick gestures extra dramatically towards the refrigerator. "I know work sucks, so why not volunteer on the side with some adorable children?"

"Do they have milk?"

"Probably. You could ask them."

I sigh. Nick follows me to the dining room and sits down next to me. Mmm, black coffee and dry cereal for breakfast. I take a sip.

"Ugh, disgusting. Tell Nate to stop putting the coffee through the filter twice."

Nick smiles as if I didn't say anything. "I can call them if you don't want to."

"Stop!"

"Ok, sorry. But I hate seeing you like this. I know how much you miss doing shows."

"Yeah, you're the kind of person who needs a creative outlet," Cricket adds.

"Well, apparently I really suck at it."

"No! Howard's not your advisor anymore, so who cares what he thinks?" Nick says.

"Yeah, fuck that guy!" Cricket's chair scrapes as she stands up. "Sorry, I gotta run to class. I'll get more milk at Village Mart on the way home." She adds her bowl to the precarious pile in the sink, which now extends above the height of the counter.

Thinking on how disgusting the house has become lately is depressing. I wave goodbye to Cricket and fight the strong urge to lay my head on the table and never get up again.

"I can't shake this feeling that I can't do anything right."

"That's categorically untrue. Bob should be on his knees thanking you for reorganizing the shelving so customers can actually find books and not just guess."

"Yeah, but that doesn't stop him from yelling at me whenever the till is ten cents off."

Undeterred, Nick again brings the subject back around to theater. "I thought your performances were so cool and brave."

"I'm pretty sure Howard described them as creatively bankrupt."

"Kids won't care about any of that! Just let them jump around and be weird and loud. At least call and see what they say. I promise I'll never bring it up again."

I agree, if only to put an end to this excruciating conversation.

I can't call right away, not after Nick harassed me about it. But he keeps his promise not to mention it again. After seeing that program on the fridge every day for weeks, I finally call. Before I know it, I've gone through the application process, background check and minimal training. Honestly, I think they're desperate for volunteers and not too picky as long as you're not an actual criminal.

I'm assigned to an afterschool class for first, second, and third graders. They come in to the community center for an hour once a week, and I get them to make up stories and act them out.

The first day, I'm so nervous. But I don't need to worry. They're all super eager to please and excited to do whatever theater games I ask them to try.

Supposedly we're working towards a performance in a few months, but I realize almost immediately that they can't do anything the same way twice, so why bother? I decide that the performance will be mostly improvised. Instead of trying to write down a script and stick to it, every week I push them to make up more and more wild stories.

And man, these kids are lunatics. I could never imagine the bizarro nonsense they come up with. I'm blown away by their effortless creativity. This, I realize, is real theater. Everything they do is so real, or at least real to them, and that's what matters.

At work in the bookstore, I've been having long conversations with Tanya, the aspiring sci fi novelist, when I'm supposed to be stocking shelves and she's at the register. We have long, rambling conversations about what is ART. I tell her all about my disastrous senior thesis, although it's so humiliating I can't say it all at once, but instead let it out in oblique bits here and there over the course of many conversations.

"I wanted to do something radical," I complain to her over a stack of unsold Paul Reiser memoirs. "But I feel like no one got it at all."

Tanya stares out the plate glass window to the street. "Sometimes the most radical thing you can do is be yourself."

At time, I may have rolled my eyes, but now I think more about what Tanya said. These kids are too young to try to be cool or pretentious. All they know is how to be themselves, no matter how weird. They're excited about everything, because it's all new to them. Watching them be so intensely themselves is magical.

For the first time in months, maybe more than a year, I feel excited about being in the theater.

43

NICK

Abby is so much happier after she starts teaching the kids' theater class. Instead of stomping grumpily around the house, now she's singing musical theater tunes when she's in the shower or cooking. It's so cute. And every once in a while I catch sight of that smile, when the light hits her just right. I ask her to tell me all the crazy things the kids think up each week and we laugh and laugh.

Cricket starts dating a girl named Laura from one of her lit classes, and she transforms into a happier version of herself too. I like Laura. She's tall and soft-spoken but kind of effortlessly cool, and Cricket is clearly smitten with her. Laura comes to more and more of our poker nights and *Star Trek* nights. I'm so glad Cricket has found the right person finally.

The only one who's still stomping around grumpily is Nate. As we get closer to the end of classes and the start of exams, I slightly dread having to go home with him for the holidays. The thought of putting up with his sullen silence for three weeks with no one else around is depressing.

But wait, what if Abby came with me?

Once I get the idea in my head, I have to make it happen. I can't bear the thought of being apart from her for so long, or her being left alone in this big rundown old house.

Abby likes the idea.

"Your parents won't mind?" I ask her as we're lying on her futon together in the dark.

"It's fine," she says. "The advantage of being Jewish is that nobody in my family cares about the 25th. My parents will be just as happy to see me any other time of year."

I give her a squeeze, and we twine our bodies together. God, she feels so good. I'll never get tired of doing this.

It should be simple, to bring my girlfriend along for vacation at my parents' house which is a little more than a two hour drive away. But it's surprisingly complicated. First, it occurs to me that I haven't actually told my parents that I'm dating this girl I'm living with named Abby. Dad met Carson and Cricket when he helped us move in, but not Abby.

It takes me three phone calls home before I finally manage to say the words "Abby" and "girlfriend" in the same sentence. Not that I'm embarrassed of her, but I hate how my parents get all super into any girl I bring home. They always feel so fake, the way they act.

"Ooooohhh, Abbyyyy," Mom says in this forced tone that tells me instantly that they already know. Nate probably told them months ago. Jerk.

"Yes, of course she's welcome to spend Christmas break with us," Dad says.

Now here is problem two, which is that Abby can't take three weeks off work, and she certainly can't skip the busiest time of year. But the bookstore will be closed on Christmas Day and New Years Day, so she used all her leverage with Bob to get that week off.

"Sure, that's fine! She can drive up whenever she wants," Dad says when I explain the situation.

Which brings me to problem number three. I hesitate for a long time. "Um…she doesn't have a car."

I might have added, she doesn't even have a driver's license. It's like a weird point of pride with her, that real New Yorkers don't know how to drive.

"Ah," says Dad, and in that one short syllable is a whole sentence. *So you, an adult man, need your parents to make an extra round trip back to Allenville to pick up your girlfriend for a sleepover.* People ask me all the time what it's like to go blind, and expect me to give some sentimental answer like how I miss seeing the sunset or something but the truth is the thing that fucking sucks the most is not being able to drive a car myself like a full grown human.

I sigh as these thoughts race around my head. I thought it was a quiet sigh, but Dad must have heard me. Before I can say anything, he jumps back in.

"It's fine. Just tell me the date, and we'll come get her."

"It'll be Christmas morning." I'm dying on the inside as I say it.

There's another weighty pause, then Mom says too cheerfully, "Great! We're looking forward to meeting her. Really."

After this phone call, I feel even worse. I almost wish they had said, *no way, what are you thinking?* Or something. I mean, it's awesome that they're being so nice about this person they haven't even met, but I can't help but wonder if it's partly out of pity. Maybe they're just like *thank goodness a human female has agreed to spend time with him, we'd better go along with this no matter what.* If I could see, would they have agreed to spend four hours in the car on Christmas Day?

I have to take a few days after this for the icky feeling to clear before I can even tell Abby about my plan.

"Are you sure?" she asks.

No. "Yes!"

"Well, ok, I guess."

Maybe because she didn't grow up celebrating Christmas, this doesn't seem like a big deal to her. Our family has never been the type to go all out for Christmas, especially now that we kids aren't little anymore. But still, I can't shake the uncomfortable feeling that I'm getting something I shouldn't have asked for.

"Is it this street or the next one?"

On Christmas Day, it's my sister Emily who drives with me back to Allenville to pick up Abby.

"How should I know? What do the directions say?"

Dad wrote out a detailed map for her.

"I don't know, I think it fell down beside the seat." The car swerves slightly as she gropes around trying to find the map.

"No, stop! Keep your eyes on the road!"

For a second I wonder which would be worse, flinging myself out the door or staying put as she skids into oncoming traffic. Great, as if it wasn't terrifying enough to be driven by my seventeen year old sister, now we're lost. To be fair, she seemed fine the whole way here. It's only when we hit the maze of one-way streets around campus that we run into problems.

I take a deep breath. "Just tell me what street we're on now."

"I don't know!"

"Is it University Ave?"

"Oh wait, yeah!"

"Ok, go straight then turn right on Micsawbee Ave."

After a year and a half, I have a pretty good mental map of Allenville, the names of all the streets around Calstock State, how they connect, the campus building names and some of the shops, punctuated with some of the bigger visual landmarks I can see, like the big glass windows of the school bookstore.

We make a few wrong turns when one-way streets force us to go around unexpectedly, but we make it to the house eventually. I feel pretty good about giving Emily the directions. I'm not totally useless after all. It takes some of the sting out of being driven around by my kid sister.

It's all worth it to see Abby, though.

44

ABBY

I'm kind of nervous about meeting Nick's parents. Not only because it's a big relationship step and I'm still keeping this secret. But also I never know when someone from one of these little suburban towns is going to hit me with some unexpected antisemitism. I've lost track of how many people at Calstock told me I'm the first Jewish person they ever met. What the hell? Before I left New York, I didn't think that was even possible. And it's not like there are no Jews in the Midwest, actually there are a lot.

But as it turns out, his parents are super nice, extra kind and accommodating. They're typical clean-cut Midwesterners, his dad in a Calstock sweatshirt and his mom in a Christmas sweater. His sister Emily is nice too, and peppers me with questions about college. She's so cute, how eager she is to go there herself.

It's interesting to see Nick and Nate in their childhood home. Nick immediately runs upstairs to dump my bag in the guest bedroom, while I linger in the front hall. Nate is helping in the kitchen. The way they move around here is different than at our shared house—smoother, more assured. We need to make more of an effort to keep our house tidy.

I stare at the photos lining the walls, years of school pictures from kindergarten through high school graduation, complete with cap and gown. Nick and Nate are identical but seeing them side by side, there are a few tiny differences: the shape of the smile, the way they style their hair. But mainly the way Nick makes eye contact, and Nate never does. In the photos, Nick is looking straight at the camera, while Nate's gaze is directed slightly downward. Even so, in the photos neither of them look blind. I know how much they hate when people say that, but it's true. People shouldn't make comments like that, though.

Nick comes back downstairs a few minutes later and we sit down to the huge meal. I apologize several times for disrupting their Christmas lunch or dinner or whatever, but they genuinely don't seem put out.

"Are you sure you don't mind eating ham?" his mom asks, not for the first time. "I can defrost some chicken nuggets real quick. Or maybe you don't want meat at all? I think we have some veggie burgers."

"It's really fine," I say for what feels like the millionth time as we sit down to eat. "When I lived in Probus Hall, I ate bacon in the dining hall every single day. I never knew what I was missing, had to make up for lost time, haha."

Everyone laughs.

"So how did you two meet?" she asks.

"We were in the same lit class last year," I say.

"Yeah, my note taker didn't show, so she helped out," Nick adds.

I know he means well, but that extra fact fills me with guilt and dread. Would I have made the offer to help if I weren't a devotee? Who knows. Would he have accepted my offer if he knew? I'm sure he wouldn't. Shit, I have to tell him. But every day that goes by, it gets harder and harder. And now here I am meeting his parents like a normal couple. Like they wouldn't all hate me if they knew.

"You can borrow the car if you kids want to go see a movie or something," his dad says.

I swallow hard. "I don't have a driver's license."

No one says anything for a beat. To their credit, his parents don't exchange a look although I imagine they want to.

"I can take you!" Emily says excitedly. "If you want to go out, I mean."

"Yeah, welcome to the bustling nightlife of Chesterford Hills," Nate jokes. "It's like a graveyard with lights."

Of course, Nick's parents don't invite me to sleep in his bedroom. They're open-minded, but not that open-minded, he whispers to me as he takes me upstairs. I get the guest bedroom, decorated in shabby chic by way of Meijer, all fake flowers and too many pillows on the bed.

I get ready for bed as fast and unobtrusively as I can, then lie awake in the darkness listening to everyone else doing the same, low voices, doors opening and closing, water running. Just as I'm feeling like I will never be able to sleep in this springy, floofy bed, I hear soft knocking at the door.

"Hey," I say in a low voice as Nick slips in.

He stumbles slightly over the pillows I threw to the floor, his arms flung outward. Seriously, who needs so many pillows?

"Hey," he whispers, falling into the bed and giving me a full body hug. "Thanks for putting up with my weird family."

I hug him back. "They're not weird. They're like the most normal people I've ever met."

"I still think they're weird. But I'm really happy you're here."

"Thanks. I'm glad I came."

He wraps one arm around my waist, and cups my breast with the other. I'm only wearing a t-shirt and underpants, not exactly sexy lingerie. But sexy lingerie wouldn't be appropriate to wear at his parents' house. Also I don't own any.

Nick doesn't seem to mind. He runs his hands all over me and it feels amazing. We've been apart for two weeks and I missed him so much. But I'm painfully aware that his parents' bedroom is right down the hall.

"Is it ok?" I whisper.

"We'll have to be quiet."

Oh lord. I'm a loudmouth theater kid. I don't know how to be quiet. Yes, I'm a screamer.

I bite down hard on my lower lip as Nick scoots down to the end of the bed and pulls off my cotton panties. My back arches as he runs his hands over my thighs, around my hips. Then he buries his face between my legs, circling his tongue around and around. Being together again, knowing we shouldn't be doing this, that we might get caught, is the extra spice that drives me over the edge. He grips my hips tightly as I hold my breath, whimpering with the effort not to make too much noise. He makes me come like a freaking freight train, over and over.

Nick hangs on until I take my shuddering last breath. I push him away gently, letting him know it's his turn now. I push my ass right up in his face as I take his cock in my mouth. I love how he lets out these little moans, like he can't help how turned on he is. Right at the end he gives a ragged gasp, I hope not too loud.

As much as I want to fall asleep curled up together, we can't. Nick tiptoes back to his own room, leaving me uneasily alone in the too-soft guest bed.

The week goes by slowly, since we're basically trapped in the house. We can't even walk anywhere as we're miles away from anything other than gas stations and fast food.

Most of our outings consist of accompanying Nick's parents to the supermarket or going out to dinner with them. His parents are nice, and I appreciate how they go out of their way to make me feel welcome. At home, I notice they don't let Nick or Nate get away with any nonsense. They both have to help out with housework and chores, the same as their sister. In restaurants, if a server is rude and doesn't talk to them directly, their mom gives a polite but pointed correction. Actually, this doesn't happen often because usually their dad cues them by announcing when the server comes by, and Nate starts talking without waiting to be addressed. It's a clever system. I'll have to try it when we get back to Allenville.

The one outing we have without parents is to the movies. Emily takes us to see the latest *Star Trek* movie, which we actually already went to see on opening night last month. But everything else at the Chesterford Hills cineplex sounds terrible, so we watch it again, hooting and hollering whenever Kirk and Picard are onscreen together. The whole audience is rowdy like that, and no one cares that Emily and I narrate the action on screen for Nick and Nate.

The rest of the time, Emily is off with her friends, and we lie around the house, watching TV and helping out with minor chores and errands. Nick is relaxed and seems to be enjoying the vacation, but Nate is checked out as usual, distant and cranky.

With his parents and sister, Nate is polite, and sometimes I see a flash of sarcastic humor. But when he talks to Nick, he's terse, almost rude. I can't be the only one who notices this, but no one says anything about it. I get the impression that this is not a family where people talk about their feelings.

I stare at Nick and Nate as we sprawl on the couch in front of the TV, watching a *Kids in the Hall* marathon. Nick is laughing at the jokes and making comments, talking back to the TV. Nate is laying with his head back and his eyes closed, frowning slightly. I don't think he's asleep. I wish there was something I could do to fix this problem between them, but I also feel like maybe I'm part of the problem. And who am I to tell Nate to come out when I'm in the closet myself?

Nick and I take a few walks around the subdivision, even though there's nothing to see but other identical faux colonial houses.

"You know you don't have to live this way," I say as we trudge down to the end of the cul-de-sac and back.

"What way?"

"This suburban, car-dependent existence. I know everyone thinks the way they live is normal and the best way, but there are places where you can get around without a car."

Nick smirks at me. "Like New York?"

"Yes, exactly!"

"Ok, so when are you going to invite me to your parents' place?"

Oh right. I still haven't told my parents about Nick. Why does everything have to be so complicated? I guess I take too long to answer, because the smile fades from his face.

"I see how it is," he says.

"No! I want to invite you over. It's just, well, it's further away and harder to get there..."

"Uh huh."

Shit! Now he thinks I'm embarrassed of him or something. Ok, now! Just tell him! But I can't have this conversation at his parents' house, can I? Once again I chicken out, then we're back at the house and I've missed my chance again.

45

NICK

Having Abby at my parents' house is awesome but also slightly weird. She belongs to college life, where I'm a grown up. Sort of. It feels out of place to hear her voice in a place filled with childhood memories. As I expected, my parents do the overly-nice thing that makes me cringe so hard but I guess it's better than the alternative.

At the end of the week, we celebrate New Years by watching TV then going to bed, like when we were kids. When am I going to move on from this?

I can't believe it's already 1995. Only five more years until the millennium, so crazy.

Dad drives us all back to Allenville, to the house on Micsawbee Ave. It feels more like home than my parents' house.

My last semester already. It's a good thing I don't have time for anything except studying because the weather turns unbelievably cold at the end of January. The temperature dips into the negative double digits and the local news issues dire warnings about instant frostbite, but I'm still expected to show up for eight AM classes.

Walking across campus, I feel icicles form on my eyelashes and inside my nose. The air feels strangely still in the frigid silence, the snow absorbing all the sounds. The snow on the ground is the texture of sand, blowing away before my swinging cane and heavy boots as I trudge across the quad. The classrooms smell of wet wool and sandy, salty puddles of melted snow. The heaters struggle and wheeze, and I can feel the cold blowing in from the locked windows.

One afternoon, when I return home from class I'm greeted by the sound of rushing water as I swing the front door open. I stand there confused for a second. Is someone taking an epic shower? Why is the running water sound so loud? And why does the whole house smell so wet?

"The pipes froze!" Cricket shouts.

"What? How?" I struggle to peel off my hat, scarf, gloves, coat, and boots. I can barely hear her voice over the noise.

"I don't know! I came home a few minutes ago and it was like this. There's water everywhere!"

My heart starts racing as I think of my computer in my bedroom, the hard drive full of half-finished assignments.

"Did you call Dwight?"

"Yes, he said he's on his way over but we need to turn off the water main."

"Ok, where is it?"

"I don't know, the basement?"

I follow Cricket through the house, and as we pass through the kitchen, I feel water dripping on me. And not a little bit either, it's like being outside in a storm. It's raining in the kitchen. What the hell?

We clatter down the basement stairs, me with my hand on Cricket's shoulder because it's too dark to see anything at all. It's raining down here too. Jesus.

"Do you see it?"

She spins around, then heads to one corner.

"Yeah, there's a big red lever here. I think that's it." She pulls at it but nothing happens. "Ugh, it's stuck! I can't move it!"

I grope around, and she guides my hands to a metal bar covered in a soft plastic handle. I brace my feet and yank upwards as hard as I can. For a second, nothing happens, then it pops up with a loud snapping noise.

"Did that do it?"

We both listen as the sound of gushing water subsides. I high five her, feeling unusually manly for having solved this domestic crisis.

My feeling of accomplishment deflates quickly, however, when Dwight arrives and notices that I broke the valve when I turned it.

By this point, Nate and Carson have returned home as well. There's a long argument as we all stand around the main in the basement. Of course Dwight wants to blame all of this on us.

"When it's this cold, you need to leave the taps dripping," he insists.

"You never told us that," Nate says.

As they argue, Carson goes upstairs to investigate and discovers the rupture happened in his bathroom on the third floor, a tiny jury-rigged closet where Dwight had covered over the pipe against an outside wall with plywood, so it stayed much colder than the rest of the house. No one says out loud that this is clearly Dwight's fault, but he stops insisting we have to pay the repair bills. Luckily, the water damage missed the big furniture and our computers.

The broken valve is my fault, though. Well, maybe. Dwight probably should have kept it better maintained. I'm the one who turned it, but even though he mutters a lot of swears to himself, Dwight doesn't blame me directly. I'm pretty sure it's because he doesn't want to yell at a blind guy. It's not the first time some asshole who normally would try to be the big swinging dick goes easy on me. I'm not sure how I feel about that.

The conversation shifts to how soon Dwight can get a plumber over to fix the main and the burst pipe so we can have water again. It's not looking good, since it's already late in the afternoon, and with the frigid weather there are frozen pipes all over town.

When Abby comes home from the bookstore, I give her the news: no water until tomorrow. The plumber will come by in the morning, if we're lucky.

"It could have been worse," Abby says thoughtfully as we eat delivery pizza for dinner. "At least now I don't feel bad about not cooking dinner or washing the dishes."

"Thanks for buying us bottled water," Cricket says to Carson.

"No prob."

"Way to play the crip card, bro," Nate says. "You saved our security deposit."

So I was right. Dwight backed off out of pity. I toss a pizza crust on my paper plate.

"Dwight can kiss my ass."

"I know it sucks, but at least we can take advantage of his shitty attitude to save some money." There's the brother I've been missing, not the cranky asshole, but the one guy in the whole world who gets it, who's on my side. I didn't realize how much I've been missing the old Nate. Maybe it's just the stress of the whole day catching up with me, but I almost feel like crying.

"I thought you would tell me I'm perpetuating stereotypes or whatever," I say.

"Nah, you were taking advantage of his ignorance," Nate says. "Never hesitate to use someone's stupidity for your own benefit."

This good feeling with Nate doesn't last, though.

46

ABBY

The water gets turned on the next day, but the house doesn't recover so quickly. The musty smell lingers and part of the waterlogged ceiling falls down in the dining room. We try to ignore the hole while we wait for Dwight to arrange repairs. Life goes back to normal, or what counts as normal for us.

Watching *Star Trek: The Next Generation* together on the couch every evening has become a house tradition, a way for all of us to relax after I get home from work and they're all procrastinating on their homework. Cricket's girlfriend Laura has started joining us too. I'm so relieved Cricket finally found someone. It would have been a freaking tragedy if that girl graduated from college without living her lesbian dreams.

Laura is objectively hot. Freckles, brown hair, fierce undercut, wears '70s style thrift store finds that look really good on her. Damn, Cricket has good taste.

So *Star Trek* night should be a chill hang but the tension between Nick and Nate is threatening to ruin my good mood.

We're watching reruns, and the station has cycled back around to the inferior first season, the episode where Geordi explains how his visor works and whines about how it's not like seeing a real sunset.

"Again with the fucking sunsets!" Nate bursts out. "Why are sighted people so obsessed with blind people not seeing sunsets?"

"They look nice," Nick says stubbornly.

This sends Nate into a full-blown rant.

"This is such bullshit! Not only the sunset, but that stupid visor and all of it! The whole purpose of *Star Trek* is to imagine a better future! So why are we so obsessed with imagining a fake magical cure for disability, instead of a future that's really inclusive?"

"Yeah!" I can't help but chime in. "And in the first season, the visor is literally just a hair clip spray-painted silver. The prop department should be ashamed of themselves."

Picard continues pitying Geordi in the background as Nate talks over him. We've seen this episode at least five times, to give a conservative guess.

"I can't believe this is what passes for disability representation. Geordi! Why is he the one character with a little kid nickname? And his whole personality is Data's boring sidekick. He's even more of a social misfit than the literal robot."

"Right on!" I don't want to make things worse, but I can't help agreeing with Nate. This is something that's been on my mind about this show for years. "How come he's the only character who never fucks? Everyone else gets laid all the time, even Data."

"Only the once," Carson corrects me.

"Whatever! Nate is right, Geordi is like a child, especially with women," I say.

"I thought it was nice that they included a character with a disability in the crew," Cricket says quietly. "They could have cured him and not ever mentioned it."

Nate snorts. "With that magic visor, it's basically the same thing."

"Can't we just enjoy a stupid TV show and not over-analyze everything?" Nick has clearly had enough of Nate's attitude.

"No! When you're bombarded with these shitty messages all the time, it matters! Maybe then you wouldn't have such a shitty attitude."

"What are you even talking about! You're the one with the shitty attitude."

Laura and Cricket look appalled and embarrassed. Nate ignores everyone. I stare meaningfully at Carson, hoping maybe he can do something about this, but he just turns up the volume on the TV louder.

We watch the rest of the episode in silence.

47

NICK

For spring break this year we decide to take a road trip to New York City. Our plan comes together because Abby has to go to her cousin's bat mitzvah and she complains that she doesn't want to and I say that I'll go with her and she says no you can't, you're a goy. Then Carson says he's always wanted to see New York and suddenly we have this plan that Carson will drive us, Abby will go stay with her parents, while the three of us stay in a hotel and when Abby isn't busy with her family she'll show us around.

We ask Cricket if she wants to come with us but she says no, she wants to go hiking with Laura. That's fine, but I suddenly realize that I wanted to spend spring break with Abby but instead I'll be squashed in a hotel room with just Nate and Carson. I'm already slightly regretting my plan, but I promised Abby we would take her, and I'm not going to let her down.

The day before our trip, Carson wakes up in the morning to find his windshield iced over. The previous night we had a big rainfall then the temperature dropped suddenly, now everything is coated in a thick layer of ice.

We all stand out on the porch in our pajamas, breathing in the frigid air.

"There's icicles hanging off the tree branches," Abby says. "It's beautiful!"

I get a strange sense of intense sunlight, glittering reflections thrown off the snow and ice-covered lawn.

"Careful, the steps are slippery," Cricket says as Carson goes to inspect his car parked at the curb in front of the house.

"Shit! The ice on the windshield is really thick." He comes back up the steps.

"I'll help you scrape it," Nate offers.

"No, I'm sick of it! I've been scraping the windshield every day this winter. Why did I pick a house with no garage? Forget it, I have a better idea."

He disappears into the house, while the rest of us stay on the porch, sipping coffee and enjoying the fresh air and sunlight. Even Nate, I assume. He can tell when it's light or dark.

Carson bangs around in the house for a few minutes then comes back out again.

"What are you doing?" Nate asks as we hear Carson go back down the creaky porch steps. He doesn't answer.

"He's got a big bucket of hot water," Abby says.

"No wait," Nate calls out. "I don't think that's—"

Before he can finish the sentence, we hear a splash then a tremendous crack, followed by a howl from Carson.

"FUCK!!"

"Oh no, the whole windshield shattered!" Abby's voice sounds kind of strangled, like she's not sure whether to laugh or cry.

There's stunned silence for a few seconds. We hear Carson come stamping up the stairs again and into the house, then upstairs. The slam of his bedroom door can be heard even out on the porch.

"Holy crap," Cricket says softly.

"That fucking idiot!" Nate bursts out. "And he's an engineering major! How could he not know that would happen?"

Silence again. I mean, Carson is kind of an idiot but saying so feels like piling on. Then something else occurs to me.

"Guys, I hate to say this, but how are we going to get to New York tomorrow?"

"We gotta get this fixed today," Nate says angrily. "I'll go talk to him."

"Maybe give him a minute," Abby suggests.

"Yeah, go easy on him," Cricket says. "It was an honest mistake. Please don't get in a big fight over this."

We go back in, feeling cold and anxious, and help ourselves to breakfast. I have another cup of coffee. I need some sort of emotional fortification and it's too early for beer.

We eat in silence. As I'm putting my cereal bowl in the sink, I hear Carson come back downstairs.

"I found a repair place in the phone book," he says. "They promised they can replace the windshield today. I'm gonna drive over now."

"What! You can't drive it like that," Nate says.

"Yeah, the seat is covered in broken glass," Abby adds. "Your ass will get cut to hell."

"I'll brush it off."

"There's no way you'll get it all," Nate says. "Just call a tow truck."

They argue back and forth for a while but in the end Nate wins and Carson calls a tow truck.

I go back up to my room and start packing for the trip, thinking this is all taken care of. My bedroom faces the street, so I can clearly hear the tow truck come and take the car. I take a shower, pack some more, then make myself a sandwich for lunch, and wonder if we should throw out some of the food in the fridge before we go, or wait to see what it smells like when we get back.

In the afternoon, the phone rings. Carson picks it up in the living room.

"Yes. … Ok… I see… Ok thanks. Bye."

Nate comes running down the stairs when the phone rings.

"Was that the shop? Can we go get the car?"

"No…" Carson sounds dazed. "They said the tow truck driver got in an accident. As he was pulling into the garage, someone rear-ended him and pushed the car up against the tow. They said they'll file an insurance claim but the car is totaled."

"What the fuck!" I'm not trying to make him feel worse. It just slips out.

"Are you sure it can't be repaired?" Nate asks.

"Yes, I'm sure!" Carson shouts. He's been relatively calm until this moment but now he loses it. "This is all your fault! I knew I should have driven the car there myself."

"Don't blame me for your dumbass mistake. I tried to tell you not to throw hot water on glass but you wouldn't listen."

"Yeah, well, I did listen to you about the tow truck and look where it got me!"

"Please don't fight," Cricket whispers.

"Now what?" Abby's voice comes from the stairs. She must have come down right after Nate.

"Now I wait for weeks to find out if their insurance will pay me for a new car," Carson says sourly from the couch.

Abby comes down into the living room. "No, I mean about the trip. We're supposed to leave tomorrow and this bat mitzvah is the day after we arrive." When no one replies, she goes on, "I mean, I guess it's fine if you all decide not to go but I've gotta be there. I already feel like the family fuckup. I don't want to ask my parents for money, and there's no way I can afford a last minute plane ticket. What am I gonna do?" Her voice goes up with a note of panic at the end.

"No," I say. "We're still going! We have a hotel room booked and everything. I promise, we're going to get you there."

"How," Nate says flatly, but at least he's not arguing.

"Rent a car?" I suggest.

"No," Carson says. "I've tried before, no one will rent you a car if you're under twenty-five."

Of course by "you" he means him, because no one is ever renting me or Nate a car no matter how old we are.

As we're all sitting in the living room thinking our own dark thoughts, the doorbell rings. It's Laura. Of course. Cricket's been hanging out on the couch waiting for her to come over. They give each other a quick greeting. I can't tell if they kiss or not. Are they too embarrassed for PDA? Or worried? They shouldn't be. We're all super happy to see them together.

Laura immediately senses the heavy atmosphere, and Cricket fills her in. As Laura is making sympathetic noises, I suddenly get an idea.

"Hey, don't you have a station wagon? How'd you both like to come along with us?"

"What!" Cricket sounds taken aback. I can see the golden blur of her short hair against the window behind the couch. I move my eyes around, trying to see her face but I can't make out her expression.

"Come on, it'll be fun, all of us together! The hotel room is already paid for."

"But we were going hiking," Cricket says.

"The hotel room only has two double beds," Nate adds.

"I'll sleep on the floor. You guys can have the beds." I'm feeling slightly desperate to make this plan work. We have to get Abby there in time.

"Ok, why not?" Laura says, to my surprise. "We can go hiking any-time. I've always wanted to see New York."

"Are you sure?" Cricket also sounds surprised.

"Yeah, let's do it!" Laura is getting increasingly enthusiastic. "What's the point of spring break if you can't make a road trip? Let's go!"

"Yeah! Spring break!" I put up my hand for a high five but she must have been standing further away than I realized because it's an awkward few moments before her hand connects with mine. At least she doesn't leave me hanging.

48

ABBY

We learned from spring break last year not to leave too late in the day. This time we do a lot better. Laura drives up early in the morning and we're off. Cricket sits up in front. Nick is relegated to the rumble seat in the wayback, squashed in next to the bags, since this trip is his dumb idea. That leaves me sitting on the hump in the middle of the back seat in between Nate and Carson.

Terrific.

As if it hasn't been bad enough sharing a house with the gay disaster couple, now I'm inches away from them. The whole time they've been alternating between horny ass-grabbing when Nick is out of the house, and pretending they don't know each other when Nick is at home. It's freaking exhausting.

Laura drives through town and out to the freeway heading east.

"Ok, now what?" she asks as we leave Allenville behind.

Oh my God, no one planned the route. Never mind finding places to eat or sleep, no one even knows where we're going.

"Just keep going east until we get there!" Nick calls cheerfully from the wayback.

Laura has a big spiralbound atlas in a backseat pocket. I pull it out and flip through it.

"Look." I show the page to Carson. "This route here is the interstate, but see how it goes way out of the way? If we take this highway instead it's a straight line."

"Yeah, but that's a smaller road," Carson says.

"So? It's also a highway. Even if we have to go a little slower, it'll still be faster because we won't have to make this big detour."

Carson disagrees, but I show the atlas to Cricket and Laura, and they agree with me, so that's the way we go.

By the time we realize I've made a terrible mistake, it's too late.

Technically we're on a state highway, but in fact it's no more than a road going right through the center of one small town after another, so basically a city street with stop lights and a speed limit far below the interstate. But now we're stuck on this road, and the only way to get to the interstate would be to double back, which would take even longer.

We knew this trip would take more than a day but we didn't book a hotel room on the way, because we weren't sure how far we'd get before night. The original plan was to drive until Carson got tired, then find a motel somewhere and stop. While there are surely motels on the interstate, there are none along the state highway, only houses and farmland.

"Fuck it," Laura says. "We'll just drive until we get there."

Sometimes Laura speeds up, until Cricket reminds her she's over the limit.

"Sorry, babe," Laura says. "I just feel like at this rate it's going to take days."

"I'm sorry!" I burst out, not for the first time. "I didn't know!"

I apologize several more times, but it doesn't change the fact that this is my fault, and I can't even take a turn at the wheel because I don't know how to drive. Nick and Nate don't say anything, but I can tell they're frustrated too at not being able to help out. Freaking car life, man! Why does this keep happening? I feel doubly guilty that once again I've put them in a situation where they feel bad about not being able to drive.

At least there are gas stations along this road. We stop at one to re-fill, use the bathroom, and grab some food. We waited too long to stop for dinner and now the few restaurants we passed have closed.

"They didn't look good anyway," I inform Nick. "I'm not that hungry."

Nick holds my elbow and Nate takes Carson's as we stock up on chips, candy bars, and soda. Or pop, as everyone else calls it. Laura gets an extra large coffee. I try not to listen to the sighs and groans as we pile back into the car.

Nick twists around in the wayback so he's facing us even though it's dark now. Even I can barely see anything as the streetlights strobe through the back seat. I'm sure he can't see anything at all, but still he puts a giant grin on his face.

"We just have to get there, and this will all be worth it," Nick says overly loudly to no one in particular. "I promised Abby, and we will get there for her."

"I'm sorry," I say again.

"It's not your fault," Nick says.

Nate, who's been quiet most of the trip so far, suddenly squirms around in his seat. "No, it's both your faults! I should never have let you talk us into this. Your girlfriend should have taken a plane."

"Hey!" Nick is almost shouting even though his head is inches from our ears. "Why do you have to be such an asshole? At least say her name. She's sitting right next to you."

"Ok." Nate's voice drips with sarcasm. "Abby should have taken a fucking plane. Now you've even dragged Laura into your stupid rescue fantasy bullshit."

"I'm fine!" Laura calls from the front. "Please don't fight over me!"

I've been trying so hard not to cry, but Nate's comment drives me over the edge. Tears spill down my face. I'm hoping like crazy that no one will notice. I give what I consider an unobtrusive sniff, but Nick hears me.

"What the fuck is your problem, Nate!" he shouts. "I don't care if you're a dick to me but you can't talk to Abby like that."

"Don't," I whisper, desperate to stop this.

"Like what?" Nate sneers, ignoring me. "Like telling you the fucking truth? Someone has to. You think we're the same person, you and me, but we're not. You just drift through life oblivious to everyone but yourself. Everything is so easy for you and all you do is complain. I'm sick of it!"

"What the hell are you talking about?"

"Nothing, never mind."

The whole car is silent. Beneath the hum of the engine and the buzz of the tires I can sense everyone in the car holding their breath. Probably wishing they were anywhere else, not trapped in this tiny metal box hurtling down a back road in the middle of the night, unable to escape Nick and Nate arguing again.

Up at the front of the car, Laura has the radio tuned to a local top 40 station but turned down low. Strains of Van Halen filter faintly to the back, distorted by static and engine noise.

"No," Nick says, too loudly, given that we're sitting inches apart. "It's obviously not nothing! I'm sick of the constant attitude from you, sick of feeling like a chump. You accuse me of not knowing what's going on with you but you never say anything. So what is it?"

Silence, except for Nate compulsively cracking his knuckles.

"What is it!"

I whisper, "Just tell him."

"Tell me what!" Nick and Nate both look stricken. If I hadn't said anything, they probably would have both tried to pretend it was nothing, but now Nick knows there is some big secret.

"C'mon, man," Carson says, reaching across me to grasp Nate's hand.

Nate takes a deep breath.

"I'm gay."

"What?"

"Do I have to spell it out for you, butthead? G-A-Y gay."

"But..." Nick seems like he's about to spew out a string of dumbass questions but catches himself in time. "Ok," he says stiffly. "Thank you for telling me."

After that, it's quiet for hours as we drive through the back of nowhere in the dead of night. Carson and Cricket take turns driving. Nate snores softly. At least someone is getting some sleep.

49

NICK

I curl up uncomfortably on the hard wayback seat, my mind racing. I feel like my life is flashing before my eyes.

So to speak.

I still have a lot of visual memories from our childhood, and some are so vivid. Going to the beach on Lake Michigan. Our sixth birthday party, when we both ate too much cake and threw up. All the times our other grandmother got us matching outfits as presents and Dad forced us to wear them for photos. I can still remember the nauseating smell of her perfume as she pinched our cheeks and said we were like two peas in a pod.

You think we're the same person but we're not.

When we were in elementary school together, we were always trying to be different. Teachers and even our friends got us mixed up all the time so we were always trying to pull apart. When Nate was into *Star Wars*, I was into *Transformers*. Thinking back, I realize what a weak strategy that was, but at the time it felt important.

But then in middle school Nate's vision got worse and suddenly everyone stopped thinking we were the same. Grown-ups kept telling me in patronizing tones that I had to watch out for my brother, be his eyes and help him. Our parents never said that, thank goodness. They knew how we really felt, which was that Nate was the one helping me because it would be my turn next. As the gray static-y patches got bigger, the only way to cope was to be more like Nate.

Was that what he meant, me thinking we're the same person? I wasn't aware I was doing that. It's just, well, he's so much better at everything. Of course I have to be more like him. Right?

But it turns out there's this big difference that I never knew about. I must be the world's shittiest brother. He could tell all of our friends but not me.

I drift off to sleep without realizing it. The next thing I know, Abby is shaking me and saying we're making another gas station pit stop. As I tumble from the car, nauseated and stiff, I realize from the sound of traffic and the gray light that it's morning and we've finally reached I-80 that will take us to New York.

"Ugh, this is the kind of experience you have when you're young so you know never to do it again," I hear Cricket mutter as we pile back into the car.

It's afternoon again before we reach what Abby calls the outer boroughs. Finally we go into a tunnel, and at the end of it, Abby says, "Welcome to Manhattan."

"It doesn't look like I expected," Carson remarks as we careen through traffic and Abby yells directions to Laura.

"What did you expect?" Nate snaps at him.

"I dunno, skyscrapers. All I see are a lot of brown apartment buildings."

"Well duh," Abby says. "Did you think people live in the offices? Don't worry, you'll get to see the skyscrapers."

Our hotel is in a neighborhood called Clinton, and it must be closer to what Carson was expecting because he starts exclaiming as soon as we get out of the parking garage. I wish someone would describe it to me but I'm too tired and dazed to ask. Abby is busy giving directions and making plans as we stagger to the hotel, me clutching her arm and trying not to hit her with my bag or cane. I get a vague impression of tall buildings and gray concrete. The air smells of pigeons and car exhaust, but after being in the car for so long, the warm breeze on my face feels good.

The plan is that Cricket and Laura will go look around for a while then sneak in later so we won't have to pay for extra guests. Abby will take the subway to her parents' place and meet up with us again in a few days.

"Wow," she says, dumping Cricket's and Laura's bags on the bed.

"What 'wow'?" I seriously might die if I don't get some sleep soon. The room feels small and smells musty. It must look even worse, I can tell from her voice. That wasn't a good wow. That was a I-can't-believe-you're-staying-here wow.

The other bed creaks as Nate flops onto it. Carson rattles the door to the closet, or maybe the bathroom.

Abby says, "For the price it ain't bad. Just, you know, watch out for cock-a-roaches."

"I'm starving," Carson announces. "I'm going to get us some dinner."

"That's my cue to leave too," Abby says as the door clicks shut behind him. She gives me a peck on the cheek. I squeeze her hand. I desperately want her to stay but I don't say anything. I'm not a child.

"You two need to talk," Abby says as she walks out the door. "Really talk. Don't be all Midwestern stoic." Then she's gone.

I stretch out on the bed. I can hear Nate on the other bed but he doesn't say anything. The longer the silence drags on, the faster my heart goes.

"You could have told me sooner," I say at last.

Nate snorts. "Oh yeah? You think it's that easy?"

"No, I just mean...I'm sorry if I ever made you feel like I wouldn't accept you."

"Thanks." His voice is low and rough. "I know you're not a homophobe. But the way you assume we're the same about everything, that we think the same way or have the same feelings, I dunno, how could I say anything?"

"Have you told Mom and Dad yet?"

"No."

I feel an unexpected surge of relief. I still feel guilty that he could tell our friends before me, but at least I'm not the very last to know.

"I think they'll be ok with it too."

"Yeah." He doesn't sound convinced, but I'm sure he doesn't have to worry. We're not religious and I've never heard our parents say anything prejudiced about gay people. Not like Laura's mother, who has her whole church praying for her daughter to marry a man.

"Watching you with Abby has been fucking killing me," he says. "It's just, it's so unfair that you have a partner and everyone thinks it's great only because she's a girl. Meanwhile, I can't even kiss my boyfriend without worrying what strangers might say. You could bring her home for Christmas like it's nothing but I can't do the same."

"Yeah, it is unfair," I say. But wait, rewind. Did he just say boyfriend? What is he talking about? Oh my God, him and Carson? No way. I was sure that was a joke. For real?

At that moment, the door clicks open again.

"There's a place across the street that sells pizza by the slice so that's all I got. Sorry I'm too wiped to get anything fancier."

It's Carson.

"Thanks, man." I listen to the rustling of plastic bags as he comes in. The hotel room furnishings consist of two beds, a TV and a coffee maker on a rickety stand with a few musty drawers. We'll have to eat sitting on the beds.

He goes over to Nate's bed, and I hear the unmistakable smack of a kiss.

"Is that ok?" Carson asks in a low whisper.

"Yes," Nate replies more loudly, that one word a challenge to me to say anything.

How long have they been together? All those noises and Abby saying the house was haunted, was that a joke? I think back over the past year and a half, and everything shifts. That time at Halloween last year, when Nate slept in his room, then Carson disappeared for a few days. Then the way he started acting when Nate was dating Cricket.

The way Nate dated girls in high school but never seemed to care about any of them, except as a friend.

One of the things Nate picked up in his disability studies class was about ableist language. He goes on and on about how many words we use every day reinforce the idea of pitying people with disabilities, and the word he talks about the most is *blind*.

"Why does blind have to be a synonym for willful ignorance?" he says. "All it means is that I'm lacking one sense. It shouldn't also mean stupid or clueless, or be a metaphor for anything else." Even though I find his rants annoying, I have to agree with him on that.

But dammit, I was blind to the real Nate. No, even if I had perfect vision, I probably still wouldn't have noticed him and Carson because I didn't want to. I wanted to feel like at least I was more successful than him at this one thing, having a girlfriend. And I was so sure that we were exactly the same so I never had to think about anything. I let him do the heavy lifting of figuring out how to live as a blind person, how to be a person in the world, and all I had to do was follow him. No wonder he's been so angry at me.

"Want a slice, Nick?" Carson asks.

"Yeah." He pushes a greasy paper plate into my hands. Carson is kind of a dumbass. I mean, he did shatter his car's windshield by throwing boiling water at it. But he's more considerate about blind stuff than anyone I know except Abby. Actually they're probably tied for not being weird around us, and for helping in a way that's genuinely useful and not patronizing. Like now, he said my name instead of trying to get my attention with eye contact, and he put the plate right in my hand instead of waiting for me to take it from him. No wonder Nate likes him.

"Thanks," I say. "You don't have to hide anything. I think it's cool that you two are together."

Nate gives a tiny sigh, but I still hear it. I'm not good with words or feelings talk but I have to say something.

"Sorry...sorry I made it hard to tell me."

"S'ok," he says around a mouthful of pizza.

For two days, we do all the usual tourist things, like the Empire State Building and the Statue of Liberty. Cricket is concerned that Nate and I will be bored but it's still fun to go to these places even if we can't see the view. On Abby's recommendation, we go to the Museum of Natural History where we can touch some of the exhibits, like meteorites and dinosaur bones. That's really cool.

On Sunday morning, Abby finally rejoins us and we all go to Chinatown for dim sum. Carson shouts at the waiters coming by with carts and orders all kinds of things I've never had before, steamed bread with barbeque pork, shrimp dumplings, braised peanuts, egg tarts. The best is something he calls carrot cake which is neither carrot nor cake. It's a slab of pounded rice with chopped radish which sounds terrible but it's fried and salty and delicious. I draw the line at chicken feet but Carson convinces Nate to try some.

"Not bad," Nate says. "Chewy."

I don't even attempt chopsticks, but Nate does, even though he flings food around the table. Carson shows us how to request more tea by flipping the lid of the teapot. It's fun, hearing him explain everything. He tells Nate and me what every dish is and where it is on our plates like it's a clock face, and tries to keep us from accidentally knocking things off the lazy susan. I do anyway, but it's only a little dish of soy sauce. He orders vegetarian dishes for Cricket and Laura and makes sure everyone has enough.

I realize why Nate likes him. Not just like, but *like* like. He's a good guy, oh and also totally ripped, I can tell from the few times he's put his arm around me. The idea of them having sex still feels a little weird, but whatever, I try not to think in too much detail about my brother doing it with anyone, male or female. Why shouldn't they be together?

50

ABBY

Now that I'm freed from the enormous burden of keeping Nate's secret, spending time with all of my housemates is actually enjoyable.

After an enormous meal, we waddle back to the hotel room and crash on the two beds. Cricket and Laura have perfected a method of circling the block then blending in with other people going up in the elevator so the front desk doesn't notice.

As we lie on the beds crosswise, I ask the question that's been weighing on my mind all through lunch. "Did you two idiots talk yet or not?"

"Not that it's any of your business," Nate says, "but yes, Nick is now on Team Ally. His PFLAG membership should be arriving in the mail soon."

Nate's words are sarcastic as usual but everything about him is different, more relaxed. It takes me a second to realize that I'm seeing him smile for real for the first time. When his face splits with a genuine grin he looks even more like Nick, if such a thing were possible.

"Wait!" Nick half sits up as if something just occurred to him. "How come I'm not gay? It's not just a choice, right? Being gay? So if it's something you're born with, and we're genetically 99% identical, why wasn't I born with it too?"

"I've been reading up on that," Nate says seriously. "No one really knows. Maybe it's that 1%, or maybe epigenetics."

"What does it matter? There's so much we don't know about why people are attracted to each other." The words slip out of me, and I instantly regret them. Ok, so one secret is out but there's still the other one.

Nick wants to meet my parents. I couldn't say no because I already met his parents and if I make up some excuse he'll think that I'm not serious about him or embarrassed of him or something, when actually the opposite is true. I'm not embarrassed of him, I'm embarrassed of me.

So I say I'll take Nick over to our apartment after everything with my cousin's bat mitzvah is over. But bringing him over meant I had to tell my parents about Nick which I hadn't done yet. I mean, I had sort of dropped hints for a while that I was seeing someone but I left out the main details, that we're living together and that he's blind.

The part about living together is not that big a deal. My parents are pretty open-minded. But it is an indication that things with Nick are kind of serious.

The part about him being blind, though, oh man, that's a lot harder. I have to force myself to say the word, as if my mouth doesn't even want to make the sounds. Because they know. They know all about Ted, that Nick isn't my first blind boyfriend but my second. One is just a coincidence, no explanation needed. I get congratulated on being such a good person. Two is a pattern, and I get weird looks.

Scratch that. Jen gave me weird looks but I never felt compelled to explain anything to her. My parents, on the other hand, give me the third degree, and I have to explain everything to them.

Dad's first reaction is that this is due to some self-esteem issue on my part. I have to tell them no, I'm not seeking out blind guys because I think I'm not attractive enough for a sighted guy. I want to tell him how freaking insulting that is. Nick isn't some consolation prize. I'm not settling for him. He's the sweetest, kindest guy I have ever met, and his blindness makes him out-of-this-world attractive to me, to the extent that I can barely keep my hands off him. But these are not things

I can say to my parents. I bite my tongue and remind them that I have a lot of flaws but low self-esteem isn't one of them.

Mom gives me this long, hard stare, like she's re-evaluating every bit of evidence from my childhood and realizing she knew all along. Even more than Dad's ignorant questions, the realization that younger me was not as sneaky as I thought opens a pit in my stomach. Did Mom find that copy of *See You Thursday* that I kept hidden in the back of my closet? I used to pretend to love books and movies I didn't care about so no one would notice that my true favorites all featured characters with disabilities.

I lay down what I hope is my winning card. "Dr. Goldberg says it's perfectly normal and not something to be ashamed of."

Dr. Goldberg is the psychoanalyst I've been seeing since I was in high school. I still try to fit in a visit when I'm in town. She's awesome. Talking to her turned my head around on the whole devotee thing. At least until Ted made me doubt myself. But I still never told my parents, because why should I have to share the details of my sex life with them? Jen loves it when a guy spanks her but she'll never need to have a conversation with her parents about it.

Invoking Dr. Goldberg's name works. My parents exchange a look and Dad shrugs.

"If that's what makes you happy, ziskeit."

Whew, at least Dad is on my side. I think of what Tanya said, that the most radical thing you can be is yourself. It feels good, knowing I can share this part of myself, let them see my authentic self without hiding.

Mom still looks unconvinced. "And this boy, this Nick? Is he ok with this too?"

"Yes," I lie.

As we walk the four long blocks from the flophouse where he's staying to the Q train, Nick goes on and on about how much he loves the city and how awesome it is to get around without a car. I keep up my end of the conversation but inside I'm freaking out.

Are my parents going to say something about Ted? Or even worse, will they ask Nick how he feels about me being a devotee? Why oh why did I have to lie about it?

Now, I tell myself. Just tell him now before it's too late.

I look over at Nick, half a step behind me, holding my elbow with one hand and his white cane with the other. We're going at a normal pace but he keeps slowing down.

"Are you ok?"

"Yeah, it's nothing. My knee is still a little sore."

"Your knee? What happened?"

"Oh, I tripped and fell on it yesterday on the way back from the museum."

"Let me guess. It was Cricket, wasn't it?"

"Don't blame her! I should have been paying better attention. We were walking under the scaffolding by some building and there was plywood all over the sidewalk from the construction."

That girl! I swear she would lose her ass if it wasn't attached to her legs.

"It's nothing," Nick insists. "Happens all the time."

How can I be attracted to this? I berate myself, not for the first time. This thing that makes his life more difficult, that he would change if he could. I don't love that he fell down. I don't want to see him suffer, be hurt. That's not it at all.

Why can't you be normal?

I can't get Ted's voice out of my head. I lose my nerve. We descend the stairs into the subway, but I can't tell him, not now.

The train ride is fast, only three stops to the Upper West Side. The car is a little crowded, so we're standing next to each other hanging on the straps. Nick leans up against me and puts his arm on my shoulders.

The doors open and close, and people jostle around us.

"Two more stops," I tell him.

"So have you told them…?"

"That we're going out? Yeah, they know we live together with a bunch of other friends, and that I spent the winter break with you."

"No, I mean the other…"

"Yeah, I mentioned about you being blind."

"And they weren't weird about it?"

"No, not at all." Shit! Why can't I stop lying? "Honestly, I thought they might be more upset that you're a shaygetz."

"A what?"

"A goy. Not Jewish."

"I never even thought about that!" Nick looks stricken. "Oh no, do they follow the whaddaycallit, the food rules?"

"It's called keeping kosher, and yes, they do."

"What if I mess it up? I don't want to do something offensive by accident."

I give his arm a little shake. "Chill out, dude. It'll be fine."

Nick accidentally using the wrong dish or fork is literally the last of my worries.

51

NICK

The trip through the subway, down the street and up to Abby's parents' apartment is dizzying, but I try to stay calm as I hold her arm. I catch a glimpse of black and white checkerboard tile on the lobby floor. The building is so old that the elevator door isn't automatic, just a kind of chain gate that rattles as Abby pulls it shut.

Abby is right, I didn't need to worry. Her parents are nice. I've learned to tell instantly when someone is feeling awkward or weird around me—the long silences, nervous laughter, overly careful language. But they don't do that at all. I had imagined them as formal and proper, like some of my professors. But no, they're loud and funny.

"How are you?" her mom says in a brassy, nasally voice. "Abby said the drive out here was horrible!"

"It wasn't so bad. At least I didn't have to drive."

Everyone laughs, a genuine, not forced laugh, and I relax. Abby leads me to the couch in the living room. Do all apartments here have this musty smell? Even with the windows shut, I can still hear a lot of street noise. But I don't mind it. It's kind of exciting, a reminder that there's always something going on.

Abby's parents ask me about our trip, what we've been up to, about school, my major, all that usual small talk stuff.

"Last semester, huh?" says Dr. Adelstein. "Any plans after graduation?"

"Dad! That's rude!"

"No, it's ok." I shake my head. "Actually, I've been putting together my resumé and cover letters for jobs in my field. The CSD, that's the Center for Students with Disabilities, a counselor there is helping me to target companies that have inclusive hiring practices."

Saying all this makes it sound much more of a big deal, and not that I just talked to someone at the CSD one time, but I do have another appointment when we get back. At least I have a real answer to this question, unlike last summer. That feels like progress.

"Good! Maybe you can give our little slacker some pointers."

"Morris!" I hear a whack, like Mrs. Adelstein gave her husband a little smack. "Leave her alone."

"Who you calling a slacker?" Abby sounds more amused than annoyed. "At least I'm paying all my own bills."

They banter back and forth like this for a while, and I get the sense that this kind of teasing is normal for them. She tells them all about the afterschool theater program, and they love how crazy the kids are.

"Sorry dinner is nothing special, just cold cuts from Katz's Deli," Mrs. Adelstein says.

"What do you mean nothing special? It's the best pastrami in the whole world!" Dr. Adelstein shout-speaks. "People come from all over and wait in line for hours to taste it!"

"I got some nice knishes too," his wife adds. I love them already

He's right, the pastrami sandwich is amazing. I concentrate extra hard on not knocking over anything on the table, or dropping food in my lap. I hope the mustard isn't dripping on my shirt. Every few minutes, I run my fingers over my chest to check.

After dinner, I ask to use the restroom. Abby leads me through a series of rooms. I realize the apartment is set up in a weird way with no hallways, just one room connecting to another. The bathroom is between the bedroom and the kitchen.

Abby leaves me in privacy, but a minute later I can hear her talking to her parents in the kitchen. The sound travels through the wall as clearly as if I was standing next to them.

"Well?" Abby says over the sound of running water and dishes clattering in the sink.

"What's not to like?" her father says. "So long as he treats you good, ziskeit. That's all that matters."

Oh my God, they're talking about me. I die a little as Mrs. Adelstein says, "And so handsome!"

I wash my hands quickly before I hear anything more embarrassing. I exit the bathroom but realize I've made a tactical error. Inside the bathroom the light was bright, reflecting off the little white hexagonal tiles, and I could make out the facilities well enough. But now the room I'm in is pitch dark. I have no idea where the light switch is, or where the door is, and I left my cane by the front door.

I take a few hesitant steps. Is this Abby's childhood bedroom? Or is it her parents' bedroom? Oh God, I might actually die of embarrassment right here. Ok, remember your training. I put my hands out but I can't find a wall. There's too much furniture. I try to make what I think is a circuit of the room, but there's no door. I come back around to the bathroom door but I can't find any other door. What is wrong with me?

For a second I feel like my dinner might come back up again. No, there has to be a door. I just have to circle around again. I take a steadying breath and start out again, moving to the right from the bathroom, one arm in front of me. I've already been gone too long. Time to hurry up.

I take a bold step forward, then another. Too fast. My shoe hits a metal radiator cover with a clang. I stumble forward, and my flailing arm connects with something hard and cold that immediately crashes to the hardwood floor with the unmistakable sound of shattering ceramic.

"Nick, are you …oh!" Mrs. Adelstein flips on the light.

Now I'm in total whiteout and I still can't see anything. What did I knock over? Was it a priceless Ming vase? It felt like a vase or something, definitely valuable, maybe an heirloom.

I bend down awkwardly as if I'm going to clean up. "I'm sorry! I'll replace it!" I mean, maybe if I win the lottery.

Mrs. Adelstein pushes me back gently, laughing. "Oh, that! Don't worry about it!"

"What was it?" I'm almost too afraid to ask.

"It's nothing, really. A life-size china cat that Morrie's parents gave us years ago. It's fine, the ear just broke off."

I hear her pick it up as a wave of relief washes over me.

"To be honest," she continues, "I never liked it. The eyes always followed me around the room. Now maybe I'll have an excuse to get rid of it."

I trail behind her out of the room. I swear that door appeared out of nowhere. I'm certain I passed the spot and it was just a wall a minute ago.

"You get lost?" Abby says as I return to the table.

"Actually, yeah." We all laugh, and it feels pretty good. I mean, if I can't laugh at myself, the rest of my life is going to be a bitter, hard slog. I might as well lean into the absurdity.

The next night, Mrs. Adelstein gets rush tickets and takes us to see a revival of *Guys and Dolls* on Broadway.

I can't exactly see the stage, just a kind of patchwork of flashing lights and colors, but Abby narrates the action in a whisper. It's so fun but the best part is how into it Abby is. Her narration includes a lot of commentary on whose performance is on point and who is emoting less than the scenery around him. I feel like I'm finally getting what she says about theater, how anything can happen. Not that anyone in this show messes up, to the contrary, it's all perfect. But I can't help thinking about how all these people are all pulling together, not just the actors on stage, but the orchestra in the pit, and everyone backstage. It doesn't even matter that I can't see the dancing. I can feel the energy coming off the stage.

"That was amazing," Abby says as we walk out of the theater toward the subway. I thought it was amazing too, not just the show, but her enthusiasm for it. I can't help teasing her a little, though.

"I thought you didn't like 'risk-free theater'? Isn't this the most risk-free there is, just doing the same show over and over for years?"

"Ah, whatever." The musky scent of her hair rises up as she tosses her head. "It's ok to have fun too."

"I'm glad you enjoyed it, darling," Mrs. Adelstein says. On the subway back to my hotel, she asks how I've been enjoying my trip.

"I love it," I say honestly. In the week we've been here, we haven't used the car once. I've been all over the city just by walking and taking the train, sometimes a taxi. If I memorized the route, I could have done it on my own. I don't mind the crowds. Walking down the street surrounded by other people is exciting, like on campus but so much bigger. I know New Yorkers have a reputation for being rude, but so far people have left us alone. Maybe I just haven't noticed, but I feel less stared at here than at home.

"He loves it!" Mrs. Adelstein says to Abby. "So how about moving back?"

"Forget it, Mom. I'm not moving back in with you like a child."

"I didn't mean that. So touchy! But you know, if you two wanted to live here, we could help you find a place. Remember Rebecca from Hebrew school? Her mother was telling me she moved into an apartment on the Lower East Side where the rent is very reasonable."

"Whatever."

Abby doesn't say anything more, but I can't stop thinking about the possibilities. Why not move here? I can't think of anywhere else I want to be. Or anyone else I want to be with.

52

ABBY

I got through that entire visit without being outed, but somehow I feel even worse about it than before.

The drive back to Allenville is faster than the trip out. Carson gets a proper map with decent directions. As we sail down the interstate, Laura, Cricket, and Carson swap driving duties every few hours. The others doze but not me. I'm still too worked up to doze off.

Somewhere upstate, we stop for the night in a motel.

We split up in three rooms, instead of trying to cram everyone into one room. In the end, the ploy in Manhattan to sneak Laura and Cricket in didn't work. When the guys checked out, there was a charge for two extra guests on the bill. So at the motel we don't even try.

We get pizza delivered, and Carson comes back from somewhere with a case of beer. The motel rooms don't have tables, so we all sit on the curb by Laura's car to eat dinner.

Laura clinks her beer can against Nate's. "I didn't get a chance to say it before, but congratulations on coming out. I know it ain't easy, but it feels good, right?"

Nate looks surprised. "Thanks. I'm sorry it took so long."

Cricket leans around at the end of the line. "Don't apologize. You take the time you need."

At the opposite end of the line, Nick squirms around uncomfortably. "Yeah, you don't have to apologize. I...I really am sorry I made it hard for you to tell me."

"Ah, s'ok." Nate takes a swig of beer. "It wasn't just you. I felt like everyone had this image of me as one thing, and it's hard to break out of that. Plus I was so focused on being super blind dude, my-disability-doesn't-define-me supercrip. How could I be disabled and gay? It's … too much all at once."

"Shit man, I'm sorry I didn't know you were going through all that. I wish I had been there for you."

"I know. I should have told you. It wasn't until I took that class last year that I realized it's not like these are separate labels slapped on me. No, it's all just fear of not measuring up to the same bullshit male ideal. Once I let that go, it wasn't so scary anymore to be myself."

"So you gonna tell your parents now?" Carson asks. He doesn't say it, but it's clear from his tone that this has been a sore point between them.

"Yeah, I'll call them when we get back. Promise."

"I'm sure they'll be fine with it," Nick says, then turns to Carson. "Have you told your parents yet?"

"Of course I told my parents," Carson snaps. "What, do you think that only white people can be open-minded? Just because they're Chinese they'll be homophobic?"

"I, uh, no..." Nick turns red. That probably is what he was thinking.

"Fuck you. Taiwan is the most liberal country in Asia. I came out to my parents in high school."

"Must be nice," Laura says bitterly.

"Ok, I admit there were a few rough years at first but they came around. I've been lucky. I'm sorry it's been so hard for you."

"Ah, screw 'em all." Laura puts her arm around Cricket. "Her mom offered to adopt me."

Cricket laughs. It's so sweet to see them like this.

"What about you?" Cricket says to me. "Have you come out to your parents yet?"

I almost throw up my pizza in the parking lot, before I realize she means come out as bi, not come out as a devotee. After a far too long pause, I say, "In my freshman year." Carson gives me a funny look like he knows I'm lying.

Shit! I can't keep living like this. I have to tell Nick, and the rest of them. But not right now. This moment is about Nate.

I'll tell Nick when we get home, I promise myself.

The day after we get back I'm downing black coffee in the kitchen because we still haven't had time to go to the store for milk when the phone rings. I leave my gross coffee on the counter in the kitchen and run to the extension in the living room.

"Hello?"

"Hiya, Abs! How are you?"

It's Ted. Fuck my life.

"How did you get this number?"

"Your mom gave it to me. When did you move?"

I've moved twice since I last spoke to him, but I don't tell him that. I'll be having words with my mother about this later.

Ted continues as if he's announcing that I won the lottery. "Guess what, I'm coming to Allenville next week!"

"What for?"

"The Calstock Writing Prize, duh."

Oh right. There's this big prestigious literary award the university gives out every year to undergrads. Ted won for fiction in his senior year. The winners get to be on the judging committee in following years and are invited to the awards ceremony.

"You're working at Dark Island, right? I'll stop by and say hi."

What can I say to this? *Lose my number, pretend I never existed.* But even if I said that, I can't exactly stop him from bothering me at work if he really wants to.

And that's exactly what he does. I'm at the register by myself when the door opens and there he is, like a ghost resurrected from my past. Or maybe I'm the one who died and came back as a ghost. Seeing him in front of the counter of the bookstore makes me feel like my soul is leaving my body.

"Abs?"

"Yeah, I'm here." I'm literally trapped. I can't leave the register or Bob will plotz and then fire me.

Ted's face brightens and he puts his arms out but there's no way I'm letting him hug me. He looks exactly the same: long dark hair in a ponytail, mustache and goatee. His prosthetic eyes have a fixed, glassy look, but not in a bad way. He's striking. I find him attractive, even after everything that's come between us. I try not to compare him to Nick, but fail. Everything about the way Ted moves is different, because he lost his sight so much younger. His whole demeanor is more stiff, uncertain. His arms drop and he reaches out to feel the edge of the counter. I hate myself for the way seeing how he moves still affects me.

Ted launches into a monologue about the prize, what an honor it is, how impressed everyone in his MA program is with him, blah blah blah. It is genuinely a big deal. I remember how excited we both were when he won. And his lingering doubt that he was given the prize out of pity, not on merit. I get it. Being taken seriously as a blind person, it's fucking hard. But then he got accepted to that MFA program and he doubled down on fronting with a giant ego.

"Glad you're doing well," I say tersely when he comes up for air. I'm hoping he'll hear my tone and get a clue, but no such luck.

"I *am* doing well! Iowa State is terrific, just terrific. Although the accessibility could be better. But you can see for yourself. I thought maybe since you're done with school now you might come visit."

"Why would you think that?"

"You promised you'd think about it. C'mon, why not?" His voice has a whining, childish tone, and that drives me right over the edge.

"Are you high?" The two or three customers browsing the shelves sidle away uncomfortably as my voice rises, but I don't care. "Why not? Ok, here's why not. One, we haven't spoken in almost a year and I've moved on with my life. Two, I'm not your personal assistant. Hire someone if you need help. Three, you broke up with me, and in a particularly shitty way, I might add."

"I'm sorry! I was wrong, ok? I want to try again."

"No." I lower my voice to a hiss because I don't want anyone hearing this part. "What you said about me being a devotee messed me up. I don't want to be with someone who can't accept me for who I really am, all of it, not just the parts that are convenient to you. I'm not going to spend my life hiding my attraction, worrying that I might say the wrong thing and be criticized by you."

I wish you were normal. This sentence has been stabbing me over and over, like a splinter in my heart but now finally I've drawn it out and the pain vanishes.

Ted's mouth opens and closes in surprise. "Whatever." His voice is tight. "God, you're such a bitch. Your parents must've really messed you up. There *is* something wrong with you, and I'm not sorry for saying it."

He swings around toward the door, wrenching it open so the bell at the top jingles crazily. Just as Ted is leaving, Nick suddenly appears in the doorway. What the hell is he doing here? He sometimes comes to meet me at work as my shift is ending, but I wasn't expecting him today.

Nick and Ted get kind of caught in the doorway. I guess neither one is paying attention, and they can't seem to get past each other. Their canes get tangled up, knocking against each other, then they both seem to realize what's happening at the same moment. I stand there like an idiot, wishing for a bolt of lightning to strike me dead.

"Excuse me." Nick tries to move to the side, but Ted stumbles against him. For a second, Ted starts to fall over, a look of panic on his face. In that second, I feel sorry for him for the first time. He never wanted anyone to pity him, and I don't, or at least not because he's blind, but because he's so preoccupied with what people think of him. All that showing off, to hide how insecure he feels inside. I used to think Nate was like him, but he got over himself long enough to let Carson in, and eventually his brother.

All this goes through my mind in a flash, then the moment is past. Ted flails out with the hand not holding his cane, finds the doorframe, and rights himself. He's gone like a shot.

"Abby?" Nick swings his head around. My heart speeds up and I'm so grateful that he's nothing like either of them. I've never been so happy to see anyone.

I find my voice at last. "Hey Nick, over here. Let me clock out then we can go."

"Was that…? Did I just crash into another blind guy? Wait, why was there a blind guy in the bookstore? Have you started stocking Braille books?"

"I'll tell you on the way home."

In a daze, I cash out of the till and go to the back to clock out. Jesse emerges from the break room to start his shift.

In a strange way, I'm grateful that Ted said those horrible things as he was leaving. I get it now—he was trying to hurt me. All those things he said were about him, his own insecurities, not about me.

And I meant what I said to him. I don't want to be in a relationship if I can't be honest. I've chickened out about telling Nick because I was afraid he would dump me, but if being together means constantly hiding and lying, it's not worth it. My heart is still hammering as I grab my purse, though. This is not going to be easy.

Nick takes my arm and we head up University Ave then left on Micsawbee, down the hill to our house. He doesn't say anything. Once the crowd thins out as we walk away from the center of town, I take a deep breath.

"That guy you bumped into, that was Ted, my ex."

Nick looks blank. "What?"

"I dated another blind guy before I met you."

"Oh, is that why you know so much about Braille and O&M and all that? Does he have RP too?"

"No, he had ocular cancer when he was little."

Nick is taking this all better than I expected, which makes me suspect he still doesn't get it. We've reached the house, but I don't want to go in yet. It's late afternoon, and everyone else is probably back from class. We go up the rickety porch steps, but instead of going in we sit on the decaying sofa on the porch. This monstrosity is even uglier than the living room one, a dingy brownish orange. It's been rained on and snowed on, and I'm pretty sure squirrels have hidden nuts under the cushions. It smells gross but at least it's dry at the moment.

"We have to talk."

Nick rubs his hands on his thighs. "Ok. About what?"

I take a deep breath. "Have you ever heard the word devotee before?"

"What, like a religious fanatic?"

"No, nothing like that. It's a term for um… someone who finds disability attractive. Me. I'm a devotee."

I can practically see him slowly putting the pieces together in his mind. "Ok… but why?"

"Why? I don't know why. Why are you straight and Nate's gay? There's so much we still don't know about human sexuality. These things are hardwired. I remember thinking about it when I was really little, long before I even knew what sex was. It's just the way I am. I didn't choose it. It chose me."

Nick looks thoughtful, taking it all in. I can tell I've caught him by surprise, but he isn't frowning. That has to be good, right? My heart is still hammering in my chest, but slows with every second that goes by and he doesn't get angry or run away.

I take what my theater profs call a calming breath, in deep through nose and out through the mouth. "I'm sorry I've taken so long to tell you, but it's not easy to talk about. I've been dumped over it twice already."

"Twice?"

"Yeah. Number one, that asshole Ted who you bumped into. He kept saying I was messed up, that I liked him for the wrong reasons. Number two, Catherine. I was trying to be honest and real with her, and she flipped the hell out. Called me a sexual predator."

"What! That bitch!"

"Yeah, I was so stunned I couldn't even stick up for myself. I mumbled something about how it's not like that at all but I could tell she didn't believe me."

"Man, that sucks! I'm so sorry. If you're a predator, then what am I? A victim? Like a child? Does she really think I can't consent to a sexual relationship? See, I was paying attention to the sexual harassment lecture we got when we moved into the dorm."

"I know there's nothing wrong with me. It's just... it was hard to grow up this way, you know? With desires I didn't understand. I used to feel guilty about it, but I don't anymore."

"Guilty? Why?"

"Obviously, because I'm getting off on something that makes the person's life more difficult. The thing they hate most about themselves, or the one thing they wish they could change."

"If it makes you feel better, I don't hate having RP. I mean, it does make my life more difficult. Sometimes a lot more difficult. But it's just the way it is. I can't change it, so hating it is a waste of energy. Wait, are you crying?"

I let out a hiccupping sob. "I was so sure you'd hate me if I told you."

He puts his arm around my shoulders and pulls me in close. I bury my face in his chest and let the tears out, releasing months of tension.

"Abby, you know there's nothing you can do that would make me hate you, right? I love you."

"I love you too."

I kiss him hard, my tears wetting both our faces. We've been together for so long but this is the first time we've ever said it.

The most radical thing you can be is yourself. I think again of what Tanya said. Letting people see your authentic self is hard, way harder than getting up on stage and shouting a bunch of nonsense. I didn't need Nick to tell me that there's nothing wrong with being a devotee. I knew that already. But letting him know how I feel about him, that I'm not looking past his disability but looking right at it and loving every part of him, that makes me feel whole.

I sigh, letting the tension out of my shoulders. I feel better than I have in months, maybe years. Nick's arms are still around me, holding me tight, so solid and real. For the first time, I can imagine a future for us together, not as wishful thinking or a fantasy I hardly dare imagine, but actual reality.

Nothing's ever felt so right.

53

NICK

Abby's confession surprises me, but what surprises me more is how worked up she is over it. I've never heard her cry like that before. I feel bad for her, thinking she had to bury part of herself for so long.

I would never have planned to tell her I love her on the stinky porch sofa while she was sobbing, but there we are. She's the most amazing person I've ever met, and knowing that she loves every part of me, that makes our connection even better. I always knew there was something different about her, not like anyone else I've ever met. And as it turns out, I was right.

That kiss feels like a deeper, truer connection even than sex. I hold her for a long time, running my hand over her springy hair, enjoying the closeness of her.

"I won't tell anyone about you being a devotee if you don't want me to," I say.

She shakes her head under my hand. "No, it's ok. I'm sick of keeping it hidden from our friends. And I'm sure you want to tell Nate."

"Yeah, kinda, only if it's ok with you."

"It's fine. But tell him if he gives me any shit about it, I'm going to kick his ass."

Abby doesn't need to worry about that. Much later, long after we rejoin the others inside, have dinner, get ready for bed, after all the lights are out, I knock on Nate's door. He's sitting at his desk, listening to a tape at super fast speed on his headphones.

"Oh yeah, I figured," is his only response when I tell him about Abby.

"What? What are you talking about? I never even knew that was a thing."

"That guy Tim at O&M mentioned it to me one time, that there are people who are turned on by disabilities." Tim was an instructor at the training program we attended. He was one of the ones who's partially blind.

"What! I can't believe you knew all this time and you never even mentioned it to me."

"It didn't seem important. Everyone has their thing, especially when it comes to sex."

"She was really worried that we would be upset about it."

"No, why would I? I'm not going to judge anyone for their desires. Or for taking time to talk about it. You're ok with it, right?"

"Actually, I think it's kind of awesome. If there's something about my body that I can't change, it's nice to know that my girlfriend finds it attractive." I don't add, and the sex with her is incredible, better than any other girl I've met. I'm not going to say that to my brother.

"Good. Try not to mess it up, ok?"

"Thanks for the vote of confidence, asshole."

"I mean it. You're...I don't know how to say it... more yourself around her."

It feels good to hear him say that. I think the same thing about him and Carson.

Something suddenly occurs to me. "Can I ask you something?"

"If it's any sex questions, you can fuck right off."

"No! Jeez! I'm trying to have a serious moment here."

"Ok, sorry." He laughs. "What?"

"Is Carson a devotee too?"

"No, man!"

"Are you sure? Did you ask him?"

"Not that it's any of your business, but we did talk about it. Not everyone who dates a person with a disability is a devotee, you know."

"Yeah, I guess that's true." I'm quiet for a long time, thinking all this over.

"Does it ever bother you that you've never seen Carson's face?"

"No! I keep telling you, you gotta let that shit go. Have you been hung up on that with Abby?"

I can see glimpses of her face, like pieces of a puzzle. Her dark eyes, her wide, dazzling grin. So what if I can't help trying to put the fragments together into a portrait in my mind?

"I guess I'm just more of a visual person than you. You're the one who said we're not the same person, right? So I gotta figure out my own way to be."

Saying it all out loud to Nate is strangely momentous. Even though he doesn't say much in reply except, "Yeah, you're right."

"Thanks." It feels good to hear him say that, knowing he's really listening to me without arguing.

As we near the end of the semester, I pull more than one all-nighter trying to get through my data management class. I've had Professor Agarwal in four classes now, and I don't want to let him down with bad grades in my last semester. Also he's helping me with my job search, so I feel extra pressure to step up.

"You look tired," he says to me after class. "Don't pull too many all-nighters. Sleep is important too."

"Thank you. I know." I nod with what I hope is a serious and not sarcastic expression.

"So I wanted to ask you," he continues as he puts his things into his bag, "would you be ok with expanding your job search out east?"

"Yeah, I could."

"One of my former students started a company that makes educational software, to sell to schools, and he wants to add accessibility features for special needs kids. I want to send him your resume, but he's based in New York. Is that ok?"

It's more than ok. But only if Abby wants to come with me.

I spend the whole day wondering how to bring it up, but somehow there's no good time until we're lying in bed together in the dark, squashed together on my narrow single mattress in the dark.

"Oh. Ok. Um. Wow." She squirms around in my arms.

My heart drops. I was certain she would be excited about this.

"If you don't want to move with me, just say so."

"No! That's not it! I want to move in with you, more than anything." She kisses my forehead. "It's just that my mom has been pressuring me since last year to move back home and take a job she has picked out for me. I feel like a brat saying no, but I don't wanna!"

"Yeah, I know." The thought of moving back to Chesterford Hills fills me with dread. "But I thought you wanted to go back to the city, right?" I've picked up this habit from her, of saying "the city" instead of New York, like there's only one city in the whole world.

Abby sighs, resting her head on her hands on my chest. "I do. But on my terms. I had this fantasy of moving to the East Village and doing one-woman shows that would blow people's minds. But that'll obviously never happen. I feel stupid even saying it out loud."

"No!" I wrap my arms around her tightly. "Don't say that! You've been enjoying the kids' theater so much. Why not do more with that? There's gotta be a way to go back on your own terms."

Abby kisses me on the mouth, and I kiss her back. I want to make this happen more than anything. That week we spent in New York was the most fun I've ever had.

"You know," she says after a long time, "maybe that's not a bad idea."

"Graduation ceremony is for our parents. The graduation party is for us," Carson says, and I have to agree.

The ceremony is long and annoying. I grit my teeth through the interminable, boring speeches, the endless lists of awards and names. The cap and gown is plasticky and hot, like wearing a giant garbage bag, with a square of cardboard on our heads. There's no escaping the early summer heat, crammed into the folding chairs on the football field. I'm squashed in next to Nate and Carson. Abby, our parents, Emily, and

Carson's parents are somewhere up in the bleachers, but all I can see of the audience is a few bright, blurry spots.

Nate and I each get a commendation from the CSD, which feels suspiciously like a participation prize to me, but whatever. There are too many students for anyone to walk across the platform, thank goodness, so we only have to stand up and wave when they call our names. There's a weak smattering of applause.

"They should've said we're graduating despite their so-called assistance," Nate mutters as we sit down.

Carson laughs. "Within five years, you'll be running that place."

"Damn right," Nate says.

He's already been accepted into an MA program in social work, in Seattle of all places. Carson landed himself a job there too. So they're moving in together, just signed a lease and everything.

Nate called up our parents and came out to them right after our trip to New York. I tried not to listen in, but according to what he told me after, they were a little awkward and weird about at first but eventually said the crucial line: "We'll always love and support you." It's been the same since they showed up for graduation, kind of nervous but going out of their way to be extra nice.

I met Carson's parents very briefly at the house before heading out to the ceremony. Carson introduced Nate as his boyfriend, and his parents seemed happy to meet him. Actually, they were more chill than our parents.

"They're just glad I'm going to be earning money instead of costing them money," Carson says. "Everything is a distant second after that." But I can tell he's pleased.

Nate's not the only one leaving. Abby and I are moving to New York, to a tiny fifth floor walkup on the Lower East Side. We're flying out in two weeks. Abby got another bookstore job, but it's just to pay the bills. She plans to do more volunteering with kids' theater, and next year she's applying for an MFA in theater education.

I got a job too, the one Prof Agarwal hooked me up with. I interviewed over the phone, he wrote me a recommendation letter, and I got hired. The pay isn't much, but it's a real job.

I was expecting our parents to hover, to ask me and Nate if we're sure, if it's a good idea to be in a new city. But they don't. No one says anything about the two blind guys, striking out on our own. They assume we can do it. And that makes me feel like maybe I really can. I can walk or take the subway wherever I want to go. I already got in touch with a guide dog training program. Being matched with a dog is a long, complicated process, but who knows. I'm finally starting to feel like an adult.

The graduation party, that's for us. The day after the ceremony, our parents head back home, and for the first time ever, we're not going with them. I feel more sad about leaving the Micsawbee house, to be honest. Cricket and Laura have one more year until they graduate, but they found an apartment on the other side of campus.

For one last time, before we all move out, we have a party and invite everyone we know. People start showing up in the afternoon, because we're still totally uncool nerds. The weather is warm, really warm finally, not only by comparison with the dead of winter. We fling open the windows and the front door and blast Camper van Beethoven to the neighborhood.

Nate and I sprawl on the living room sofa while Abby and Cricket run around setting out bowls of chips and candy. Carson is at the store buying bags of ice which we forgot to get earlier when we bought the food and drinks. I look at Nate's blurry form at the other end of the sofa. He leans back and I see the top left corner of his face, that face that's exactly the same as mine. It's always slightly jarring to be reminded of how old we look. My mental image of us is still around thirteen or so. I wonder if that'll ever change. I know Nate would tell me to stop thinking visually. But I don't have to, I realize. We're really not the same person.

"You're awfully quiet," Nate says.

"I was thinking how this'll be the first time we're living apart. Opposite sides of the country, even."

"That's what being a grown-up is, right? Did you imagine we'd live in the same house for the rest of our lives?"

"No," I lie. Honestly, I never gave it much thought. I assumed we'd be together, but I realize he's right. "Bet you're glad to get away from me, huh."

"Yeah, aren't you? Come on, we're starting our lives finally. Aren't you excited to move to New York?"

"Yeah." That's an understatement. Even though it means learning a whole new city, memorizing new streets, new habits, it's all worth it. To live with Abby, just the two of us, with jobs like real adults.

"I'll miss you, asshole," Nate says.

I scoot over closer to him on the couch and put my arm around his shoulder, like we used to do when we were little.

"Me too. We can still talk on the phone."

"Of course. Anytime."

Later, I dance with Abby, the two of us shimmying and swaying in the cluttered living room of our run-down house as the stereo plays "Last Splash" by the Breeders. I can feel the floorboards vibrating slightly and I know that Nate and Carson, Cricket and Laura are dancing too. I fling my arms up in the air. I probably look like an uncoordinated penguin flapping my flightless wings, but who cares.

There's just enough light that I can see a few flashes of Abby's curly hair, her earrings, her wide grin. I put my arms around her, pulling her close. She's warm and solid in my arms, and returns my embrace tightly, putting her head on my shoulder.

We're going to go to the big city together, just the two of us.

I can't wait.

54

Epilog

Nick

2015

"Mom, are you sure this is the right way?" Rachel calls from the back seat of the rental car.

"Relax! I still know this town like the back of my hand," Abby replies.

The car swerves wildly and I grip the handle above the door more tightly. I don't mention that Abby didn't learn to drive until years after we lived in Allenville.

Abby mutters to herself about how she doesn't remember all these one-way streets. Then she shouts, "Oh, we're on Micsawbee Ave!" The car slows down. "There's the house we used to live in."

"Ok," Rachel says, all bored teenager. "Wait, we're not going in, are we?"

"Nah, it was a dump." Abby speeds up again. "Still is, by the looks of it."

I smile, but I still don't say anything. The only way I could "see" the old house would be by walking around inside, but I don't want to bother the students living there now. Anyway, we're not here for me and Abby to relive the past. We're here for our high school senior daughter Rachel to visit Calstock and decide if she wants to go here.

She has her heart set on a small liberal arts college but her mother convinced her to at least make Calstock her safety school. So here we are, back for the first time in twenty years.

Abby finds an overpriced parking garage in the center of town, and we walk towards campus together. According to Abby's running narration, Allenville has changed. It's all trendy new storefronts now. Dark Island Books is still there, but we don't go in. Bob retired a few years ago and someone else took over, but Abby has no interest in seeing the renovated store. She's more excited about meeting with the community outreach program she used to volunteer at, but that's more of a professional than a social thing. She's visiting them tomorrow as artistic director of the largest youth theater in the triborough area.

"Campus looks the same though," Abby remarks as we walk across the quad.

Rachel grudgingly admits that the Midwest Gothic buildings and leafy trees of the quad look cool.

I have to admit, though, nothing feels familiar to me. My mental map of campus is gone, replaced by Manhattan and the neighborhood in Queens we moved to when Rachel was little. I hold onto the rigid harness of my golden lab guide dog, Clover, trusting her to keep me from bumping into the students rushing off to class.

It's not until we walk through the echoing stone archway by the engineering buildings that I finally match up my present location with an actual memory.

"Hey sweetie, remember recording your senior thesis here?" I call out to Abby as we come out on the other side of the archway.

"Don't remind me!" Abby says with a laugh. "I was such a pretentious little shit."

"No, you were passionate," I say. "It was sexy."

"Ugh, you guys! Gross!" Rachel protests.

"I can't help it," I tease her. "Your mother's a hottie."

Rachel groans dramatically.

"Oh look, there's Probus Hall," Abby says as we continue down the street. "Wow, it really looks the same. Man, just seeing that old building reminds me of frigid winters."

"Way to sell it, Mom," Rachel says.

"We'll go visit the English department later," Abby says, undeterred. I wondered for a time if Rachel would rebel against her artsy mother by going into science or something, but no, she wants to major in literature. That's fine with me. Taking a literature class was the best decision I ever made.

We drop off Rachel at Probus Hall for a tour and leave her to form her own impressions without her parents hanging around, and head out to get coffee while we wait for her. The locations of the cafés around campus are basically the same, according to Abby, but the names have all changed. We settle into a tiny marble-top table by the plate glass window with our oat milk lattes. Clover lies down at my feet with a little sigh. I give her some reassuring pats and a treat. She's been a champ in unfamiliar territory.

"I think this is the same place we used to come after class," Abby remarks. "It's hard to tell, though. Everything's been renovated."

I reach over and find her hand, giving it a squeeze. "I'm glad to be back here with you."

"Me too. Crazy to think how long it's been."

I keep squeezing her hand, so warm and solid in mine. It's been years since I could see even the puzzle pieces of her face. Losing that last bit of vision was hard, especially not seeing Rachel's face. But like with everything else, we all just muddle through somehow. I still remember every detail of Abby from when we first met.

"I thought for sure you would never go out with me." I can't help teasing her a little. Even after all this time, I can still hardly believe my luck that such a smart and sexy woman wants to be with me.

She pushes against me playfully. "Come on, you know I wanted to from the start! I was just scared to tell you about, you know, the whole devotee thing." Even now, she drops her voice when she mentions it because we're in public.

"You didn't need to be scared."

"I know." She squeezes my hand again.

Honestly, what she calls "the whole devotee thing" almost never comes up. It just kind of faded into the background of our lives. Our careers, family, day-to-day life. I feel so lucky with all of it. I got in on the ground floor with software engineering, and worked my way up through a decent company. Raising a child has been way more of an adventure than I ever could have imagined but I couldn't have picked a better partner. She's so much more than just a devotee, just like I'm more than just that blind guy.

I think we've done pretty well so far. Rachel's an amazing kid. She may have her sullen teen moments, but she's as smart and passionate as her mother. I feel a little twinge of jealousy thinking of how much fun she'll have at college.

"So do you think she'll decide to go here?" Abby asks.

"Probably not. But that's ok, she should make her own choices, even if it's different from what we did."

"Yeah, you're right, I guess."

"Why are you so sad about that? When we were students, you complained about this place all the time. You kept saying what a crappy school it is. So why are you pushing her to go here?"

"Because it's where I met you! I know, when I say it out loud it sounds stupid, but I just want her to have the same chance at happiness that we did."

I slide my arm around her shoulder. "It wasn't this place I fell in love with. It was you."

Abby lays her head against me. "Soon it'll be just the two of us again."

"There's no one else I want to be with."

And I do what I always wanted to, back when we were students, but I was always too shy. Now, nothing is holding me back. I find her lips with my fingers, and kiss her right there in the coffee shop.

www.ingramcontent.com/pod-product-compliance
Lightning Source LLC
Chambersburg PA
CBHW071305140726

47996CB00005B/1642